Marielle gazed directly and teasingly in~~to his eyes, reminding~~ him of noth~~ing~~ ... woman whe~~...~~

"Perhaps I'm w~~rong about you,~~" she said. "Perhaps—"

"You *are* wrong about me."

Dylan wanted to say more. He wanted to say that he was a drifter by necessity, not by choice. He wanted to say that he already wanted to stay in Morrow Creek and she was the reason. He wanted to say that he would have given anything to believe things could be good and lasting between them. But that was unthinkable. That would only ensure, as it always did, that everything unraveled in the end. So instead he let his need for her say everything. He let his need for her—so long denied—move his hands to her face, cradle her jaw and pull her nearer.

"You're wrong about everything about me," Dylan said.

She *was* wrong—because he'd made damn sure she would be.

He'd made sure everyone would be. For so long now.

Marielle hauled in a breath—probably to argue. B~~...~~ ~~al~~ready mee~~ting~~

Author Note

Thank you for joining me for another Morrow Creek story! I absolutely love sharing my little Arizona Territory town with you. I'm so thrilled to bring you Marielle and Dylan's adventures, too! I hope you enjoy reading about them.

There's more for you in the rest of my Morrow Creek series, too! It includes *Notorious in the West*, *The Honour-Bound Gambler*, *The Bride Raffle*, *Mail-Order Groom*, and several others—including some short stories and an eBook exclusive—all set in and around my favourite corner of the Old West. I hope you'll give one (or all!) of them a try.

If you'd like a sneak peek first, you can find complete first-chapter excerpts from all my bestselling books at my website: lisaplumley.com. While you're there you can also sign up for personal new book alerts, download an up-to-date book list, get the scoop on upcoming books, request reader freebies and more. I hope you'll stop by today!

As always, I'd love to hear from you! You can follow me on Twitter @LisaPlumley, 'like' my Facebook page at facebook.com/lisaplumleybooks, circle me on Google+ at google.com/+LisaPlumley, visit me online at community.eharlequin.com…or just send an email to lisa@lisaplumley.com.

Best wishes, until next time.

MORROW CREEK MARSHAL

Lisa Plumley

Published in Great Britain 2015
by Mills & Boon, an imprint of Harlequin (UK) Limited,
Eton House, 18-24 Paradise Road, Richmond, Surrey, TW9 1SR

© 2015 Lisa Plumley

ISBN: 978-0-263-24824-1

Harlequin (UK) Limited's policy is to use papers that are natural,
renewable and recyclable products and made from wood grown in
sustainable forests. The logging and manufacturing processes conform
to the legal environmental regulations of the country of origin.

Printed and bound in Spain
by CPI, Barcelona

USA TODAY bestselling author **Lisa Plumley** has delighted readers worldwide with more than three dozen popular novels. Her work has been translated into multiple languages and editions, and includes Western historical romances, contemporary romances, paranormal romances, and a variety of stories in romance anthologies. She loves to hear from readers! Visit Lisa on the web, 'friend' her on Facebook, or follow her on Twitter @LisaPlumley.

To John, with all my love.

Chapter One

April 1885, Morrow Creek,
northern Arizona Territory

At Jack Murphy's popular saloon, cowboys bellied up to the bar alongside newspaper editors, mercantile owners and railway workers. Miners and lumbermen tested their luck at the gambling tables, hoping to best gullible greenhorns or visiting card sharps—or simply to suss out which men fell into which of those two categories. Music plunked out at two cents per song—but only if those bits were tipped directly into the musician's overturned bowler, which he customarily placed atop his upright corner piano. Overlying it all came the tang of whiskey, the rich haze of cigarillo smoke and the earnest hum of business being conducted, gossip being told and men being men.

Among those men, Marielle Miller felt both comfortable and celebrated. For the past twelve of her thirty years, she'd been spending her nights

in places just like Murphy's saloon, kicking up
her skirts for profit and honing her skills at dancing—and managing the men who watched her
dance. Being both applauded *and* respected by
those men was a tricky business. It was one Marielle had mastered, too. Unique among her fellow
dance hall girls, Marielle excelled at making sure
no one man stepped his spurred boots or battered
brogans out of line—or got wrongheaded ideas
about the smiles she tossed out while performing, either.

Her smiles were for show, meant to charm and
entice. As near as Marielle could tell, they rightly
did both of those things. But her smiles were all
performance, approximately as genuine as the
horsehair padding cleverly sewn into her costume
to augment the curve of her hips and the swell
of her bustline.

It wasn't that Marielle didn't enjoy dancing.
She *did*. Especially with her current close-knit
troupe and especially for a generous boss like
Jack Murphy. But she didn't particularly enjoy the
artifice involved. Or the wariness, either. More
than most girls, Marielle knew she could not
afford to invite the attention of a scoundrel. Or
any man, really. She had too many responsibilities to see to. Until those responsibilities were
properly sorted, there would be no offstage flir-
tation for her.

That's why, as Marielle stepped onstage in the

full saloon early one ordinary Thursday evening, she began by sweeping the boisterous crowd with an assessing look. It was easy to spot the infatuated ranch hand, new to Morrow Creek, who nursed a single ale while casting lovesick glances at Jobyna Lawson, Marielle's fellow dancer and closest friend. It was similarly simple to identify the high-rolling faro player who believed his string of luck at the gaming table would also assure him feminine company for the night. Fortunately, Jack Murphy's faithful barkeep and cook Harry would correct that misapprehension quickly.

The dance hall girls at Murphy's saloon weren't disreputable. Their company wasn't for sale, either.

They were all—like Marielle—entertainers, first and last.

Handily proving her proficiency at her profession, Marielle high-stepped across the stage in unison with her troupe, lit by blazing lamps and accompanied by rollicking piano music. She swooshed her skirts and then skipped to the side, executing a perfectly timed move—all while continuing her customary study of the saloon's patrons, both regulars and strangers. Alertness benefitted a dancing girl, Marielle knew. More than once, she'd been forced to duck flying bottles, shimmy away from shattering chairs or retreat to the back of the house to avoid gunfire.

At Jack Murphy's saloon, in peaceable Morrow
Creek, such antics were almost unheard of. Certainly, newcomers to town sometimes tested the
tranquility of the saloon—and the resolve of the
townspeople to keep it that way—but those ruf-
fians never got far. Typically, one or more of the
brawnier locals stepped in before disagreements
could progress to full-on brawls. When that approach failed, Sheriff Caffey and his deputy Winston were available to handle problems—at least
notionally—but most of the time, the lawmen's
intervention wasn't necessary.

It was a good thing, too. Almost everyone
in town knew that Sheriff Caffey and Deputy
Winston were too busy enjoying the privileges
of their positions to actually work on behalf of
their badges. In a less tranquil town, they would
have been ousted long ago. But in Morrow Creek,
the need for a lawman arrived as infrequently as
snow in the low country and lasted about as long.
More often than not, the members of the Morrow Creek Men's Club found a way to deal with
wrongdoers themselves.

Raising her arms and smiling more broadly,
Marielle sashayed to the opposite side of the stage,
her footsteps perfectly timed with her troupe's.
From her new vantage point, she surveyed the
men playing cards at a nearby saloon table. As the
eldest member of her company, Marielle was responsible for seeing to her fellow dancers' safety.

Even as she winked at the audience and then went on dancing, she went on watching, too.

Atop her head, her feathered and spangled headpiece bobbed with her movements, secured to her dark, upswept hair with multiple pins. Around her skipping feet, her costume's fancifully adorned skirts swirled. Her ensemble was of her own design, made for free movement and utmost prettification. It provided flash, flattery and—unlike ordinary dresses—necessary if minimal modesty during high-stepping kick routines.

Thanks to her skill with a needle and thread, Marielle augmented her income from dancing quite conveniently. Along with supplying costumes to her hardworking fellow dancers, she also took in ordinary mending, tailoring and other seamstress's work for her neighbors. Between the two—her dancing and her sewing—she'd amassed a sizable nest egg...which was undoubtedly providential, given that Marielle had begun feeling a little less excited than usual by the prospect of stepping onstage.

Just once, Marielle imagined, she'd have liked to have gone home at the end of a late evening *not* smelling of cheroots, Old Orchard and Levin's ale. She'd have liked to have had a more amenable schedule—one that didn't bring her to work at a time when most women were settling around the hearth with their families. She'd have liked to have had a family of her own, for that matter, with children to care for.

She'd have liked *not* to be required to notice—and deal with—the one dance hall girl in their troupe who was inevitably behaving foolishly.

This time, it was Etta, a girl who was newly arrived from cattle country. Unfortunately, she appeared to have about as much gracefulness and common sense as a dolled-up heifer from her hometown. Plainly unaware of the need to retain a certain sensible distance from the saloon's customers, Etta was flirting with one of them instead. Even as their current dance reached its finale, Etta broke routine to pout and pose and toss pantomime kisses at the man while bawdily tossing her skirts.

Seeing those shenanigans, Marielle groaned inwardly. It was true that they needed another dancer in their troupe. Jobyna was getting married soon to her beau, Gordon "Snub" Sterling, so she wouldn't be performing anymore. That meant replacing her was a necessity. All the same, Marielle had recommended against allowing giggly Etta to try out tonight. She knew a calamity in the making when she saw it. Softhearted Jack Murphy had seen things differently. So had his wife, infamous suffragist Grace Murphy, who believed every woman deserved a chance to shine.

Currently, Etta was shining in the direction of a particularly disreputable-looking saloongoer.

Dark haired, shadow bearded and broad shouldered, the man in Etta's sights packed eight feet of manliness in a six-foot package. He was brawny, relaxed and curiously uninterested in the glass of whiskey Harry had poured him. He was also, Marielle couldn't help noticing, wearing a gun belt with his clean and pressed dark clothes. Overall, the man had trouble written all over his attentive expression...only Etta was too dense to realize it.

Given a saloon full of potential husbands—because doubtless that's how foolish Etta saw those men who watched her dance with their tongues all but lolling—their troupe's giggly cattle country upstart had singled out the worst possible choice. He looked, to Marielle's dismay, like a typical territorial drifter—albeit, an absurdly handsome one—ready to pick up and pull foot with no notice and no cares for anyone he left behind.

But if she were honest...didn't all men look that way to her?

There wasn't a man alive who could be counted on, Marielle knew. Not the ones who wooed her with raw gold nugget tips. Not the ones who shyly stared at the saloon's sawdust-covered floor rather than meet her measuring gaze. Not the ones who proposed debauchery and ruination and an end to her wonderings about exactly what went on between cajoling men and the unwise women who loved them during a single scandalous evening at the nearby Lorndorff Hotel. Not even the ones who were related to her.

Marielle had never lacked for opportunities to give away her heart. She'd simply refused to accept any of them. Only a very reckless woman would have allowed herself to believe a man was the answer to her prayers—at least not those involving heavy equipment, exacting machinery or ornery animals…and maybe not even then. Only a woman like silly, still flirting Etta would have risked her potential employment with the company for the sake of trying to catch the eye of a wandering gunslinger.

Even as Marielle danced closer to Etta, trying to gain her cohort's attention without breaking rhythm, the drifter proved his fickleness by letting his gaze meander away from seductive, overpainted Etta…directly to Marielle. Confidently, the stranger watched her dance. His dark-eyed gaze took in her swooshing skirts, her self-assured steps and her lace-adorned bosom, each in turn, then traveled up to her face. Shockingly, his attention lingered there. It was almost as though he truly saw *her*. Not her flashy costume, not her titillating movements, not her fan or her lightly painted lips or her spangled hips. Just…her.

Deeply unsettled, Marielle faltered. On her way to silently but pointedly confront Etta, Marielle missed the next step. She could have sworn the rascal at the front row table actually quirked his lips in amusement at her mistake—but a moment later, she had larger problems to deal with. Literally. Because as she stumbled, Marielle accidentally veered in the direction of a drunken stageside cowboy who wasted no time in grabbing her.

"Yee-haw!" he whooped, clutching a fistful of spangles. "Lookee here, boys! I done lassoed myself a dance hall girl!"

More annoyed with Etta than with the cowboy—who really couldn't be expected to behave himself under the influence of that much mescal—Marielle attempted to dance away. Her exuberant admirer held fast, almost toppling her off the stage.

All right, then. The time for being accommodating was over.

Nearby, the piano player helpfully kicked into a new song, obviously noticing Marielle's predicament and trying to distract the cowboy into releasing her. Likewise, the other dancers around her sashayed into a new routine. They stepped in unison, twirling their fans. They gave winsome smiles. Their high-buttoned shoes flashed beneath their swirling skirts, providing ample entertainment with color and movement...but the cowboy held fast, even as Marielle gave a determined yank away from him.

Fine. Fed up with being patient, she flashed

him a direct, beguiling smile. Seeing it, the cowboy started. His face eased.

Any second now, he'd let her go, Marielle knew. The grabby types always did. Most of the time, they meant well. Some of the time, they even expected her to be flattered by their hamhanded attentions. Typically, when Marielle appeared to *return* their ardor, the ranch hands, cowboys and other small-time miscreants who tried to manhandle her came to their senses and behaved like gentlemen instead. Given the possibility of genuinely earning her attention, those men customarily gave up their groping.

Just as she'd known it would, the power of her smile worked its magic. The cowboy blinked. He grinned. He started to let go…

… And an instant later, all tarnation broke loose.

The drifter from the next table stood. Sternly, he said something to the cowboy. Marielle had the impression he'd been speaking to the man before then, but she hadn't heard him above the piano music. The cowboy shook his head in refusal. Then belligerently, with his fellow cowpunchers' encouragement, the cowboy shouted something back. Prudently seizing the opportunity provided by his distractedness, Marielle pulled away again.

Before she could free herself, the drifter's demeanor changed. He looked…*fearsome*. That was the only word for it.

Taken aback by the change, she gawked. Several other saloon patrons stood and shouted, rapidly choosing sides in the developing melee. Marielle had a moment to examine the newly disorderly saloon, belatedly realize that most of Morrow Creek's unofficial town leaders—including Daniel McCabe, Adam Corwin, Griffin Turner and others, weren't in attendance—and worry that things might go terribly wrong. Then the stranger pulled back his arm, grabbed the cowboy and punched him. With authority.

Dylan Coyle wasn't sure where he found the authority to deliver a sobering sockdolager to the grabby knuck who'd been manhandling the watchful, dark-haired dance hall girl. He wasn't part of Morrow Creek's self-appointed slate of local honchos. He had no duty to fulfill. In fact, he'd deliberately chosen *not* to embroil himself in a position of authority while in town.

Folks tended to want to rely on him, Dylan knew. But he was a wandering man. He wanted no part of putting down roots—especially not in a town like Morrow Creek. As a community full of like-minded homesteaders, traders, workers and families, it was as wholesome as apple dumplings and as cozy as flannel sheets. It was the wrong kind of place for a no-strings type like him. That hadn't always been the case, but it was now.

In fact, now that he was done with the job he'd

taken on in Morrow Creek—working as a security man for the mysterious proprietress of the Morrow Creek Mutual Society—Dylan was on his way *out* of town. He'd only stopped in Jack Murphy's saloon for a parting whiskey before catching the next train farther west.

But there were some things a good man couldn't put up with. Allowing a pie-eyed cowpuncher to inconvenience a woman was one of them. Letting that same knuck upset Dylan's glass of good whiskey as he'd stumbled toward the stage was another. Now, Dylan realized with a frown, every time he put on his favorite broad, flat-brimmed black hat, he'd smell like a distillery.

"Just remember," Dylan told the cowboy as the liquored-up fool swayed in his grasp, "I asked you nicely to let go. Now I'm going to ask you nicely to apologize to the lady. If you don't—"

The dupe shouted something that was *definitely* not apologetic. It wasn't suitable for ladies' delicate ears, either. Hearing it, Dylan deepened his frown. If there was anything he believed in more than the necessity of savoring a good whiskey when it came his way, it was the sanctity of women. Evidently, here in the Western territories, they brewed up cowboys on the wrong side of sensible.

"You're going to want to apologize for that, too."

As the knuck glanced up at the dance hall girl,

Dylan gave the cowboy a mighty yank, aiming to surprise the man into properly squaring off with him instead of catching hold of her sparkly skirts again. Just as he'd intended, the cowboy reeled. He gave a blustery wheeze that stank of ale, then staggered and waved his arm, too goose jointed to quickly regain his balance.

With his usual sense of fairness, Dylan waited the few ticks it would take for the cowboy to get his feet under him. He didn't want to take advantage of the man's inebriated condition. All he wanted was for the cowpoke to leave alone the dance hall girl—not the least because he'd be damned if she wasn't the oldest such female entertainer Dylan had ever encountered.

He wasn't sure she could withstand too much rough handling. Not that any woman could be expected to keep her feet when the legless cattleman who'd been clumsily pawing her staggered again, lurched, then fell plumb backward with much greater velocity than Dylan had intended.

Damnation. He hadn't thought he'd grabbed him that hard. Perceptibly, he had. He'd accidentally tipped the last domino, too. Because the cowboy *had* managed to catch hold of the damn near elderly dance hall girl again. Now Dylan's well-intentioned protectiveness had put her in an even more precarious position.

With a surprised whoop and a flurry of skirts, she fought against the sudden frontward jerk caused by the cowboy's fall. She pinwheeled her arms in a search for balance—and almost found it, too. For a single, breath-holding moment, she tottered at the stage's edge. Then her ankle buckled at an unmistakably sideways angle. Crying out, the dance hall girl pitched forward.

She was falling. Instantly seeing her predicament, Dylan lunged toward her. He held out his arms, ready to catch her. Before he could think twice about his decision, he received the gift he hadn't wanted and had no present use for: an armful of sweet-smelling, silky-haired, caterwauling female.

It all happened in an instant. With an *oof*, they both collapsed beside the cowboy on the sawdust-covered floor, saloongoers scattering to all sides of them with shouts of surprise.

Ouch. Dylan winced, still cradling her. Stupidly, as it turned out, since she'd landed atop him like a hundred-pound sack full of nothing but elbows and knees. She'd obviously been gifted with multiple sets of each—or at least that's what it felt like. He wondered where the hell her admirably curvy hips and delectably full bosom had gone. He held fast anyway.

Their ignoble pileup defused the developing saloon fight. Instead of throwing punches, saloongoers hollered, pointed and laughed. The piano music kept on tinkling. Chairs scraped backward, then were settled back into place. Dylan had a moment to register the soft roundness of the dance hall girl's rear end in his cupped hand, to experience the feathery, sneeze-inducing interference of her sparkly headpiece in his face... and then to tardily understand that she was trying to get *away* from him.

That was unusual. Most women tried to get closer to him. Given any excuse, they snuggled nearer and flirted—just like the other garishly painted and less interesting blonde dance hall girl had done earlier. But this one was different. Also, Dylan observed amid the ruckus, while parts of her body might be soft, her gouging knees and prodding elbows most certainly *weren't*.

Even as Dylan came to grips with that, the dance hall girl kneed him again, coming dangerously close to his manly bits.

Involuntarily, he loosened his hold on her. Just by a fraction, but it was enough for her to take advantage of.

That was all right with him. *Argh*. Chivalry was one thing. Volunteering to be made a functioning eunuch in an unexpected dancing girl tussle was another. Dylan valued his masculinity.

Even if *she* didn't. Clearly. With a determined final effort, the dance hall girl rolled sideways, adding a vicious and maybe not accidental belly squash to her initial blow as she went. She scrambled onto her hands and knees, then sat on her backside instead. He glimpsed her annoyed pro-

file, heard her murmured grumble of exaspera-
tion as she adjusted her feathery headpiece, and
briefly entertained the idea that she might not be
as properly grateful for his intervention as he'd
hoped.

Gingerly, Dylan moved a fraction. Everything
seemed fine in the downstairs department. He released a long, pent-up breath.

He couldn't believe he'd come to her rescue and
almost gotten himself a banged-up set of punters
for his trouble. Was she going to apologize? Or
thank him? Or even acknowledge him?

"I'm so sorry, ma'am." The cowboy's thick
drawl reached Dylan at the same time as his sense
of being affronted did. Obliviously, the knuck
kept talking. "Are you all right?"

"I was wondering the same thing about you,"
the dance hall girl had the gall to say—*to the
cowboy.* "Are you hurt bad?"

Dylan glanced up in time to see the fool's shy
smile.

"I'm just fine, ma'am. It's yourself I'm worried about."

The cowboy's weathered hand—sporting a
full set of predictably grime-encrusted finger-
nails—entered Dylan's field of vision. Evidently,
the cowhand had discovered gallantry. He was
trying to help the dance hall girl up off the floor.
She seemed to be hesitant about that. She also

seemed, as she frowned anew, concerned about putting too much weight on her injured ankle.

Rightly so, Dylan reckoned. That onstage crumple had looked serious. Ankles, feet and legs weren't meant to go in contradictory directions— not while connected to the same person. Thanks to her whirling skirts, he'd had a clear enough view to know that's exactly what had happened to her a second ago.

"I didn't mean to trip you up." The cowboy offered dubious encouragement by waggling his filthy fingers at her. "I'm awful sorry about that, ma'am. It's just that you're so pretty. I plumb couldn't help myself. Catching ahold of you was like catching a beautiful, sparkling star, right here at Murphy's."

Still on the floor, Dylan rolled his eyes. Then he got to his own hands and knees, counting on getting upright in time to help the dance hall girl to her feet himself. As he should.

"Well, aren't you sweet?" she cooed to the cow-puncher while she cautiously tested her ankle's strength, speaking just as pleasantly as though the fool *hadn't* caused her to fall offstage. "It's only too bad that I never, *ever* go spoony over men who frequent saloons. It's my one ironclad rule, you see."

"You…what?" The cowboy whined with confusion. Then regret. Then resignation. "But if I weren't here at the saloon, I wouldn't never have seen you in the first place, now, would I? So you wouldn't have needed any rules about me to begin with."

"No." She sighed, then pulled an elaborately regretful face—a markedly pale one, probably on account of the pain. "Isn't that the devil of it? It's a conundrum, all right." She panted. "You're awfully clever to notice that. I do *very* much appreciate your kindness, all the same. I sincerely do."

As Dylan nimbly got up—the whole endeavor having taken a few seconds at most but feeling like much longer—he glimpsed the cowboy's crestfallen expression. It was evident that the man didn't know how to begin arguing against the dance hall girl's convoluted logic. She was being so all-fired sugary about it that he couldn't very well object outright, either. She actually seemed…*disappointed* not to have those grubby hands on her.

Against his will, Dylan admired her gumption. Her fortitude in withstanding the discomfort of her injury. And her cleverness in making her turndown of the man both impersonal and final, too. Most likely, she'd had years—given her advancing age of probably twenty-eight or so—of disarming unwanted suitors. She'd learned to do so capably and kindly, without stirring up unnecessary rancor in the process.

Also without damaging her saloon-owning boss's business, Dylan couldn't help noting. Given a fair choice, no man would choose to forgo the whiskey and companionship available at a good saloon—not even in favor of wooing a woman. Doubtless, Jack Murphy would applaud that tactic—then ask her to teach that technique to the other dancers, besides. A few of them looked as though they needed more than a thimbleful of her good sense.

As he shouldered forward to help her stand, then to let her lean sideways on him, Dylan found himself appreciating her unexpected gentleness in letting down the cowboy almost as much as he admired her ingeniousness in doing so. But he'd rather be hog-tied and left wearing nothing but boots in a blizzard than admit it. First, because he wasn't a man who went all mush-hearted over other people's business. Second, because...well, where in tarnation was the damn appreciation she owed *him*?

He was the one who'd saved her from that blundering, overeager cowpuncher in the first place. He was the one who was holding her upright at that very moment! He deserved a smile at the very least—and a whole passel of thank-yous at the most.

Instead, the dance hall girl teetered in his arms. Setting his mouth in a straight line, Dylan half held, half hauled her to a marginally quieter spot away from the stage. There, she tried to put her weight on her right leg. She grimaced. Her face turned even ghostlier. With growing concern, Dylan steadied her.

"You're hurt!" Predictably two steps behind the situation, the cowboy rubbernecked. He scrambled to rustle up a chair for her. Lickety-split, he shoved it under her caboose. "Here."

Gratefully, she sank onto that support. Gamely, she beamed up at that troublemaking bootlicker of a cowpuncher, just as though he deserved her gratefulness for getting her injured.

She didn't say a solitary word to Dylan, kind or otherwise. She only compressed her pretty lips, then frowned at her ankle while the saloon's usual hurly-burly proceeded just beyond them.

"You'd do best to elevate that sore ankle," Dylan advised gruffly, mindful of the need for quick action. He knelt at her skirts, then expertly delved his hands beneath their spangled hems to test what he suspected was grave damage to her ankle.

Before he could do more than graze her high-buttoned shoe and skim his fingers up to her stocking-clad ankle to gauge the swelling he expected to find there, the minx *kicked* him.

Instant pain exploded in his knee. "Ouch!"

Her eyes narrowed. "Next time, I'll aim higher."

Her gaze fixed menacingly in the vicinity of his gun belt. Ordinarily, Dylan didn't wear it. Not anymore. But when traveling alone across multiple states and territories, he did.

As much as he didn't like it, sometimes he needed…backing.

Feeling provoked, Dylan glared back. He nudged his chin at the cowboy. "How come *he* gets a spoonful of sugar from you, and *I* get a big dose of vinegar? I'm the one who helped you."

"Near as I can tell, *you're* the one who made me get dragged offstage in the middle of my performance." With a worried frown, the dance hall girl glanced toward the stage, where her fellow dancers were currently high-kicking in the glow of the lights.

The show had to go on, Dylan guessed. That seemed fairly coldhearted to him, though. He'd thought his line of work was hard-nosed—and it was—but there was more to skirt tossing than he'd first realized, it seemed. There was more to her, too.

Contrariness, for instance. Also, plenty of obtuseness.

"I was protecting you!" Dylan objected. It was past time to set her straight. Maybe, he reasoned, the pain had made her light-headed. That would explain her poor grasp of the situation.

"No, you were picking on poor—" She broke off, glancing at the cowboy for his name. After what felt like enough time for Dylan to turn gray-haired and stooped, the befuddled cowpoke finally blurted it out. "—Rufus, here, when your intervention was entirely unnecessary. I had matters well in hand."

"Near as I could tell, *Rufus* had matters well in hand."

"A miscreant like you *would* concentrate on the disreputable side of things, wouldn't you? That is a very rude comment."

"Very rude," Rufus put in, looking belligerent.

The dance hall girl put her hand on his mud-spackled wrist in a calming gesture. Unreasonably, Dylan resented her caring.

At the same time, grudgingly, he admired how well-spoken she was. How indomitable. How courageous. He knew good men who would not have dared to speak to him in the tone she'd used.

"I didn't require your 'help,'" she informed him further.

"She *didn't* require your help," said myna bird Rufus.

Dylan gave him a quelling look. Sensibly, the man cowered.

"What you require is treatment for that ankle." He cast her gaudy skirts a concerned look. "If you'd just let me see—"

"Are you a doctor?"

"I promise you, I'm better qualified than whatever backwoods sawbones you're going to find in Morrow Creek."

"Then you're *not* a doctor." She eyed Rufus.

"I'm terribly sorry to impose on you this way, Rufus, but would you mind very much fetching Doc Finney for me? Harry can tell you how."

The cowboy hesitated. It was evident that he wanted to linger—that he was having second thoughts about her avowed "no saloongoers" courtship policy. Helping him along the path of a true believer, Dylan scowled at him. "Good idea," he growled.

While the knuck was gone, *he* would settle things here. Starting by getting her *out* of the noisy saloon and into someplace more conducive to a proper medical evaluation.

He hadn't spent years as a Pinkerton detective, then more years as a lumberman doing dangerous work in largely unmapped territory, then more years as a private security man for hire, without acquiring a necessary quantity of medical knowledge. In his time, he'd extracted bullets—sometimes from himself—set broken limbs, stitched up knife wounds and kept at least one man from bleeding to death in the middle of nowhere. To him, treating a turned ankle—no matter how serious—was a walkover.

Not that he meant to tell anyone that. He wasn't a medical man, per se. He was just a man who didn't like leaving loose ends. From the moment the dance hall girl had tumbled offstage, she'd temporarily become his responsibility to see to.

Noticing that Rufus hadn't left yet, Dylan gave

him another glare. Obediently, the cowpuncher scurried off, hat in hand.

The moment he'd gone, the dance hall girl aimed a self-assured look at Dylan. "See? Rufus is doing exactly as I asked him to. I had this situation perfectly under control all along—until *you* blundered in with your fisticuffs."

She hadn't had anything "under control." Dylan knew damn well that Rufus had only done as she'd bade because *he* had intimidated the man into compliance with that final scowl. How that fact had escaped her notice was beyond him—although she was in obvious discomfort, so she probably wasn't herself just then.

"I'll thank you to leave me alone now," she added.

Her imperious tone wrested a rueful grin from him.

He'd wager *that* was her true self, despite everything.

"All right. I'll go." Contrarily, Dylan pulled up an empty chair. He sat across from her, rested his forearms on his thighs, then gave a carefree nod. "Just as soon as you get up from that chair and get yourself back onstage."

Chapter Two

Sucking in a deep, pain-filled breath, Marielle met the stranger's gaze dead-on. He knew full well she couldn't just get up off that chair and get back onstage. Not in the condition she was in. She'd tested her ankle. It hadn't borne her weight.

Instead, it had made agony shoot clear up her leg and nearly overwhelm her. Reacting helplessly, she'd clutched the stranger's muscular shoulder so hard that she knew by now he must be developing fingertip-size bruises beneath his fancy coat and collared shirt. He knew she couldn't just gallivant onstage.

What's more, he knew that she knew that he knew that.

People didn't typically challenge Marielle. She'd been born charming her mama and papa and all the stagehands at the New York theater where they'd worked. She'd grown up knowing how to finagle her way…and, more important, how to make people *want* for her to get her way. It was a knack she had never questioned.

"Or," the stranger went on in that selfsame blithe manner, his tone belying his handsome face full of concern, "you can come with me to the back of the house, let me fix up your ankle and maybe have a snort of applejack brandy for the pain, too."

That sounded…tempting. But she refused to give in. She didn't even know this man. He looked like a scoundrel to her.

A scoundrel was the very last thing she needed. Over the years, she'd turned down the assistance of several reputable men. Why would she abandon her practical path for a rake like him?

She managed an airy wave, trying not to betray that her ankle was throbbing. "I'll wait for a proper doctor, thank you."

"I'm *better* than a 'proper' doctor," he assured her with a steady look, occupying his chair with assurance and vigor. He looked as though he could have whittled the dratted thing. Possibly with a huge bowie knife…which he kept strapped to his person like the bad man he was. "And you're wasting time."

"I don't need your assistance, Mr.—"

"Coyle. Dylan Coyle."

"—Coyle. I don't even know you. Except to know that I find your air of nonchalance and entitlement completely irksome." Earlier, privately, she'd found his steady and sure touch as he'd boldly examined her ankle downright...*galvanizing*. But she was certainly not going to inform him of that. She'd found the wherewithal to deliver him an aptly discouraging kick, and that had been that. Marielle Miller was no pushover. "I'd thank you to leave me alone. I'm injured. *You* are the cause of that. So—"

"That," he said patiently, "is why I'm trying to help."

"Aha." She didn't want to be small-minded. But she *did* want him to admit his obvious wrongness. Between being hurt and being upset with him, Marielle wasn't her most clear-eyed and generous self. "Then you admit that *you* were at fault? Good. Thank you."

His brown eyes flared. Arrestingly. "I said no such thing."

"Humph." Why on earth was she noticing his eyes at a time like this? Determinedly, Marielle went on. "Of course you did. Just now. And the fact remains that I had things under control—"

His interposing snort was infuriating. So was the way she couldn't help noticing how finely honed his jawline was, how masculine his nose was, how intelligent his demeanor was.

Good-natured yokels, she was used to handling. A man like him? He was another beast entirely. She wasn't sure she knew what to do about him. But she knew backing down wasn't possible.

For her, it wasn't even an option.

"—until *you* interfered and got me dragged offstage," Marielle went on, deliberately transferring her gaze away from his eyes…only to notice how attractively his dark hair swept back from his face. An errant wave tumbled over his forehead, lending him a newly boyish look that she understood to be false.

Dylan Coyle was all man. Tall. Handsome. Not to be trusted.

"Your fall was an accident," Coyle assured her, seemingly sincerely. His husky tone soothed her, despite everything. "I never meant for you to get caught up the way you did. I saw that cowboy manhandling you. I set out to put a stop to it. I did."

"I wish you hadn't." Purposely, Marielle glanced away from their semisecluded corner. Rufus the cowboy was still nowhere in sight. She hoped he really had gone to fetch Doc Finney, the way she'd suggested. If not…well, she'd be stuck with her unwanted, self-appointed protector—at least until her younger brother, Hudson, turned up to assist her. He ought to be someplace inside Murphy's saloon. They'd come there together. "As I said, I was handling it. Of the two of us, *I* have the most experience, expertise and aptitude at discouraging suitors."

His grin flashed. "I wouldn't be too sure about that."

She flicked her gaze over his broad-shouldered form, neat clothes and open, self-assured posture. Most likely, women did pursue him. Not that such brazen behavior mattered to her. Marielle inhaled. "Aside from which, I have my own protectors—"

At that, Coyle had the audacity to scoff. He emanated certainty, strength and outright authority the way some men—like poor, misguided Rufus—exuded confusion and bodily odors.

"—who can come to my aid," she went on, wincing as a fresh wave of ankle pain struck her, "so I certainly don't need—"

"You're hurting," Coyle interrupted, suddenly out of forbearance for their conversation. As she opened her mouth to protest, he shook his head. "Don't try to deny it. Just let me take a look. Please. I'll wrap it up for stability, then..."

As he went on describing a potential treatment for her injury, he sounded startlingly knowledgeable. More surprisingly, he sounded caring. Despite his rough tone and imperious manner, Dylan Coyle appeared to be both bright and kind. Darn him.

All the same, Marielle didn't want him probing under her skirts again. No good could come of that. Even if, in that single shocking moment, she'd been tempted to let him continue.

Purely for the sake of good medicine. Of course.

"I've been hurt before." *Not like this, though,*

she knew. Something in her ankle had snapped. She'd felt it give way beneath her. That was part of the reason she was so infuriated with him. Thanks to him, she was in a verifiable pickle.

If she couldn't dance, she couldn't earn a living.

Still, Marielle didn't want Dylan Coyle's help—or anyone else's. Except Doc Finney's. Even his, only reluctantly.

She knew better than to become reliant on other people. Growing up backstage, she'd seen how frequently people came and went, leaving her behind with typical bonhomie. Taking care of herself was nobody's business but her own. Mustering another airy wave, she assured him, "I'm stronger than I look. I know what I'm talking about—dancers get injured fairly often."

Coyle gave her an evaluative look—one she fancied included *him* enjoying *her* appearance in the same way that she'd mooned over his a few seconds ago. Why was she so addlepated, anyway?

Doubtless, she reasoned, her nonsensicalness owed itself to the pain. All the same, it would be only fair if Coyle dished out a compliment for her bravery. Or offered up some praise for her dancing. Or composed a sonnet to her "cerulean blue" eyes, the way a ranch hand from Everett Bannon's place had done last year, with the probable help of a thesaurus and memorable—if doomed—romanticism. If not for Hudson needing her, in fact, Marielle might have given in to that ranch hand. Eventually.

Her unshared secret was that she *adored* all things dreamy and sentimental. Maybe because she didn't expect to enjoy them for herself. Not for years and years yet.

"Hurt fairly often, eh? Hmm." He rubbed his stubbled jaw, examining her carefully. "Especially at your age, I'd imagine."

"What?"

"You're getting on, that's all," Coyle clarified in a blasé tone. "After all, you must be…what, thirty-three or so?"

"Thirty-three?" Marielle gawked at him. He'd aged her by three years in an instant! A moment ago, she'd been feeling woozy with pain. But now her clarity was fully restored. "I'll thank you, Mr. Coyle, *not* to comment on my age. Or anything else about me! I am not interested in your opinions. What I *am* interested in is having your apology and maybe some recompense for this disastrous incident. Because this is all your fault—"

"I'm sorry. I've gone and made you angry."

"Indeed, you have!" Of course he had. *Thirty-three?*

"I didn't mean to disregard your experience." Coyle gave her a keen look. His eyes sparkled. "Your *vast* experience."

That was more like it. Proudly, Marielle lifted

her chin. "For your information, I am *not* thirty-three years old."

"Ah." He roamed his gaze over her again with nearly the same perceptiveness he'd employed while she'd been onstage. He rubbed his whisker-stubbled jaw. He nodded. "You're thirty-five. I have to say, ma'am, that while *you* are a very fine specimen of womanhood, it's no wonder your feeble ankle snapped so readily."

Speechless, Marielle stared at him. Had he said…*feeble*?

He actually grinned, looking pleased. Intolerably so.

"I am *not* feeble," she informed him. "*You* are deluded."

"I've never seen a dance hall girl with so much…maturity," Coyle opined. "No wonder you're the one pictured on the fancy painted sign in front of the saloon." He gave her a look full of wonderment. "You make those other girls look like novices."

Confused, Marielle squinted at him. He sounded pleasant, but… "That's hardly complimentary—to me *or* my fellow dancers."

Not clarifying, he studied her…probably looking for the old crone's wrinkles he expected to find. Of all the audacious—

"*You're* older than me," she shot back. "By a year or more."

Coyle raised his brows. "You think I'm forty?"

She earnestly considered kicking him again. Harder than before. It wouldn't be polite, but he did deserve it.

Before she could do so, he laughed. That act transformed his whole being. It turned him from a very attractive man to a downright fascinating one. Drat. How did he keep doing that?

He was enjoying himself so much, Marielle almost wanted to join in the frivolity. Instead, she gave him a peevish look.

"I'm thirty-two, Miss Miller, plus a month or six."

Hearing her name on his lips, Marielle frowned. "How do you know my name? We haven't met. If you expect me to believe—"

"That I divined it? If you must. Be my guest."

His teasing didn't deter her. "The sign. My name is on it."

She'd negotiated strictly for that with Jack Murphy.

"Right alongside your likeness," Coyle confirmed. He tilted his head to observe her. "Paint doesn't do you justice, though."

"*Hmmph*. It didn't lead you to expect geriatric dancing?"

"It didn't lead me to expect to be helping a stubborn dance hall girl quit thinking about her injury. But that's working out all right." He nodded toward her ankle. "I bet it doesn't hurt as much now, does it? Outrage cures everything."

Marielle was startled to realize it did. It had. At least momentarily. Her expression of relief clearly revealed as much.

Charitably, Coyle let his small victory go unremarked upon.

"I've already apologized," he said instead. "I'm very sorry you got hurt. But as far as reparation for your injury goes, I doubt that your cowboy has the means to pay for the damage he's done here tonight. So if I were you—"

"I meant *you* should pay, you cretin! Thanks to you, I won't be able to dance for days, if not weeks." Judging by the growing throbbing in her ankle, her injury was indeed serious. She doubted she would be able to remove her dancing shoes when she got home tonight. They would have to be cut off. Then replaced. That would cost money. So would food. Housing. Fuel for her stove. Tallying her expenses, Marielle grew ever more alarmed at her predicament. "The way I see it," she said, "you owe me."

For the first time, Coyle seemed taken aback.

Could he…did he truly believe he'd been *helping* her? As far as she could tell, he'd been spoiling for a scuffle. Men often were when imbibing. She had unfortunately provided an impetus.

Now here they were, deadlocked on what to do next.

"I don't owe anyone anything," Coyle disagreed darkly. "That's the way I like it. That's the way I intend to keep it. I'm going to fix your ankle. Then I'm leaving Morrow Creek."

Leaving. That confirmed all her misgivings about him. It was too bad, really, Marielle thought. She almost liked him.

It wouldn't pay to let him know that. Quite literally.

"I am not interested in your travel plans, Mr. Coyle." With a purposely regretful look, Marielle glanced from their position in the very back of the saloon to the crowded saloon floor itself. There was a ruckus near the front doors as several men entered. She'd need to make this quick, in case Doc Finney was arriving and this was her last chance to be heard. "I'd hoped that further... encouragement...wouldn't be necessary for you to do right by me in my predicament. But now that I see it is..."

Meaningfully, she let her threatening statement linger.

"You expect your neighbors to force me to pay? Is that it?" Coyle gave a knowing headshake. "I see you looking to them for help, but I promise you, I know most of these men. They know me. They won't go against me. Not even at your insistence."

Undoubtedly, he'd scared them into that stance, Marielle guessed. Above all else, Dylan Coyle was intimidating.

"You don't know my brother, Mr. Hudson

Miller. I'm afraid he'll be *very* unhappy to hear that you won't help me."

Doing her utmost to appear apprehensive over what Hudson might do to assuage his unhappiness, Marielle bit her lip.

Thankfully, Coyle appeared to swallow her pretense.

"Are you suggesting your brother will force me to pay you for your lost work time?" he asked. "Because if you are—"

"Hudson is awfully large. And strong. And *very* mean."

Uttering that last outright fib, Marielle all but expected to be struck by lightning. If Hudson ventured closer, her threat would fall apart like crepe paper on a rainy day. Because while Hudson was indeed big and burly, he was anything but malicious.

That's why Marielle had dedicated herself to caring for him, all by herself, from before they'd arrived in Morrow Creek. Hudson needed her. He was a sweet, softhearted soul who had a sense of fun where his ambition ought to have been. Hudson would have been lost without her. She'd supported them both for years. She didn't aim to quit now. She'd made promises to that effect.

"Is Hudson 'mean' enough to make you agree to have your ankle treated?" Coyle inquired. "Because if he is, bring him over and let him supervise while I tend to it the way I tried to before. That injury is only getting worse the more you dally."

She couldn't do that. Hudson was approximately as menacing as a gamboling puppy. He was probably inebriated, what's more. That was the cost of having her brother at Murphy's saloon to watch over her. He drank. He gambled, smoked and caroused, too. But he didn't exactly terrorize bystanders, even with his size and his strength. He would greet Coyle like a long-lost friend.

Caught, Marielle swallowed hard. She looked away.

"I told you, I don't need anybody's help!"

She never had. She refused to now. Period. But her outburst was as good as an admission of defeat. Her erstwhile "protector" didn't let it pass unnoticed, either. His expression hardened.

"You are confusing obduracy with strength," Coyle told her in an unyielding tone. "Everybody needs help sometimes."

Exasperated and hurting, Marielle glowered at him. "I also don't need some drifter with a ten-dollar vocabulary and a gun belt telling me what to do and how to do it. If you're too skint to make good on the trouble you've caused, just own up to it."

"This isn't about money, and you know it." His gaze wandered to her face. Held. "It's about getting what's coming to you. Having the ledger squared. We're the same in that way. Trouble is, we're going about it from opposite directions."

The same. Could they be? All Marielle knew was that at those words, the raucous saloon fell away, pushed like daytime before night. She frowned at Coyle, struck by his perspicacity.

She did want fairness to prevail. She didn't want to be disadvantaged. If he was speaking truthfully, he felt the same way. No one had ever truly understood her. Yet here he was…

…Trying to manipulate her into granting him his wishes. Which she didn't need to do. Doc Finney would deal with her ankle, very soon now. Letting a stranger tend to it—especially now—felt like surrendering. Marielle refused to be cowed.

For Hudson's sake and her own, she'd always been strong.

"We're *not* alike," she objected in no uncertain terms, vexed at his nerve. "You're nothing but a drifter, and I'm—"

"Allergic to a man with a wandering foot?" Coyle guessed. His eyes sparkled again, making him seem absolutely unlike someone who would start a saloon brawl with a cowboy. "You say *drifter* as if it's poisonous. I like *traveling man* better. It sounds jaunty. Nobody can object to that."

"Whatever you call it, it means leaving someone behind."

His smile dimmed. Thankfully for her. Because seeing its brilliance had made Marielle feel…captivated. Also, disinclined to press the issue of her fair compensation for lost work with him. But she was the one who charmed people into forgetting themselves and their goals. Not him. It couldn't be him.

"Not putting down roots isn't a crime. It's freedom."

"It's selfishness," she disagreed. "And it's cruel."

"Cruel? Look here, Miss Miller, this is getting a mite too personal for my taste. Whatever somebody did to you, you can't pin it on me. Like you said, we've never met before tonight."

"And yet you claim to know me so well."

"I—" On the verge of disagreeing, Coyle stopped. He squinted at her with far more astuteness than she liked. "I am letting myself be diverted by you, just like you were by me." He seemed oddly impressed. "You don't want me to look at your ankle again, so you're concocting a cockamamie theory to dissuade me."

She had been. But she'd gotten carried away with her own hyperbole. A flair for the dramatic did run in her family, but Marielle saw life lightly—much more lightly than she'd let on just now. Coyle didn't know that about her, though. "Aha." She nodded. "There's another one of those pricy words of yours."

"You understand them all, and you know it," Coyle told her. "You're a dancing girl on the outside, but you're a damn poet on the inside. That's why you keep watch up there onstage."

"I 'keep watch' because men like you start fights!"

"You keep watch because you want more. Why wouldn't you?" He aimed another knowing look at her. "You can't very well let it sneak on by when you're not on the lookout. So you watch."

He was right. Of course he was. Because after all, the other dance hall girls were grown women who could take care of themselves without her. Even Etta. But she refused to say so.

Marielle wasn't even sure what more she wanted. Only that it felt hazy and essential…and eternally out of her grasp.

For a heartbeat, they only looked at one another—two people pulled together in a boisterous, plain-hewn saloon in a faraway, lonesome territory. Two people who were surprisingly the same.

Marielle liked *that* even less than her ankle injury.

"You want a husband and a passel of babies," Coyle went on, "which would be only fitting and natural for an older woman."

Argh. He was, quite possibly, the worst know-it-all she had ever encountered. Why had she even entertained the notion that he understood her? Commiserated with her? *Needed*…like her?

He was a blowhard and a tyrant, born to boss people around and take charge. She was through inveigling him. She would find another way to support herself until her injury healed.

But Coyle wasn't done deciding her future for her yet. Musingly, he studied the saloon. "I reckon there are several men here who'd suit you. You look like the settling down type. You should pick one of them, retire from dancing and start having babies."

That sounded like heaven. *Except* coming from him.

Marielle cast him a scathing look, only to see him grin unrepentantly in response. He was enjoying baiting her.

"Oh, why won't you just go away?" she grumped.

"Because you're a woman who won't admit she's wrong, and I'm a man who won't leave his responsibilities behind him." Coyle stood. He held out his arms as though entertaining every expectation she'd jump into them. "Come to the back room. I'll look at your ankle in private. We'll see what can be done."

Marielle was hurt. She was tired. She was confused and worried and unsure how far her nest egg of savings would go.

Given all that, she wanted to concede—to give up trying to make him settle with her and just let him tend to her ankle the way he wanted to. On the verge of doing so, though, she spied more movement from the saloon's floor. Doc Finney was headed her way, having evidently spoken with a few of the men around him to discern her location. He was accompanied by Jack Murphy, Daniel McCabe, Owen Cooper and several other leaders of the town.

Wearing a frown on his lined and weary face, Morrow Creek's longtime physician scanned the crowd. He spied Marielle. He walked faster, carrying his hat and physician's bag.

Finally. She was about to be well quit of Dylan Coyle.

Alertly, Marielle sat straighter in her chair. She thought she could make it to the saloon's back room, if she had a little help. Since several of the town's burliest men had accompanied Doc Finney to the saloon, she could ask someone she knew to help her. Then she could see the back of Mr. Coyle. For good.

Unexpectedly, the notion made her feel…almost wistful.

Her melancholy didn't last long, though. Because to Marielle's surprise, even as she prepared to make that arduous journey to the saloon's back room, Doc Finney did not rush to her side. He did not open his physician's bag, extract a miracle cure and fix her. He didn't even *try* to do those things.

Instead, he spied Dylan Coyle—who stood

with his back to the room and thus couldn't see Doc Finney approaching—and hurried nearer. He raised his arm. "Coyle! There you are!"

Coyle turned. "Doc!" His jovial greeting extended to the other men. "McCabe. Cooper." They all shook hands. Heartily. The others—men Marielle had known for years now—gazed at the drifter through respectful eyes. "Murphy, you owe me a new hat," Coyle teased. "One that's not soaked clean through with whiskey."

"The hell I do!" Marielle's boss returned. "When you drink in my place, you can't expect to come out looking like a dandy."

They went on joshing with one another, trading back slaps and jokes. Taken aback by their good-humored meeting, Marielle frowned. She adjusted her feathered headpiece, then pointedly smoothed her skirts. Any second now, they would come to their senses and properly tend to her injury. Surely they would.

She cleared her throat, attempting to make sure of that.

"We thought we might miss you, Coyle," Daniel McCabe, the town blacksmith, was saying. "I'm glad to see we didn't."

Cooper agreed. "You were supposed to come to the Morrow Creek Men's Club meeting. We needed you there. There's been a certifiable emergency in town." The livery stable owner eyed his friends. "I told you we should've hog-tied him and brought him."

They all guffawed. A few more men drifted nearer, drawn by their boisterous conversation. Marielle sat alone, all but hidden behind hotelier Griffin Turner, detective Adam Corwin and lumber mill owner Marcus Copeland, each of whom took their turns greeting Dylan Coyle. At the center of their attention, Coyle ably held his own with handshakes and rough-edged banter.

For a self-professed wandering man, Marielle couldn't help noticing grumpily from the shadows, Coyle had certainly managed to forge some strong connections in Morrow Creek. Her friends and neighbors seemed to hold him in very high regard.

"Excuse me!" she called. "Doctor Finney? A word, please?"

The town's curmudgeonly physician didn't hear her.

Frustrated, Marielle tried again. More loudly.

The only person who heard her was Hudson. He broke through the ring of men surrounding Mr. Coyle, all of them chattering away, then spied Marielle on her chair. Her brother shouted.

"Mari!" Almost six and a half feet tall, possessed of a powerful build and a headful of shoulder-length dark brown hair that matched his coffee-colored eyes, Hudson lumbered forward. He was neither graceful nor formidable, but he *was* beloved by Marielle. At the sight of her brother, she sagged with relief.

"I heard you were hurt!" He knelt at her chair, looking her over for what he plainly expected to be calamitous bumps and bruises. He grasped her hand. "I'm sorry I wasn't here sooner. I, uh, stepped outside for a while. The next thing I knew, some cowboy was rushing by, shouting for Doc Finney like a darn fool." Hudson scoffed, sending ale fumes wafting toward her. He smelled of cheroot smoke, too. "Everybody knows Doc was at the men's club meeting, but I guess that broke up. Anyway, I—"

"Can you get me out of here, please?"

Hudson balked. "You aren't done dancing already, are you?"

His disappointment was palpable...and understandable, too. He didn't want to cut short his evening of fun. While she was dancing onstage, Hudson always promised to linger nearby for her "protection." In actuality, her brother spent most of his time drinking and carousing. Sometimes gambling. Marielle knew he meant well. After all, if not for her profession, he would not have been exposed to so many objectionable influences at all.

Hudson's potential ruination was partly her fault.

"I'm afraid," she admitted, "that I'm done

dancing for quite a while." She didn't want to worry him by saying how long.

New concern shadowed his face. "You're hurt *bad*? Where?"

"My ankle." Ruefully, Marielle glanced in its direction. That traitorous "feeble" appendage might take weeks to heal. "If you could please just ask Doc Finney to meet us at home—"

"Of course! Of course I will." Her brother squeezed her hand. "Anything you need, Mari. You know you can count on me."

"She'd better be able to." Jack Murphy separated himself from the crowd. Judging by his solemn expression, he'd been informed of Marielle's situation—and had heard her own gloomy pronouncement of her prognosis, too. He pushed a glass in her hand. "Drink this. I'll send the doctor to you straightaway."

"This is a double whiskey!" Marielle objected.

"It'll help. Trust me." Jack turned to Hudson, even as the Dylan-Coyle-centered melee went on behind him. "She'll do better at home, where it's quiet. Make sure she gets some rest."

Irked, Marielle cleared her throat. "I'm right here!"

"I'll listen to you," Jack informed her with a devilish gleam in his Irish eyes, "after you down that medicinal snort."

Expeditiously, she did. It burned all the way down. *Ugh*.

Eyes watering, Marielle persisted. "I already told Hudson to take me home, Jack. You needn't interfere. I have this well in hand." A surprising warmth spread through her, kindled by the liquor she'd consumed. "I'll be back within days. Don't worry."

Hudson took away her glass. He nodded at her. "Ready?"

Marielle murmured her assent. She held out her hand, ready for her brother to help her to her feet in a dignified fashion.

Instead, he saved time by scooping her outright into his massive arms, then cradling her to his chest. Marielle couldn't help whooping in surprise, then clutching him. She gave him a swat, feeling relieved and displeased in equal measure. She loved Hudson. She knew he'd care for her, however inexpertly. But she didn't like being treated like a helpless child.

"Days," she promised Jack sternly, desperate to make sure he wouldn't hire someone to replace her. "I heal quickly."

"You'll take as long as you need," her boss countered.

But Marielle knew she couldn't do that. "I can't afford to stay home languishing! You know that. Without a steady income—"

But Jack Murphy had an answer for that, too.

"I'll give you half pay, for as long as you're laid up—"

"What?" She was astounded. His offer went above and beyond what any dancer could expect. "That's so generous of you."

"—as long as you rest up and follow orders."

Humph. Marielle wrinkled her nose. Naturally, there were conditions attached to Jack's munificence. It was almost as if they all *expected* her to flout doctor's orders, charge ahead on her own authority and handle this situation however she liked.

It was almost as if they all knew her, Jack included.

Dratted know-it-alls. No adult man would have had to agree to "follow orders" under threat of penury. Why should she?

She could take care of herself and darn well would.

"Making a cranky face," Jack observed, "is not agreeing."

"Don't you think I know that?" Marielle asked.

Hudson chuckled. She felt the vibration of his laughter.

"That's why I'm pressing the issue," Jack said. "We've known each other for years now, remember? My saloon was just a wee upstart when I brought you and your troupe to Morrow Creek."

Marielle remembered. Daniel McCabe had built the stage she danced on with his own two blacksmithing hands. Catching a glimpse of

Jack's expectant expression, she knew what he wanted.

She wasn't ready to give him her agreement, though.

"You all think you're so clever, don't you?" she groused.

"I don't." Holding her in his arms, Hudson shrugged. He gave her an endearing grin. "But I agree with Jack about this."

"Traitor." Stubbornly, Marielle frowned at them both. But a second later, her head began swimming with the aftereffects of the whiskey. It was the only explanation for what happened next. "Fine," she agreed. "I'll behave myself! I promise. All right?"

"All right." Jack nodded. So did Hudson.

Then he swept her out of the saloon and into the night.

Chapter Three

At some point, Dylan realized that Doc Finney had left the cluster of men surrounding him. Until that moment, he'd been keeping a firm eye on the reedy physician. It was imperative to get the doctor's treatment for the dance hall girl. But between one joke and the next—between one urgent statement about the dire emergency facing the town and the next—Dylan lost him.

He hadn't expected to be swamped by Morrow Creek's take-charge menfolk, all of them eager to get his attention—and his opinion on the crisis they'd discussed at the men's club that evening. Truthfully, when Dylan had spied the group of men coming into Murphy's saloon, he'd thought they were there for Marielle Miller. Especially the doctor. It had certainly looked that way. As one, they'd turned their heads toward the dance hall girl's position, perked up, then beelined straight there.

It turned out, though, that they'd beelined toward *him*.

Since that turn of events, Dylan had been unable to avoid all the backslapping, camaraderie, jokes and gossip they'd surrounded him with. He hadn't invited it. But he also hadn't been idly jawing to Miss Miller earlier. He *did* know these men. They knew him. During his short stay in Morrow Creek, he'd taken part in some important goings-on, mostly involving his employer at the Morrow Creek Mutual Society, the conniving brute who'd followed her West and the thugs that reprobate had employed.

In the aftermath of that incident, Dylan and the other men—Murphy, Copeland, McCabe, Corwin and several more, along with his fellow security men Seth Durant and Judah Foster—had assembled a posse and seen that justice was done. Rightly so.

But if they now believed that his onetime participation in a single necessary manhunt meant he wanted to join their damn men's club and spend his days being gradually nailed down to one place, fenced in by friendship and obligation and belonging…

Well, they needed to think again.

"…Caffey is still on the loose. The bastard got away," Miles Callaway was telling everyone, explaining the emergency that faced them to those listening saloongoers who, like Dylan, hadn't been at the meeting that night. The dance hall girls had taken their usual midevening break to change costumes. The saloon had quieted somewhat, even as the faro games and drinking continued. "Deputy Winston wasn't so lucky," Callaway went on. "The federal marshals already took him off to Yuma Prison."

"He deserves it. Caffey deserves worse." Clayton Davis, the lumberman who said so, made a grim face. There was no love lost between him and the deputy—or the sheriff, for that matter.

As near as Dylan could gather, Caffey had absconded a few days ago under mysterious circumstances. The townspeople were still trying to understand what could have made their longtime sheriff leave his badge and his post. He'd skedaddled just steps ahead of the marshals who'd closed in on his hapless deputy.

None of them, though, would miss Caffey. They were right not to, Dylan knew. The lawman had abused his authority, plain and simple. More than a few of the good men present had themselves been unjustly detained by Caffey at one time or another, under one fabrication or other. Even one woman had spent copious time in the jailhouse for her rabble-rousing and protesting: Grace Murphy, the saloonkeeper's suffragist wife.

All of which explained Jack Murphy's particular zeal to attend the men's club meeting and have the sheriff's wrongdoings dealt with—whatever they were. In Murphy's position, Dylan would have done the same thing. Not that he could glimpse Murphy at the moment. He seemed to have disappeared along with Doc Finney.

Maybe they were both tending to the dance hall girl?

Wanting to make sure, Dylan looked for them.

"I don't expect much integrity from folks, generally speaking," Cade Foster was saying as Dylan searched. As a renowned gambler, Cade undoubtedly had his reasons for expecting the worst of people. "But a lawman ought to be different."

"Our lawmen *were* different," Adam Corwin said. "Crooked."

Dylan could have told them that. In fact, he *had* told Miles Callaway and his enterprising fiancée, Rosamond McGrath Dancy—the proprietress of the Morrow Creek Mutual Society and his most recent employer—that more than once. In no uncertain terms.

Until this latest incident, though, no one had been too riled up. When it came to Caffey, they'd been content to look the other way. Sometimes, in small towns, convention trumped sense. Tradition beat intelligence. Good intentions were no match for longtime connections and established ways of doing things.

As far as Dylan was concerned, those were fair arguments for not getting caught up in a close-knit community like Morrow Creek. The people here were too all-fired busy being cozy to use their heads. They hadn't wanted to see the problem at all.

Now it was too late. By Dylan's reckoning, Sheriff Caffey had never earned his job in the first place. There was evidence he'd fixed his election, wrangled himself an undeserved position of authority and gloated for years about doing both of those things. He'd also forcibly impeded the press—including local *Pioneer Press* newspaperman Thomas Walsh—from reporting on his misconduct. And that had been nothing more than his way of getting the job.

Dylan hadn't poked his nose too far into what Caffey had done after securing his position, but the man's penchant for brute force, coercion and dishonesty were known. Widely, now.

"We can't go on much longer without a sheriff." Jedediah Hofer, the mercantile owner, jutted his chin. "Already, bad men are coming into town. Damnable drifters and the like—"

Dylan objected. "I take offense to that, Hofer," he said with a smile. "Not every traveling man is up to no good."

"Not every traveling man is capable of organizing a posse, taking out Arvid Bouchard's lackeys and handling protection for a place like the mutual society." Griffin Turner gave Dylan a nod of recognition. Coming from the infamous

"Boston Beast," that was high praise, indeed. "People around here don't know what a man like Bouchard is capable of, but I reckon you did."

"You brought him in anyway," Marcus Copeland reminded everyone present. As the man who'd built one of Morrow Creek's first businesses—his successful lumber mill—Marcus was respected in town. So everyone quit nattering to listen. "You took care of it. No hesitation. That's why *you're* the only man for this job."

Dylan didn't like where this was going. *He* was the only man for what job? Tracking down the sheriff? The lawman's disappearance was none of his business. He was leaving. He should have already been gone. Just then, he wished he was.

Marcus's father-in-law, Adam Crabtree, nodded. "I'm not sure anybody else could cope with the no-good criminal types flooding into town right now." He held his hat in his hand, but stood bravely. "If the women find out what we're facing—"

"They're not going to find out." Rancher Everett Bannon said so with evident authority and resolve. "Not ever."

All the men murmured agreement. They were united in wanting to protect their womenfolk. Dylan couldn't fault them for that.

He'd accidently caused a bit of misfortune tonight for one solitary dance hall girl and had himself become obsessed with protecting her and helping her—to the point of becoming enchanted by her obstinacy and overall sense of independence...not to mention her lithesome figure and pretty, expressive features.

He couldn't stop wondering what she'd look like when she smiled. When she laughed. When she sighed after kissing a man.

Marielle Miller was beautiful, all right. But she was a handful and then some. She didn't like him much, either. She would sure as hell not be kissing *him* anytime soon.

"We already had enough on our plates, what with them no-account Sheridan brothers taking up in our town," complained Ned Nickerson, owner of the local book agent and news bureau. He cast a tardily cautious glance around the saloon, then prudently lowered his voice. "We've already got Charley, Peter and Levi. We don't need to invite every damn criminal in the territory to come here!"

The Sheridans. Dylan had a requisite familiarity with that family of felonious troublemakers. He knew they were bold. They were crafty. They acted immortal—like many men who were too young to know better—and were all the more dangerous because of it. They were best avoided by anyone sane, man or woman, who didn't want to wind up gut shot and left for dead.

He didn't know why Caffey hadn't sent that gang packing a long time ago. Instead, he'd tolerated their petty thievery and frequent fighting to the point of seeming to encourage it.

Which, Dylan mused, he might well have. What better way to ensure his lasting employment than to keep a homegrown gang of reprobates close by? Since their arrival, the Sheridans had kept some in town running scared. Now the situation had worsened.

"Sheriff Caffey picked a hell of a time to skedaddle, that's for sure," Adam Corwin agreed, pacing like the restless former detective he was. He squinted toward the saloon doors. "The weather is good. The passes are clear. There's nothing to stop more bad elements from coming here to Morrow Creek."

As pressing as that issue was, Dylan didn't see where this inbound lawlessness concerned him. He wasn't a peacekeeper. He was just a gun for hire—a man with an experienced mind who'd finished one job and was headed to the next. He'd already picked up an assignment in Sacramento. All he owned sat in the satchel he'd left behind the bar with Harry. All he'd pocketed before leaving it was enough cash to assure he had money to leave town with. That was all Dylan really needed—enough to move on.

His limited funds were the reason he hadn't agreed to pay Marielle Miller for her lost work time right from the get-go. If he'd had the greenbacks to spare, he'd have given them to her—even if he didn't feel strictly responsible for her predicament. That would have been the right thing to do. As it was, Dylan had not even considered surrendering his moving-on money.

He was pleased that he'd distracted her from the pain of her ankle injury, though—no matter how many stretchers he'd had to tell in the process. Truly. No thinking man would have taken Marielle Miller for a thirty-three-year-old woman, much less a dancer on the near side of forty. When he'd said that, she'd practically shot sparks from her eyeballs. It had been all he could do to keep a straight face and keep on riling her up.

Reminded of the dance hall girl—and beset with an entirely unlikely sense of fondness toward her, too—Dylan took a step to the side, intent on shouldering past the other men to Marielle's position. He was worried about her. Although his conversation with the menfolk had taken only moments, he hadn't wanted to abandon her. She ought to be right where he'd left her…

As he made his way, the conversation continued.

"You took down the Bedell gang just last year, Corwin," Daniel McCabe was saying, standing head and shoulders over most. "Near as I can see, you could do the same to the Sheridans. Hell, you could put up a posse and get Sheriff Caffey, too."

Amid general murmurs of agreement, Jack

Murphy raised his arms, signaling for quiet. The group of men obliged.

"We've already settled this, remember?" the saloonkeeper reminded them. "We've already chosen our new sheriff."

Adam Corwin nodded. "We have." Evidently, that's what the men's club meeting had been for. "Besides, you all know Savannah's expecting." He shook his head. "I'm sorry, boys, but if I up and took a job as sheriff now, she'd have my damn head."

"Or *I* would," rumbled Mose Hawthorne, Savannah's longtime loyal helper at the adjunct telegraph station outside town. "Ain't no way you're deserting Savannah now. Not when we've got Coyle here. The man's practically tailor-made for the job."

Hearing his name, Dylan went still. Again… "What job?"

At the expectant, confident looks that met his question, he balked. This didn't feel right. This… *hopefulness* wasn't for him.

"What job?" he repeated, wary and tense jawed.

"Why, the job of sheriff, of course." Thomas Walsh moved nearer, a pad of paper and pencil at the ready. As usual, the editor of the *Pioneer Press* wanted his story. This time, from Dylan. "Typically, the sheriff's position is filled following an election, but with all these degenerate types coming to town—"

"Drifters?" Dylan felt compelled to ask. "Like me?"

But unlike Marielle, no one seemed to believe he'd earned that moniker. A few men chuckled. More shook their heads. All gazed at him with that same damn unearned faith and expectancy.

What the hell had he done to earn *this*? Only his job.

"—we don't have time for bureaucratic paperwork shuffling," the editor continued. "We just need to get on with it."

"Uh-oh. If Walsh don't want paper shuffling," Hofer said with a laugh, "this situation is right next door to doomed."

Everyone laughed. But the newspaperman merely continued in his usual earnest fashion. "We'll have a proper election," he assured Dylan. "But while you're serving, instead of before. During your first term, rather than wasting time with campaigns and signs and speeches. It's more efficient that way. You can get started straightaway protecting everyone in Morrow Creek."

They all beamed at him, but Dylan balked anew.

Protecting…everyone? That sounded like a nightmare to him.

Resolutely, he squared his shoulders. He sobered his expression. He held up his arms. An instant hush fell.

Damnation, he couldn't help thinking. *They were serious.*

They truly expected leadership from him. Safety.

The realization was worrying. And all the more reason he had to put a stop to this before it went any further.

"Far be it from me to deny Walsh, here, the joy of organizing an emergency election," Dylan tried with a grin. "Not to mention the whole caboodle of newspaper coverage that'll go along with it. But it'll have to happen without me."

They didn't seem to understand. "We already voted," Clayton said. "At the men's club meeting. You're the man for the job."

Everyone agreed—even as, at the other end of the saloon, the piano player tinkled a few keys. It felt as though ages had passed, but it must have been only a few minutes. The dance hall girls didn't typically take a long break. They couldn't risk losing customers who would drift away during a lengthy interval.

Speaking of dance hall girls...where was Marielle Miller? As the queen of obstinacy, she should have refused to budge from her chair until Doc Finney properly saw to her injury.

Funny thing was, Dylan couldn't help musing,

in her shoes, he would have refused help, too. They were alike in that way.

They were alike in several ways, when it came to it. But he couldn't think about that now—not with a whole saloon full of people expecting him to ride to the rescue as their new sheriff.

"I already have a job," Dylan protested more strongly. "In Sacramento." He took out his pocket watch and glanced at it. "In fact, I can probably make the next train west if I leave now."

Remarkably, everyone laughed. Some men raised their ales and whiskies in apparent toasts to what they assumed was Dylan's customary joshing. Growing concerned, he glanced at the door.

He had an awful feeling he wouldn't be catching that train.

"I guess you should'a gone to the meeting, eh?" Nickerson yelled, rubicund and jolly even before receiving his first pint of ale. "So you could cast the only vote against yourself."

Everyone roared with glee. But Dylan started pacing.

Thomas Walsh noticed. "It's just the usual sheriff's job, Mr. Coyle, nothing more," he promised Dylan. "Peacekeeping, serving summons, collecting tax money, investigating crimes—"

"I'm not the man you're after," Dylan said more plainly.

"You are *exactly* the man we're after," Miles Callaway maintained. He aimed his chin at the friends he'd made since coming to Morrow Creek from Boston. "Or do you have such little faith in our judgment that you'd disagree with *all* of us?"

Each of their gazes veered to his face. Held. Stubbornly.

Glancing beyond the men for a respite from this wrinkle in his getaway plans—from this entirely unwanted obligation—Dylan glimpsed movement near the saloon's door. A huge man lumbered toward it with a woman in his arms—a woman who was pointedly directing him exactly where and in what fashion to carry her.

Marielle Miller. She was hearty enough to dispense orders. That meant she would be all right. In her wake, Jack Murphy watched contentedly as his lead dancing girl left in the man's keeping.

Evidently, Dylan's responsibilities to her had ended.

He was free to leave. Free to drift to the next town, the next job…the next person who would disappoint him in the end.

"What's it going to be?" Copeland pressed. "Sheriff?"

Sheriff. Not liking the sound of that, Dylan frowned.

But everyone else shifted and murmured, plainly het up. They wanted him for this job. Dylan knew he could still refuse.

More than that, he *had* to refuse.

But then, on the verge of turning to do so,

he caught another, more surreptitious movement near the saloon doors. As Marielle passed by, a wiry man in a long coat and hat stepped out from the shadows. He watched Marielle with avid interest.

Dylan recognized him as one of the Sheridan boys. Charley, he thought. Charley Sheridan. The wily ringleader. At the realization, Dylan's blood iced over. Why the hell would one of those criminals be interested in Marielle Miller? Or, he saw further, in trading a shifty nod with the man carrying her?

As though sensing Dylan's attention, Sheridan transferred his gaze from Marielle…to Dylan. Calculatingly, he narrowed his eyes. Whatever was going through his mind, it wasn't good.

"I'll do it." Dylan turned, saw the tin star held by Marcus Copeland and closed his fist around it. "Starting now."

Forty minutes after leaving the saloon, Marielle found herself at home with an elaborately bandaged ankle, an order to rest up with no dancing allowed for an impossibly lengthy period of at least four weeks…and a younger brother who'd been plumb tuckered out by the events of the evening.

With a sigh, she glanced at Hudson. In the glow of the lamplight, he sprawled across his cot in their small house's front room, still wearing all his clothes and boots, snoring.

His familiar snuffle rent the stillness. He snorted, then turned over and flopped on his side, facing her fully now.

Looking at his peaceful face, Marielle couldn't help giving a pensive smile. That was Hudson to a tee. Now that the kerfuffle was over—at least for him—he was oblivious to everything but his pillow. Her brother lived life as it was handed to him, neither striving for more nor complaining when there was less. Hudson was jovial and giving, simple and free.

He was as big of heart as he was massive of body, and although he hadn't strictly amounted to much in the traditional sense—having no steady employment nor a wife and family to call his own—he was nonetheless content. Hudson tried sometimes, at Marielle's urging, to find steadier work. He tried to grow up as fully as they both knew he needed to. But his every attempt ended up confirming the same foregone conclusion.

"I can't keep on with that job, Mari," Hudson would say, shaking his head with his soft brown eyes fixed on hers. "Who will look after you while you're dancing? I can't leave you."

Every time, Marielle would soften. Every time, she would see the end arriving along with the beginning and be helpless to stop it. Because all she knew were dancing and sewing, and the former was much more lucrative than the latter. Plying her needle did not support two people nearly as well as dancing did.

It would have been churlish of her to quit performing. Yes, Hudson enjoyed drinking and throwing dice at the saloon a bit too much. Yes, she regretted that her employment kept them both in such overall corrupting quarters. Jack Murphy's saloon was better than most—better than many she'd worked in during her journey westward after her mother had passed on—but it was still a place where men went to imbibe, carouse, fight and forget.

Sometimes, she thought, Hudson wanted to forget, too. Sometimes, she thought, Hudson missed New York, missed the backstage work he'd done at the fancy theater there, missed their mother and their absentee father most of all. But then her brother would make a joke or tug her hair or laugh over some memory of their time together back in the States—before it had all fallen apart—and Marielle would tell herself he was fine.

After all, he had no more to forget than she did. If her own memories didn't send her to drink and smoke and carouse to excess, then why would they do so to Hudson? Men could handle their intoxicants better than women, anyway. Everyone knew that.

Her own father excepted, of course…

A knock at the door jarred Marielle before she could fall straight into the quicksand of those darker memories. Puzzled and a mite vexed, she stared across the front room at the door.

Another knock came. Louder this time.

She looked at her ankle, duly wrapped in bandages and properly elevated on a footstool as the doctor had ordered. Doc Finney had left her with a crutch, but she hadn't tried it yet. He'd also left her dosed with a quantity of laudanum for the pain, which—on top of the whiskey Jack had pressed upon her—had made her feel quite woozy. Also, clearly, far too melancholy.

The third knock threatened to wake Hudson. That was more than Marielle would permit. Frowning anew, she grabbed her crutch and used it to lever herself out of her comfortable chair. She hobbled across the front room, paused to pull a warm blanket over Hudson against the chill that might come in with opening the door, then made her way to answer that summons.

Most likely, she knew, it would be Doc Finney, returned to offer still more instructions or admonitions or medications. He'd told her that the keys to healing her injury were circular compression, something called perfect immobilization, and a hearty dose of that flawless healer: time. It had all sounded like a lot of fancy terms for wrapping and resting, but Marielle had followed his directives, all the same. Her livelihood depended on healing her ankle, and quickly.

She couldn't take chances. She *had* to get better.

Leaning awkwardly on her crutch, Marielle worked the lock, bracing herself for the cool springtime chill that was coming. In the evenings, in this mountainous part of the territory, frostiness crept in and then sank into a person's bones. She didn't want a chill on top of everything else.

She opened the door to an unexpected visitor. Startled, Marielle leaped back.

Or at least she tried to. Instead, she stepped onto her hurt ankle, received a jolt of pain for her efforts and yelped.

Behind her, Hudson stirred. He moaned. He began to snore again.

At the doorway, the goose bumps that spread over Marielle's body had nothing to do with the weather—and everything to do with the man who lounged in her open doorway, canny and mean.

"'Evening, Miss Miller." Charley Sheridan tipped his hat. It was too big for him—probably because he'd nicked it off a larger man—but no one would have dared laugh at that. Folks had heard tell of men getting knifed for less. Sheridan roamed his gaze over her. "How's that ankle of yours doing?"

"That's none of your business." Marielle wished she had something—anything—to cover up with. Instead, all she had was the costume she'd danced in. Although she'd set aside her frothy, feathered headdress and had lost her spangled fan someplace. "It's too late for company, Mr. Sheridan. Good night."

Heart hammering, she tried to shut the door.

Charley's shoulder prevented it. "Well now, that ain't neighborly at all, Miss Miller. I come here to talk to you."

Usually—and unfortunately—the Sheridans came to talk to Hudson. To get drunk with him and gamble with him. The four of them had been…well, Marielle couldn't call them *friends*, exactly. But her brother had foolishly taken up with Charley, Peter and Levi once or twice. She hadn't been able to stop him.

Their influence had come along with his time at the saloon—another thing for which Marielle couldn't help blaming herself. If not for her job dancing, none of them would have crossed paths. Charley certainly wouldn't have been there bothering her.

With a backward glance, Marielle made sure Hudson was sleeping. A disloyal part of her wished her brother would wake up and deal with this himself. It might have been nice to have had a genuine protector to rely on. But now, as usual, she had only herself. It was up to her to protect both of them.

Wasn't that what she'd promised, when Mama had been dying?

"We have nothing to discuss." Marielle jerked up her chin. "Certainly nothing that can't wait until morning."

It was late enough there, on the outskirts of town, that no one was about. The birds were stilled in the darkened ponderosa pines. The moon provided most of the light on her front porch.

"Ah, but this here can't wait till morning." Charley looked beyond her, into her house. "Ain't you gonna invite me in?"

As he moved to take the invitation she pointedly hadn't offered, Marielle shoved him with her crutch. Charley was too surprised to object outright. He obligingly made room, looking amused, while she clumsily half hopped, half lumbered her way onto the porch. She shut the door. At this point, being outside with him felt safer than being in her own house with—she had to face facts—a passed-out-drunk Hudson as her only protection.

Admitting as much, even to herself, made Marielle's former wooziness subside, just a bit. Evidently, laudanum was no match for having a notorious outlaw appear at your door uninvited.

"What do you want, Mr. Sheridan? I don't have all night."

"Nope. What you have is…*all of that.*" His loathsome gaze traveled over her costumed form. His odious gesture indicated those dratted horsehair-augmented curves she'd given herself where the Almighty had chosen not to bless her himself. Charley's appreciation was anything but divinely inspired, though. His attention felt despicable. "Men pay good money to see you, Miss Miller. That there's the reason for it."

He meant her figure, plainly. She shuddered with disgust.

"They pay to see me *dance*," she specified. "That's all."

"If you believe that, you're dumber than your brother."

"I'll thank you to leave Hudson out of this."

At her fiery, protective retort, Charley guffawed. "There ain't no leaving Hudson out of this. It's all his damn fault."

"What is?" Newly alert, she clutched her crutch.

"You'll have to ask him about that." Plainly comfortable in his thuggery, Charley leaned on her porch railing. "Point is, and the solitary reason I'm here *talking* to a woman at all, is that I'm not the only one who's noticed you and your 'dancing.'"

Marielle knew he meant something far baser. She scowled.

"That Coyle fella—he noticed your 'dancing,' too."

Shivering, Marielle looked up at the night sky. She wished she were anywhere but here, with an outlaw's whiskey breath and overripe saddle stink washing over her. She couldn't help noticing the heft of Charley's gun belt. She wished she hadn't.

"Now that he's gonna be the new sheriff in town—"

"Dylan Coyle? The *sheriff*?" Marielle almost laughed outright, despite her alarming predicament. "Impossible. The man can't stay put long enough to use up a pound of coffee, much less see to maintaining law and order in Morrow Creek."

Unfazed, Charley spat his tobacco juice over her porch railing. "Seems you're wrong about that. I saw him pin on that shiny ole badge myself just a little a while ago."

Dylan Coyle…the sheriff? In a single night? How could this have happened? She'd known the men's club was meeting to discuss their errant sheriff and to fill his now vacant post with someone new. But…this? Dylan Coyle? In charge?

Marielle could scarcely envision Mr. Coyle with a badge to go along with his gun. Yes, she'd felt a certain…affinity toward him. Yes, he seemed to be a reasonably fair and intelligent man, if entirely too autocratic for her liking. But he was a drifter, though and through. There was no way they could count on him.

Had the whole town lost its wits?

With effort, she tried to regain hers. "This has nothing to do with me. If you're interested in the new sheriff, why don't you go speak with him yourself?" As if he would. The Sheridans were notorious in the territory. Only Sheriff Caffey and Deputy Winston had been oblivious to the dangers their gang had posed.

Now that their former sheriff had fled so mysteriously and his deputy had been duly locked up—events Marielle had learned about along with everyone else just days ago—lawlessness would obviously increase. It was no accident there was no one around to stop Charley Sheridan from harassing her at nearly midnight.

"*I* ain't gonna speak with him." Charley poked her chest. "You are. You're gonna jaw your fool head off. You're gonna do whatever it takes to get in good with the new sheriff—and I mean *real* good. After you done that, you're gonna make sure he's good and distracted while me and my boys get what's coming to us."

She couldn't help stating the obvious. "Prison?"

"Tsk-tsk." He shook his head. "If you weren't laid up—"

"I'm strong enough to face *you*, aren't I?"

"—and maybe crippled for good—"

Marielle gulped, hoping he wasn't right. Fearing he was.

"—I'd make you pay for a disrespectful remark like that."

Shaking from fright and cold, Marielle nonetheless stared Charley down. "I'm not going to do anything for you. Not now. Not ever." She reached backward for her doorknob, all but itching to turn it and escape. "I'm going inside."

Charley slammed his hand on the door before she could open it. His presence loomed over her, menacing and conscienceless.

"You Millers *owe me*," he said. "Hudson cost me something. So far, he ain't been able to pay. But tonight, when I saw you gettin' all flirtatious with the new sheriff, I figured out another way for me to get what's coming to me. I aim to get it."

Irrationally, Marielle wasn't most piqued by the threat inherent in that statement. *"Flirtatious?"* she repeated in an outraged tone. "I assure you, Mr. Sheridan, that I was not—"

"Yep. Flirtatious." Charley seemed nauseatingly pleased by that. "I reckon Coyle will do damn near anything you ask."

That was outlandish. Still…a part of her wondered if it was true. Coyle had been mighty insistent about staying by her side. Why would he have done that if he hadn't liked her…a little?

Befuddled and worried, Marielle shook her head.

"All you have to do is get the new sheriff to trust you," Charley told her coaxingly. "Get him to look the other way while Hudson helps us get what's ours. That's it. Your brother cost us. That's not something I'm prone to forget." He rested his hand on his gun belt, making his meaning plain. "Or forgive."

"You leave Hudson out of this!" Marielle hissed. "You stay away from my brother. Otherwise, I *swear* I'll—"

Charley's chuckle cut short her useless threat. "Just ask him. Ask Hudson what he cost us—cost me. You'll see. This is the only way. It's the smart way."

Mutely, Marielle shook her head. She wanted to leave, but Charley came closer, still keeping one hand on the door. His body pressed on hers, wiry and strong and scary. His whiskey breath panted against her neck. Cursing her skimpy costume, Marielle froze in place. She was in no condition to stop him.

"Unless," Charley crooned lasciviously, "you'd rather do this another way?" He put his hand on her waist, making sure she felt the full force of his coercion. "I'd be willing to take *you* as fair compensation for my losses instead. My little brothers wouldn't like it much. But I could always give them a turn."

Marielle was personally virtuous and wholly innocent. In fact, Dylan Coyle hadn't been far from the truth. She *was* the oldest dance hall spinster she knew. But that didn't mean she didn't recognize the abhorrent bargain Sheridan was suggesting.

With effort, she kept her tone even. "I don't want any man, Mr. Sheridan." She felt queasy as she added, "Not even you."

He smirked, providentially believing her flattery. "You don't know what you're missing, dancer girl."

I'm glad of it, Marielle couldn't help thinking. What in the world had Hudson done to irritate the Sheridans this way?

"You must have had Sheriff Caffey in your pocket," Marielle pointed out, still trying to sidestep this problem. There had to be another way—one that didn't involve her or Hudson helping the Sheridans with their crimes. "Why not pay off Coyle, too?"

"Don't you think I already tried that? He can't be bought. What kinda lawman can't be bought?" Seeming provoked, Charley spat. Then he tipped his oversize hat again. "I'll be in touch, Miss Miller. I'll be watching, too. You can count on that." He nodded. "You just do as you're told, and it'll all be fine." Wearing an intent look, Charley caught a hank of her hair. He wrapped it around his hand, holding her like a harnessed horse. His intention to control her was plain. "You understand me?"

Marielle jerked away. Stupidly, since Charley did not let go. He was mean enough to hurt her, casually and unthinkingly.

Eyes watering, she gave a scanty nod. "I understand."

"Yep." Charley sneered in response. "I knew you would."

Then he released her abruptly and clomped off her porch into the night, leaving her well and truly caught in a problem that was even bigger than her injured ankle…and even more worrisome than her brother's penchant for getting into trouble.

What, Marielle wondered as she hobbled her way back into the warmth of her small house, was she supposed to do now?

If Charley Sheridan would be watching, she guessed she'd better to try to make good on what he wanted—or at least make sure it *seemed* that's what she was doing until she could finagle a better way out of her predicament. Ordinarily, Marielle would have reported Charley's attempt to extort her help and been done with it. But she didn't know the new sheriff. She certainly didn't trust him. Until she could do that, she was stuck.

How exactly, she wondered further, did a woman "get in good" with a man she'd already antagonized multiple times in a single night? She hadn't exactly been friendly to Dylan Coyle. In fact, she'd outright insulted him by calling him a drifter. She'd tried to make him pay for her lost work time and called him stingy right to his face. That wasn't a promising start.

Beset with concerns, Marielle made her way across the front room. Thanks to her dancing training, she had good balance. She could manage on her crutch fairly well. But the events of

this night had more than knocked her sideways—
they'd terrified her.

Oh, Hudson, she thought. *What have you done
now?*

And how, above all, would she get them both
out of it?

Chapter Four

Marielle was sleeping fitfully when the sound of conversation reached her bedroom. Startled awake, she listened.

Hudson's deep, murmuring tones filtered through the wall separating her chamber from the kitchen. Identifying that sound, Marielle relaxed. Sometimes her brother hummed or sang while carrying out chores around the house. That wasn't unusual. He wasn't a hard worker, but he was definitely a cheerful one. That was part of his charm—part of his carefree way of enjoying life.

Probably there was nothing wrong at all.

Except…today there was something different about the sound of Hudson's voice. Today, her brother sounded…more manly?

Marielle jolted. Had Charley Sheridan returned? Was Hudson in danger? That would explain why he'd lowered his voice to a deeper, more threatening register. He was trying to be tough.

Poor Hudson was about as tough as a spring breeze. She had to do something. Pushing upright in her nightgown, with her long braid swinging carelessly down her back, Marielle grabbed for her dressing gown. She yanked it on. Then she leaned farther sideways and scrabbled for the crutch she'd left leaning on her bed table. She hated it already. She didn't like relying on it.

Necessarily doing so anyway, she hurried toward the kitchen. The unexpected aroma of fresh coffee struck her first.

Slowing her steps, Marielle frowned. Had Hudson brewed a pot of coffee for him and his no-good "friends" to share?

Why had he ever gotten mixed up with them at all?

"Morning, Mari." From the cookstove, Hudson grinned at her. He opened the oven door—at least remembering to shield his hand safely with a cloth—and withdrew a saucepan. Appearing very delighted with himself, he upended the saucepan. A slice of toast dropped out onto a waiting plate. "Did you sleep well? Would you like some toast? Or some coffee? I'll get you some coffee."

Goggling at him, Marielle shook her head. "Hudson…are you *cooking*?" He appeared to be trying to. Dear, incapable Hudson. The last time he'd tried to heat a tin of beans, he'd cut his hand, scorched the beans and all but ruined her saucepan.

"I surely am cooking!" her brother announced. "As usual," he added in a proud tone. Perplexing her further with that preposterous boast, Hudson scurried to the table. He pulled out a chair, then helped her into it. Groggily, Marielle sat and then set aside her crutch while her brother urged, "You just have a seat right here. I'll have that coffee straightaway."

With that pronouncement, he beamed in the direction of the doorway…

…at Corinne Murphy, who'd apparently come to call on them.

Seeing her, Marielle started. "Corinne! Good morning!"

"Yes. Good morning to you!" Corinne blushed but continued on with her usual capable crispness. She sat poker-straight in her place at the table. "I'm afraid we woke you, Marielle. I'm sorry. I can certainly come back later, if you'd prefer. You're not even dressed. Although I do have some rather pressing news to share, and I'm certain you'll want to be informed of it, so…"

Suddenly aware of her state of dishabille, Marielle clutched her dressing gown. With her other hand, she smoothed her hair. She liked Corinne. She was the eldest of her boss's four sisters, and—along with Nealie, Glenna, and Arleen—had relocated to Morrow Creek from Boston some time ago. All four of them seemed to have found the territory most invigorating.

"Of course I'll want to know your news." Doubtless, Corinne's news had to do with their opinionated, unstoppable, freshly appointed sheriff, Marielle thought. Not wanting to let on that she'd already been informed of that particular tidbit—by Charley Sheridan, of all people—she smiled. "I'll just go put on something a bit more suitable. It won't take a moment."

She couldn't help marveling at Corinne's presence—or at Hudson's apparent interest in making her feel at home.

Demonstrating that interest, Hudson approached the table.

"Here you are, Miss Murphy!" He delivered the slice of toast—only slightly charred—with a flourish and plenty of jam. He watched her expression ardently. "It's sweet, just like you."

Oh, good gracious. Hudson was smitten with Corinne Murphy!

But that redheaded woman merely accepted her toast with a wry smile. "Thank you. I've never seen anyone make toast in a saucepan before, Mr. Miller. It's very…enterprising of you."

"You haven't? We always do it that way," Hudson bluffed.

But as he turned back to the cooktop, Marielle saw his bravado fade. He plainly considered *enterprising* to be on the same level as *ridiculous*. His crestfallen expression broke her heart.

Bravely, he squared his shoulders for another attempt.

"I'd be happy to make you something else," he offered.

"No, no. Thank you," Corinne demurred. "This is fine."

But their guest hadn't touched her toast, and the slump to Hudson's shoulders was the final straw for Marielle. She had to do something to salvage this situation. Otherwise, Hudson's inelegant attempts to impress Corinne would come to naught.

He was her brother—the only family she had left in the world. Helping him was more important than anything else.

"Saucepan toast is *very* good," Marielle assured Corinne, wincing as she leaned on her crutch. Her ankle still hurt a great deal. Likely, there was more painkilling laudanum in her future. After last night, she didn't want to be dizzy with medication. She needed to be vigilant. There was no telling when Charley Sheridan might return. "The pan helps keep it…moist!"

"I see." Contemplatively, Corinne examined her toast. "In that case, well done, Mr. Miller! You are an innovator, indeed."

She tried a bite. Hudson nearly danced an elated jig.

Proud of herself for drumming up that bolstering fib, Marielle gave an encouraging glance to her brother. His relieved expression meant everything to her. All she'd ever wanted was for him to be happy—for him to never feel abandoned, as she had.

When Dylan Coyle had suggested that she was on the lookout for something, Marielle supposed that's what it had always been.

But why in tarnation was lasting happiness so elusive?

"Although," Corinne went on, furrowing her brow as she watched Marielle gamely struggle to get up from the table and get back to her room, "shouldn't you be helping your sister? It looks as though Marielle could use a strong man's assistance."

"Nah. Mari won't hear of it." Puffing up his chest to look extra brawny, Hudson waved off that suggestion. Insensible of this opportunity to appear even stronger for Corinne's benefit, he shook his head. "She's mighty proud of her independence."

Corinne appeared dubious. "Are you sure? At least pour Marielle some of that coffee you promised. You were brewing it when I arrived. It can't all have been for me, can it?"

"'Course not." Hudson shifted his gaze to Marielle, silently begging her not to reveal his customary postrevelry habit of sobering himself with gallons of strong coffee. He'd learned the tradition from their father. "It's just… I had

a powerful need for coffee, and Mari wasn't up
yet, so I had to fend for my—" Hudson broke off,
belatedly catching sight of Corinne's distressed
face. "I was out pretty late last night," he tried
again, "what with the need to watch over Mari at
Jack's saloon and all. I might've had a mite too
much to—" He stopped short, realizing too late
that describing his raucous night would probably not endear him to someone as reputedly upright and no-nonsense as Corinne Murphy. After
a despairing gulp of air, he tried again. "What I
mean to say is, I'm going to have to learn to do
a few things around here, now that Mari is laid
up awhile. I'm going to be taking care of her. I
can't wait!"

Corinne looked amused…and maybe a tiny bit
impressed, too. "You can't wait to learn to cook,
clean and quit carousing?"

Marielle wanted to bury her face in her hands.
Hudson's wild nights had earned him such infamy
that his propensity for riotous behavior was discussed casually? Just after daybreak?

Hudson hitched up his britches, giving every
impression of taking that question as a challenge
to his manhood. He nodded. His efforts did nothing to dispel his usual overall demeanor, though.
Her brother looked then, as always, like a moun-
tain man who'd been partially tamed and left to
babysit wayward tykes.

Which was to say careful, oversize, in dire

need of a good haircut…and entirely naive of the many challenges ahead.

"That's right, I am," he assured Corinne. "You'll see."

"I hope I do." Meaningfully, their guest arched her brows in Marielle's direction. "Beginning quite soon now?"

Catching her hint more quickly this time, Hudson understood that Corinne meant for him to help Marielle immediately.

Nonetheless, as Marielle stopped to let him make a good impression, he frowned in confusion. "You want me to *dress her*?"

Corinne laughed. "Fixing your sister some of this delicious saucepan toast while she puts herself to rights would be a better idea, I would say." Then she trained her astute glance on Marielle. "Would you like some help? Thanks to Jack's adventures in corset making, all of us Murphy sisters have more than our share of experience with an incredible variety of garments."

Marielle nodded, keenly interested in knowing more about her boss's unlikely past as a corsetry genius. "Thank you. That would be very kind of you. I'm afraid my injury has presented more of a challenge to my day-to-day routine than I'd expected."

"Given what you're facing today, it's the least I can do." With that dismal and enigmatic pronouncement out of the way, Corinne set aside her plate of toast. Briskly, she stood, then smiled directly at Hudson. "Don't clear away my toast in your zeal to clean up while we're gone," she instructed, gesturing at the mess he'd made while cooking. Coffee grounds littered the tabletop. Spilled water sat next to the cookstove. Bread crumbs spoiled the floor. The breadknife sat precariously atop the day-old loaf he'd sliced. "I'll be back to finish that before you know it." Her serious gaze leveled Hudson. "I *adore* my toast extra sweet. You're brilliant to discern so. Thank you again."

Hudson's cheeks turned an adorable shade of pink. As far as Marielle knew, no one had ever deemed him "brilliant." Under the heady influence of Corinne's praise, he appeared insensible to the fact that his potential sweetheart now expected him to make good on his previous vow. He had to truly take care of Marielle—beginning with actually scrubbing and cleaning the kitchen.

He'd never picked up a mop in his life. Marielle couldn't wait to see him try. Stifling a grin, she headed for her room.

"I'll be expecting to see this place spic-and-span when I return," she called cheekily over her shoulder. "Good luck!"

Wearing his best coat, shiniest boots and brand-new sheriff's badge, Dylan rounded the corner near Molly Copeland's gingerbread house of a bakery. As he strode down the street carrying his satchel, intent on getting some business done on his first day as sheriff, he was met by a number of masculine grins and hat tips. Women offered shy nods. Several folks tossed admiring and altogether trusting smiles in his direction.

Already, as if by magic, the whole town knew that he'd been chosen to replace crooked Sheriff Caffey. By the looks of things, everyone approved of that selection, too—even those who hadn't attended the men's club meeting last night. From the most doddering granny to the most fresh-faced youngster, everyone he met that morning seemed to believe that Dylan had matters well sorted already. He could practically feel the exhaled breaths trundling him along on a wave of shared municipal relief.

Squaring his shoulders to better manage the weight of all those unreasonable expectations, Dylan kept going. His boots rang against the raised plank sidewalk. His coat trailed on the breeze behind him. Against his better judgment, he'd strapped on his gun belt again today, just to be on the safe side of sorry. He'd also managed to remove the worst of the whiskey vapors from his favorite hat. It shaded his face capably as he moved past the mercantile and the milliner's, the butcher's and the livery stable, seeing all those businesses with a new sense of care.

He knew the way to his destination. After

last night, he'd made it his business to know the way—and not just because his security expertise required knowing the particulars of any given situation. He'd made it his business to know the way because his first day's work necessarily involved the resident of Morrow Creek whom Dylan still felt the most personally responsible for.

Still…and maybe eternally. If Marielle Miller continued to pester and needle him the way she liked to, he'd never be free.

Lord help him, but she was a challenging woman.

He only hoped she would agree to what he planned to ask. Given the antagonism she'd behaved with last night, the odds of that miracle occurring were not good. If she refused, Dylan was prepared to go another, more difficult, way. But he wasn't a man who backed down from a challenge—even one that presented itself in flounced skirts, acres of spangles and enough lush curves to make a man doubt his commitment to anything except womankind.

Dylan *loved* womankind. As far as he could discern, women were generally kindhearted, loyal and generous. They were as ready with a smile as they were with a helping hand. He'd failed a few of them in his time—more than he wanted to admit—but he couldn't help being spellbound by femininity overall. Women had less power, fewer means and more limited opportunities than men did. Yet they managed to stay upbeat in the face of their difficulties—or, like Grace Murphy, work to improve their lot.

That was admirable. So were sweet lips, feminine softness and the kind of mystery that kept a man wanting more. Faced with a willing woman, Dylan was all but powerless to resist. Weren't all men, in truth? All any man ever wanted was to be needed. Any woman who could make a man feel he was necessary to her…well, that woman was one step closer to the angels without knowing it.

'Course, she was in a good position to take that man for all he was worth, too, Dylan had to acknowledge. Stranger things had happened. Men had risked more for less than a woman's smile.

Shaking his head at his own bent for philosophizing, he reached his destination—a humble house on the outskirts of town.

It looked different in the daytime. Last night, in the dark near midnight, the place had seemed oddly vulnerable. Today, it only seemed to be what it was: an ordinary split log house with a front porch, a minimal yard, two curtained windows and a pair of occupants who likely had no idea what was on its way to them.

Still examining the place, Dylan trod past a well-tended vegetable garden situated—by the house's layout—just outside the kitchen. He admired its seedlings and noticed its low fence with curiosity. Once those pickets had been white. Now

they were spackled and worn. Why would someone take such care with those sprouting vegetables and herbs, then allow the fence to crumble?

Similarly, Dylan noted, the front porch of the
house suffered from neglect. Its top rail was dam-
aged and badly needed replacing, but the front
door was decorated with a cheery homemade rug.
The windowpanes shone spotlessly in the sun, but
their frames wanted paint. One missing pane had
been boarded up.

Still, wood smoke puffed welcomingly from
the chimney. The scent of freshly brewed coffee
drifted from the interior. Dylan even fancied he
could catch the particular lilt of one sassy dance
hall girl's voice as she called out, then began
laughing.

Wondering over that sound, Dylan stopped. He
felt pinned to the spot, lashed by the sunshine,
struck by a sense of yearning for the warm and
convivial household he believed lay inside.

For the first time since last night, he entertained real misgivings about accepting that sheriff's badge and pinning it on. Because for the first
time, it occurred to him that taking on steward-
ship of Morrow Creek might mean getting closer
to the people who lived there—much closer than
he justly wanted to be.

It had been a long time since he'd let himself be
part of anything that felt like a family—anything
that felt like a home. Deliberately, Dylan had cho-

sen bachelor's quarters for his diverse lodgings during his various jobs—the grubbier, the better. Over the past few years, he'd lived in boardinghouses and hotels, bunkhouses and lumber camps. He'd set up tents on the outskirts of mining towns and slept in the trees as a lumberman. Even during his brief time as a Pinkerton agent— when presented with the best accommodations as a part of seeing to the problems of the rich and endangered—he'd chosen modestly. When Rosamond McGrath Dancy had offered to let him stay at her fine house downtown for security, for instance, he'd politely refused.

He knew better than to get too comfortable.

That way lay disappointment. And, inevitably, heartache.

Frowning anew, Dylan listened as another peal of laughter rang out from inside the house. He pictured the scene that might have provoked such a sound and felt entirely too aware of his own solitude. He had friends, he knew. But he had no family.

He damn well didn't need one, either. Not for this. He was there to do a job. The sooner and more capably he did it, the better, he reminded himself—starting with clearing the Sheridan brothers out of Morrow Creek and ending with tracking down Sheriff Caffey and making sure the runaway lawman saw justice.

With both of those things accomplished, Dylan

reckoned, he would be able to leave town with his conscience clear. That was all he could hope for: to keep his word. Providentially, too, the salary he would earn as sheriff would help dispatch his obligation toward prickly Marielle Miller. The rest he intended to manage with hard work, close protection and expertise.

Even now, he doubted she'd wrapped her ankle properly.

Spurred by that galling realization, Dylan stomped toward the house. He ascended the porch steps. His shoulders tensed as he armed himself for the onslaught of merriment he expected inside. It wasn't that he was a gloomy man. He wasn't. At all.

He simply didn't want to feel…*anything* like the crushing sense of hopelessness he'd felt, all those years ago, when he'd dared to risk everything. He'd learned then that—for him at least—there would be no angel by the fireside at the end of every day. For him, there would only be another fireside. Then another. Then another. On and on until he scarcely knew where he was at all. It was good, he knew now, that he'd learned that lesson early. It was good that he knew better than to reach for more than he could reasonably expect to have, given who he was.

Steeling himself more firmly, Dylan knocked on the door.

Abruptly, the laughter inside ceased. At that,

he couldn't help cracking a cynical smile. He had that effect on Marielle Miller, he guessed. He stopped her laughter. Around him, she could only quibble or harangue. If that had even been her laughter, he groused to himself as he waited for someone to answer the door, it would have qualified as a real phenomenon.

Having never heard his favorite dance hall girl laugh himself, he couldn't very well be sure that had been her at all.

Waiting, Dylan stuffed his hand in his coat pocket. He touched the feathery and bespangled fan he'd stuck inside and felt a fresh wave of doubts buffet him. Why was he carrying the damn thing? Worse, why did he feel so giddy while touching it?

It was Marielle's lost fan, of course. He'd found it last night. It wasn't as though, if he'd wanted, he couldn't have been touching the dance hall girl herself instead...wantonly and freely. He had a demonstrable knack for making friends and for discreetly satisfying the intimate needs of himself and a chosen woman. If he'd wanted, he could have made Marielle Miller his. He didn't need a dancing girl's fan for...what, a keepsake?

He wasn't a sentimentalist. Yet he stood there, fraught with soppiness, during the few seconds it took for someone to clomp across the house's probably warped and unpainted floorboards. At the realization, Dylan scowled to himself. It wasn't that he planned to seduce Marielle. Of course he didn't. He might be a wandering man, but he was an honorable one, too. It was simply that thinking about becoming intimate with her was so all-fired distracting that he could scarcely summon up his own name when the door finally opened. Caught, he blinked in confusion. In his imagination, he'd been midway through his first kiss with Marielle. He'd already pulled her closer, tucked her tumbled-down hair behind her ear, breathed in her rosy scent—

"What do you want?" demanded the giant who stood there.

Suspiciously and impatiently, the man who'd ferried Marielle out of the saloon last night stared at Dylan. He looked as though he'd sooner slam the door in his face than wait for a reply. If not for Dylan's own renowned patience, he might have been tempted to issue the knuck a few choice demands of his own.

Instead, he said, "I'm Dylan Coyle, the new sheriff. You must be Hudson Miller—Miss Miller's terrifying brother."

Hudson looked confused. "I'm not terrifying."

Dylan quirked his lips. "I didn't think so." He glanced beyond the behemoth into the house. It looked tidy. Welcoming. Perfect. "Don't tell your sister. She's under the impression you're a fearsome colossus bent on vengeance and bloodshed."

"Bent on...huh?" Hudson scratched his head.

Then his face changed. Dylan could practically envision the word *sheriff* dancing its way across the inside of his forehead. Belatedly, Hudson recoiled. "If you're here for me, sheriff, I haven't done a single thing wrong."

Eyes wide, he held up his ham-sized hands to prove it.

"In my experience, folks who feel compelled to proclaim their innocence have generally misplaced it somewhere." Dylan offered Hudson a genial look. "Where'd you lose yours?"

The man paled. He glanced over his shoulder, then hastily back at Dylan, doing everything except write down a confession to prove that Dylan was right to be concerned about him. That exchange between Hudson and Charley Miller last night had not been an accidental one. *If you've got something on me,* please *don't haul me in now!* Hudson's expression begged. *Not now. Not in front of—*

"Who is it, Hudson?" Marielle stumped her way to the door with a crutch and a great deal of determination. When she saw Dylan standing there, a bewildering mix of expressions flashed over her face, one after another. Confusion. Dismay. Fear.

In the end, delight proved to be the implausible winner.

"Why, Sheriff Coyle!" she exclaimed sweetly. "To what do we owe this great honor?" She nudged her brother with her crutch. "Move along, Hudson, and let Sheriff Coyle come inside, please."

"Ouch!" Hudson shot her crutch an irate look. "You're getting to be downright wicked with that thing, and it hasn't even been a day yet," he complained. "Cut it out, Mari!"

"I'm sorry, Sheriff. We weren't expecting company." Marielle reached for his hand. "Please, do come inside."

At her touch, Dylan went entirely still. Warmth stretched from her to him, kindled by her smile and helped along by his own gullibility. Damn it all, but he *wanted* to believe that she wanted him there.

Marielle couldn't possibly want him there. Not after last night. Not after she'd wound up injured, irritated and hot for payback. From him. She'd told him in no uncertain terms that she had no use for a drifter. She'd accused him of selfishness. Of cruelty. She'd refused his help. She'd called him a skinflint!

Nothing had happened that could have changed her opinion—nothing except his being appointed sheriff…and her having met in secret with Charley Sheridan last night, of course. After seeing that criminal watching her, Dylan had trailed the man all the way across town to her house. He hadn't been close enough to overhear their moonlit conversation, on account of Sheridan having been accompanied by his gun-toting brothers, who'd lingered beyond the light thrown from the house. But he had been close enough to discern that, just as Hudson Miller knew Charley, so did Marielle. He also knew she was afraid of him.

But if he told her as much, she'd likely up and go kiss that killer, just to be typically contrary. He couldn't risk that happening. With Marielle, Dylan knew he had to be smarter. He had to stay near her—close enough to watch over her—but he couldn't let her know that's what he was doing. Not ever.

It wouldn't be easy, but he meant to do so anyway.

Whipping his hat politely into his hands, Dylan allowed Marielle to precede him inside. He stepped into her front room, feeling himself engulfed in coziness as he went. Tarnation.

Critically, he tried to catch a glimpse of the bandaging job Doc Finney had done on her ankle. Marielle caught him at it.

Uh-oh. Bracing himself for the impending explosion, Dylan directed his gaze toward her household instead. "Nice place."

That would never hold water, he knew. She'd torment him.

It wasn't as though he'd been ogling her ankles, Dylan thought in his own defense. He wasn't a scoundrel. But all Marielle did was show him a chair, then arrange herself opposite him. Nearby,

Corinne Murphy sat on the settee, watching him with what appeared to be an exceptional quantity of curiosity. She possessed the same air of competence that her brother Jack did. Only hers was spiffed up with starchiness and leavened with far more beauty than the big Irish barman could rightly claim.

Despite his alarm, Marielle smiled calmly. "Thank you so much, Sheriff. You're too kind. You know Miss Murphy, don't you? I think you both have in common that you've lived in Boston."

With effort, Dylan hid his surprise. He hadn't thought Marielle knew a single thing about him. Apparently, she did.

He exchanged pleasantries with Miss Murphy. Then he turned back to Marielle. "You've heard I'm acting sheriff, then?"

"Yes, I have. Miss Murphy made a special trip here this morning to tell me so." Marielle gave her friend a nod.

"That's…not *all* I came to tell you," Miss Murphy interjected. If Dylan didn't miss his guess, she seemed distinctly nervous. Possibly about whatever she'd neglected to tell Marielle until this point. But Marielle didn't stop.

"It's all part of the feminine solidarity we share here in town," she went on blithely, looking very pretty in a blue gown with her brown hair upswept. "You should probably know—"

"About that feminine solidarity," Miss Murphy interrupted again. "I've been awfully remiss in showing mine, because—"

But Marielle merely gave her another amiable, *just a minute* nod. "—that all the women in Morrow Creek are behind you, as well. Although they weren't allowed to attend the men's club meeting, they *did* strongly encourage their menfolk to choose you as our interim sheriff. In fact, in Mrs. Murphy's polls—because Grace did, in fact, commission polls among the members of the Ladies' Aid Society, the Morrow Creek Bicycling Association and the Ornithology Club, all of which she heads, of course—"

"Mr. Coyle is here to exercise his quartering privileges!" Miss Murphy blurted, fed up with waiting. "Don't you see his satchel, Marielle? He's here to move in with you and Hudson!"

Miss Murphy cast Dylan a rebellious look. Then she sat up straighter, most likely preparing herself for Marielle's fiery reaction. With interest, Dylan waited for the same thing.

"Move in?" Marielle blinked. "With us? But why?"

Her mild tone surprised him. She seemed… preoccupied.

"The sheriff has the prerogative to be quartered with a local family of his choosing," Miss Murphy explained. "It's part of the town charter. Grace told me so yesterday. I thought you had a right to know. I'm sorry, Marielle. I was waiting for the right time to tell you. But we got caught up choosing corsets—"

His interest thoroughly piqued, Dylan imagined the scene. Marielle, dressed only in her sheer chemise and underdrawers, picking and choosing from among various lacy, frothy things...

"I think it's a fine idea!" Hudson Miller thundered. With a jovial grin, he lumbered into the front room. He took a place beside Miss Murphy on the settee. The spoony look he tossed her could not be mistaken. "Let's do it, Mari! Welcome, Sheriff!"

For a man who'd appeared so all-fired guilty before, Hudson seemed unaccountably eager to have the long arm of the law quartered in his household, Dylan couldn't help noticing. That was not at all what he'd expected. What was Hudson up to, anyway?

Curiously, Dylan shifted his gaze to Marielle, trying to discern if her reaction would be equally perplexing. He was not disappointed. Because the woman who'd come after him last night as resolutely as a dog with a bone now merely smiled at him.

"I can't say I don't have reservations," she admitted with a glance at Miss Murphy. "Of course I do. But Hudson will be here to safeguard my propriety, and I *do* want to be helpful to the law in any way I possibly can." She sighed. "Of course,

Mr. Coyle *does* owe me a bit of recompense after last night, which I will gladly accept in the form of caretaking and occasional chores." Her gaze returned to him. "After that, I suppose we can consider our accounts settled. So yes. Welcome, Sheriff!"

Her smile beamed at him with all the radiance he could have hoped for. Her sugary tone matched it with easiness and warmth.

Both of those qualities bothered him—because they were, he knew, not reflective of her feelings about him—but Dylan couldn't fault Marielle for putting a good face on their situation. She was doing everything an upright citizen would have done.

Best of all, the next time Charley Sheridan came to call, *he* would be there to greet him. That was worth putting up with a lot of confusing, confectionary-laden talk from Marielle.

"Where should I sleep?" he asked, hefting his satchel.

Why, with me, of course, he imagined Marielle saying…and knew himself to be a fool. How had he gotten entangled in this?

"Anywhere you like," she said, unknowingly inciting him further as she spread her arms to indicate the front room. "What's mine is yours, Sheriff—for just as long as you want it."

Chapter Five

When she'd agreed to allow Dylan Coyle to be quartered at her house—after having first all but interrogated Corinne Murphy about everything Jack Murphy had ever disclosed about the man—Marielle could not have foreseen how complicated it would make things. How confusing. How surprising. She hadn't known how downright *dangerous* her everyday life had been about to become.

Afterward, she wished she had known. Not that that could or would have changed anything. So far, the provisional sheriff—for she could think of that drifting man in no other, more lasting terms—had been with her and Hudson for fourteen days and nights.

Even after all that time spent together, Marielle stood not one whit closer to understanding Dylan than she had on the day he'd arrived with a solitary satchel, a shiny tin badge and a freshly

shaved face that still made her look twice at him
every time he took a chair across from her at the
breakfast table.

It seemed beyond surreal to her that *she*, the
oldest dance hall girl in Morrow Creek and one
of its most avowed longtime spinsters, should be
living temporarily with a man like Dylan.

The whole town saw him as their savior. The
effect he had on the townspeople was, in a word,
remarkable. When he strode through the streets,
folks smiled and waved, then stopped the sheriff
to chat. They blushed and nodded. Children followed him, copying his swagger, wearing their
borrowed hats pulled down low, as he wore his.
Grown men sought his counsel on subjects as diverse as horses and plowshares; they spread his
advice far and wide on those topics, too. Women
regarded him with awestruck looks. Businessmen took off their hats and grew humble in his
presence. Even the town leaders—strong men
all—deferred to Dylan in matters of criminality,
justice and safety. They were all relying on him
to keep them secure. By extension, they were all
relying on Marielle to keep Dylan well cared for
at home, too.

Where she might have expected criticism or
inquiries for having so complaisantly agreed to
quarter him, she instead received help, hoopla and
gifts of foodstuffs and supplies. By day and evening, baskets full of cured hams, freshly picked

fruits, spring vegetables, preserves, wholemeal bread and Molly Copeland's special cinnamon buns all arrived at her house.

Her neighbors brought blankets and clothing for Dylan, hats and bullets, a variety of guns and a quantity of men's boots—even, very kindly, a new pair of shoes to replace Marielle's. The butcher delivered meats. The blacksmith brought knives and a passel of jokes. The livery stable owner offered the use of any of his horses, one of which soon came to be cared for right alongside Hudson's mare. Before long, Marielle and her brother's small house overflowed with goods... and that wasn't even counting the multiple services offered by the grateful townspeople.

Seeing it all, Marielle realized it was no wonder that Sheriff Caffey had turned crooked. Any weak man would have.

Spoiled by gifts and overrun by offers of free services, Caffey had obviously been corrupted by the privileges of his office. He'd then gone on to abuse them. Fortunately, Marielle doubted that Dylan would succumb to a similar fate. He would never remain in Morrow Creek long enough for that to happen.

That didn't mean he didn't have opportunities, though.

"Tell Sheriff Coyle he should come by any old time," said Miss Adelaide, who ran the bathhouse downtown, when she stopped by one afternoon.

The place was nearly a brothel, offering a variety of soapy, scandalous experiences. "All my girls are just brimful of excitement over the prospect of meeting him."

"I'll be sure to let him know, next time he feels dirty," Marielle had replied, surprised that Dylan hadn't already sampled the titillations on offer at Miss Adelaide's place.

It was popular with all the bachelors in town— newcomers, old-timers and passers-through alike. But she'd only laughed right along with good-natured Miss Adelaide, then gone back to the business of trying to crutch her way through the crates of goods, boxes of gifts and piles of victuals that filled her house to the brim. Her bedroom stood chockablock with those items. So did the kitchen and the front room where Dylan, along with Hudson, slept—not on a pallet but on a comfortable, custom-designed bed made to nest with its twin when not in use. The design was ingenious, but its use was startlingly problematic.

More than once, Marielle wandered into the front room, long accustomed to waking up Hudson before starting breakfast…only to find herself confronted unexpectedly with the striking sight of brawny Dylan Coyle, shirtless and clad only in his underdrawers, half exposed by his tangled bedclothes as he slumbered on.

She knew it wasn't polite to stare. All the same…heavens! The acting sheriff was as muscular as he was opinionated. He was as handsome as he was authoritative. If not for her own fear of getting Hudson in even deeper trouble with the Sheridans, she would have made Dylan Coyle leave her house and not come back.

That's what would have been the levelheaded thing to do, Marielle knew. Any right-thinking woman would not have subjected herself to the constant risk inherent in having a man present under her roof under those conditions. It simply wasn't wise.

Marielle had always prided herself on behaving intelligently. But where Dylan was concerned, she could not do that. Partly because getting Hudson out of trouble depended on placating Charley and his brothers. Partly because she really had no experience with any of what it took to win a man's favor—at least not when she was offstage. She was out of her depth and treading water for all her might, doing whatever she could to "get in good" with the new sheriff.

Her efforts were fruitful. At least she thought so. Dylan seemed to enjoy being around her... even if he *did* throw her a bemused look now and again. Mostly, he responded favorably to her smiles, her conversation, her helpfulness, her attempts to draw him out, her touches...and her tentative flirting, too.

That was the most perilous act of all. Because without the safety of a stage between them, Marielle was not at all sure how far to go—or how, in fact, to ensure that Dylan trusted her.

He needed to appear to do so to satisfy the Sheridans. Because Charley and his brothers were still watching. She needed to be ready when they returned to claim what they thought was their due. Reasoning that there was no such thing as excess in her situation, Marielle took every opportunity to compliment Dylan. To praise his efforts. To sit near him, to share a bit of herself with him…even to touch him, intrepidly and recklessly.

Doing so left her feeling beset with conflicting feelings, but Marielle had no choice except to continue. As time went on, she truly *liked* Dylan Coyle more and more. But she couldn't be honest with him. How could she? She didn't trust him herself.

She doubted she ever would. But she was entertained—by him, by their predicament, by her own seemingly unstoppable bravado.

Every time Marielle thought she was pushing things too far with Dylan, she was surprised to learn she wasn't. She gave him an opportunity to know her; he took it, but didn't offer much of himself in return. She teased and flirted; he did the same, but managed to thrill her without ever becoming serious. She touched him on his hand or his arm or once—very stirringly—his taut, squared-off jaw; he allowed her to, but never touched her back.

With Dylan, there seemed to be no end to the shocking things she could get away with. Frustratingly, though, he let her make all the advances. Marielle couldn't tell if she was succeeding, failing or floundering somewhere in between.

She was indeed "cozying up" to the new sheriff, as Charley Sheridan had ordered her to. But as their time together lengthened, Marielle was irked to learn that her pretense no longer felt sufficient. She wanted more from Dylan. Much more.

Probably, her disgruntlement owed itself more to a sense of inherent, unfulfilled competitiveness than it did to real tender feelings, Marielle told herself on the dawn of their fifteenth day together. But that didn't mean she didn't intend to have her way. She did. Since Dylan was foolish enough to give her plenty of lead, she meant to run with it—now more daringly than ever.

After all…didn't she have him right where she wanted him?

His choice of sheriff's quarters had played right into her hands, Marielle knew. Now she had only to capitalize on that.

For the sake of clarity, she privately chose getting Dylan to kiss her as her next yard mark of achievement. If he did *that*, Marielle told herself as she gussied up in her most becoming pink dress, raveled up her hair into a chignon at her neck and then dabbed on some rosewater perfume, she would know she had done all she could to fulfill her unwanted contract with the Sheridan brothers. She would know she'd done her utmost to save Hudson—even if she wouldn't know precisely from what.

She'd tried asking him. Hudson had refused to say. With uncharacteristic reticence, he'd rebuffed her every query.

So Marielle had no choice but to continue with her plan. She decided to catch Dylan before he went out to commence another day of investigating, tax collecting, summons serving and being the subject of a whole town's adulation, intending to do her best to enchant him. It was as simple and as foolhardy as that. Marielle wanted to win. She wanted to end this. If she could somehow persuade the sheriff to go utterly softhearted on her, then she could accomplish both of those goals at once.

Then the Sheridan gang would sweep in, do their dastardly worst and finally—blessedly— leave her and Hudson alone.

Drawing in a deep breath, Marielle examined her reflection in her bedroom mirror. She knew she looked appealing. She still didn't know if Dylan Coyle found her to be so, though. His continuing resistance vexed her. So did her ongoing near imprisonment in her own house. She didn't like being vexed.

Forbidden to dance, barred from taking care of anyone and helpless to influence her life and her brother's in any way except to make Dylan trust her…well, Marielle intended to give everything she had to the one thing she *could* still do.

If Providence had been sensible, it would not have forcibly focused all of Marielle's considerable determination on the single necessary goal of "cozying up" to the new sheriff. But that's what had happened. So that's what she aimed to do.

Grabbing her crutch—which now required hardly any thought to operate, thanks to her coordination and fortitude—Marielle lifted her head and then moved toward the kitchen, ready and willing and able to do whatever was necessary have this done.

For Hudson's sake. And for the townspeople's, too.

Because the longer they foolishly counted on someone like Dylan Coyle, Marielle knew, the more disappointed they would be when he left them in the end—just the same way he'd leave her.

It was a good thing, she reckoned, that she had more control over her emotions than everyone else she knew did. She might well be the only person left clearheaded in Morrow Creek.

She had to be the one to ride to the rescue.

The first step? Proving her advantage by getting Dylan to kiss her. After that, she'd know she was on top and could proceed accordingly—possibly by alerting Charley Sheridan, or possibly by convincing Hudson to tell her how he'd riled up those outlaws so Marielle could stop this, once and for all.

Heart pounding at the scale of her intentions, Marielle puckered her lips. She set her sights on the place where she knew Dylan would be, then headed straight toward it.

The last place Dylan expected to find Marielle Miller creeping up on him was outside the house, beside the shed, where the light was good for morning ablutions and he disturbed no one by being awake at his customarily early hour.

Marielle thought she was being surreptitious. He could tell by the sneaky, self-satisfied expression on her face as she made her way across the yard. He had to give her credit; she operated her crutch as though she'd been born with it in her hand. He plainly hadn't fully appreciated her strength and resolve.

Stealthy she was not, however. Not by a mile.

Grinning to himself as he watched her in the shaving mirror he'd nailed up within reach of the water pump and well, Dylan casually reached for his straight razor. He'd set a zinc basin of water on a nearby tree stump. He'd placed some piney soap right beside it, letting it keep company with his gun belt.

He still didn't like wearing it. Strapping it on made him feel like Atlas, with the mythical weight of the world on his hips instead of his shoulders. He should have gotten rid of it long ago. Because if force was available, force tended to be used. It was as simple as that. If he didn't want to hurt anyone—and most of the time, he didn't—he oughtn't to pack weapons.

Of course, his hands were weapons, too. His encounter with Arvid Bouchard's men had proved that—to Miles Callaway's eternal gratitude, too. Dylan packed his fists every day. But hands could be used for more than inflicting punishment. Hands could be used for stroking, fixing, shaving. A gun only did one thing.

It did the one thing he didn't much care to do anymore.

Shirtless in the sunlight—with his day's clean togs draped conveniently on the pump handle—Dylan went on shaving. Carefully, he drew his straight razor across his lathered-up jaw. He kept his gaze fixed on Marielle, loving the determined look on her pert, clean-scrubbed face. Without her dance hall girl's feathers, rouge, reddened lips and spangles, she seemed twice as fresh to him. Twice as appealing. Twice as dangerous.

Damnation, but it had been difficult to live with her. He'd anticipated that her obstinacy would challenge him—that her insistence on having her own way would irritate him. Instead, Marielle possessed other qualities that had knocked him off-kilter.

Her kindness should have been the stuff of legends. Her generosity toward her brother—and even toward the stranger in their midst—should have been written about in songs and poems. She was as smart as a feisty retort and as gentle as a summer's night. She was bold and indomitable, strong and silly, and although Dylan knew darn well that Marielle didn't *really* want him there in her suddenly topsy-turvy household full of bribes and bunkum and fraudulent hopes masquerading as townspeople's gifts, she nonetheless made him *feel* as though she did.

As far as he could tell, that was a near miracle, too.

Over the past two weeks, during the times he hadn't been settling disputes, looking into minor misconducts, encouraging unwanted elements to move on and going door-to-door meeting the townspeople by way of collecting their overdue tax money, Dylan had been doing everything he could not to be lured in by Marielle. So far, he had failed completely. When she spoke to him, he fell spellbound into her tales of dancing, emigrating from New York City, fending off rough audiences and baking cakes. When she teased him, he laughed in spite of his resolve not to. When she looked at him, he wanted to preen. When she touched him…he wanted to abandon every shred of self-control he had.

He had a mission to complete here. Yet all he

wanted to do was lie with Marielle in a damn field of flowers and look at the clear territorial skies sweeping past overhead. He was a fool.

To a point, so was Marielle, Dylan knew. Even now, she crept nearer—at least as well as a body could be said to creep while encumbered by a crutch—then crouched behind a rain barrel. Her eyes were wide, her posture alert, her face an enraptured oval of curiosity beneath her messily dressed long brown hair.

Had she *never* witnessed a man shaving before? Dylan wondered. Admittedly, Hudson was a hairy beast of a man. He wasn't overly concerned with matters of fashion. But even Hudson had to shave his beard occasionally. So Marielle must have happened upon him doing it once or twice. She wasn't that sheltered; she knew that men bled and sweated and shaved their whiskers. Yet whenever she stumbled upon Dylan doing so in the mornings—which she somehow managed, time and again lately—she behaved as though he were accomplishing something extraordinary.

In the mirror, he amusedly watched her gaze follow the next stroke of his razor. Then the next. More lather disappeared from his face, leaving Dylan one step closer to presentable.

What was she doing there? Why had she bothered to hide?

Did she truly believe she was fooling him?

"If the Sheridan brothers were as pathetic at

sneaking around as you are," he finally said in a lazy drawl, "they'd never have graced a single wanted poster."

At the sound of his voice, she started. Then she ducked.

At her overdue show of furtiveness, he almost laughed.

"I already saw you, Marielle." Dylan reached for a towel. He dried off his face, then slung the towel atop his gun belt. "You might as well come out and tell me what you want already."

"What I want," she huffed, staring downward, "is to find the hairpin I dropped someplace behind this rain barrel."

"I can assure you, your lost hairpin is not on my face," Dylan said. "Which is where you were looking a minute ago."

"Your *face*?" Marielle popped up from her hiding place. She pooh-poohed. "I was never looking at your face." As if proving it, her gaze dipped to his bare torso. Her cheeks turned a shade rosier. She came audaciously closer, trailing her flowery perfume, performing as near a casual stroll as she was able to with an injured ankle. "At least I wasn't, except with the intention of letting you know that you're doing that all wrong."

He laughed. "I'm *shaving* all wrong? How would you know?"

"By your results." She reached him in a breathless flurry of skirts. "They're abominable. Truly wretched. I honestly can't believe anyone accepts you as sheriff looking the way you do."

Perturbed by her suggestion that he wasn't entirely suitable for the job he'd taken, Dylan bristled. "What way?"

Her gaze had drifted again to his chest. "Hmm?" she asked.

That was when he knew he had her. Against all expectation, Marielle—for that's what she'd pleasantly invited him to call her on the day he'd arrived—had a weakness. He could exploit that weakness. He was going to have to, if he wanted to get inside her noggin, find out what she knew about Charley Sheridan and his brothers…and protect her while he was at it. So far, those miscreants hadn't returned.

Dylan knew it was only a matter of time before they did.

Trying to get to Marielle in other ways hadn't worked. He'd tried casual queries, direct questions and steady observation. He was going to have to get tougher with her. Right now.

Testing his theory, Dylan scratched his nose. Marielle's gaze dutifully followed his movements…but not to his nose, the way an ordinary person's would have done. Instead, her attention veered to his biceps, then held. She sucked in a breath. Sighed.

Marielle, Dylan realized assuredly, liked his muscles.

She liked looking at them, watching them in action—maybe she would even enjoy touching them, too. Although he was considering the matter as an issue of strategic importance, he couldn't help being caught up in the notion of her doing just that. If he let her, Marielle would touch him. Maybe all over.

He wanted that to happen in the most powerful way.

Unfortunately, she chose that moment to regain her usual assurance. "Your shave job," Marielle said, "says that you are a man with poor attention to detail and a lack of commitment."

"All that?" Wryly, he shook his head. "Tarnation."

She shrugged. "It's too late to be regretful now. You've already made the decision to look like a gypsy vagabond."

"Given the way you were looking at me just now, you like gypsy vagabonds."

"Humph. You may wish that were true, Sheriff—"

"I already asked you to call me Dylan."

"—but if wishing made reality, Dylan, my brother and Miss Murphy would already be skipping down to the church to be wed."

"Hudson does like Miss Murphy then?"

A careless nod. "He does, but it's hopeless. She's confided in me that he's a bit unreliable for her liking. She doesn't want to take a chance on a man who's not grown-up all the way."

"He's done a good job taking caring of you," Dylan allowed.

Privately, though, he gave much of the credit for that to the assistance Hudson had enjoyed—via the gift baskets, offers of foodstuffs and visits they'd had since Dylan had moved into their household. Certain of the less reputable townspeople—and even some folks who merely wanted to be friendly—had gone out of their way to be of service to his host family.

"He's learned to do a lot more than I ever thought he would," Dylan told her honestly. "He's made an effort."

Her smile beamed at him. "He has, hasn't he?" Marielle glanced to the house, which now sported newly repaired porch railings, courtesy of Hudson—with a great deal of tutelage from Dylan. "Dear Hudson has cooked and cleaned his heart out for me while I've been laid up. But Miss Murphy doesn't want a *wife*."

"She might. She's an avowed suffragist, like Grace."

"She wants a man who's virile. Capable. Tough. Qualified." Again, Marielle's attention veered to the house—this time, to the fence surrounding her vegetable garden. Dylan had helped Hudson mend and repaint the pickets, which now shined white. Marielle had been leaving those "rougher" chores up to her brother—who had not possessed anywhere near the ambition or know-how to accomplish them. "Someone skilled at manly pursuits."

Her hinting was about as subtle as a bash to the head. She wanted something from him. He wasn't yet sure what it was.

Dylan hid a smile. "You mean manly pursuits like carpentry?" he guessed offhandedly. "Painting? Woodworking?"

"Exactly!" Marielle touched his arm in approval, causing him to go stock-still with yearning. With effort, he managed not to touch her back. Again. But he sorely wanted to. "Miss Murphy wants a man who has experience under his belt." She chanced a coquettish look at him. "A good job never hurts, either."

"Ah. I see what you're driving at."

Marielle wanted him to give Hudson a job.

"You do?" She seemed thrilled. "Excellent!"

"You're telling me that Miss Murphy is over the moon for me." With a wry look, Dylan nodded. He pursed his lips, then glanced skyward. "I can see why. I fit her every qualification."

Marielle's mouth dropped open. Just as he'd expected.

"Not *you*, you egotistical mule! *Hudson!* She wants Hudson."

Dylan had guessed that much several days ago. But just then he pretended to be perplexed.

"Hudson doesn't have a job. Not right now, at least. He's scarcely learned about the existence of hammers and paintbrushes, much less how to use those things. He won't be getting a carpentry job, that's for certain."

"Don't be too hard on him," Marielle coaxed— but her eyes darkened with ferocity. In her presence, no one dared bad-mouth her brother. "He didn't have any role models to look up to. My father ran off with a visiting opera singer when Hudson was only a squeaky-voiced kid playing backstage at the theater."

She frowned and glanced away, doubtless wishing—too late—that she hadn't blurted out that family calamity. She'd shared with him the Millers' adventures as backstage workers in the New York City theater world, but only in passing. Her mother had been a seamstress; her father, a strong stagehand. Marielle herself had trained as a standby performer before striking out westward after her mother's death with only ten dollars, a dream and Hudson for company.

"Granted, our mother could have taught him to sew, as she did me, or to keep house, as she did me," Marielle added airily, "but that would have been silly. Hudson had me for that."

"Yes. And he always will, won't he?"

She blinked. "Of course he will. I'll always protect him."

Even to the point of conspiring with the Sheri-

dans? Dylan couldn't help wondering. *Or risking your own safety?*

It had been clear to him that Charley Sheridan had threatened Marielle. It had been equally evident that she'd nodded in agreement to Charley on that fateful night, promising him…something. But her winsome nearness made Dylan's responsible thoughts of his peacekeeping duties feel very far away.

"Maybe you shouldn't protect Hudson," he opined, nonetheless feeling sorry for her. After all, she'd learned from those idiosyncratic stage performers she'd known and her own feckless father that people—*men*—were not to be counted on. No wonder she mistrusted his own wandering ways. "Maybe then Hud could fend for himself a little better."

"I don't want him to fend for himself!" Marielle looked at him as though the very notion horrified her. "I promised my mother, before she passed on, that I would look after Hudson."

"That's very honorable of you." Dylan fetched the shirt he'd left on the pump handle. Making sure his arm muscles flexed almost comically with the effort, he pulled it on. "I doubt your mother meant that you should sacrifice everything for him."

She seemed puzzled—and not nearly as distracted by his muscular display as he'd hoped. "I haven't sacrificed anything."

"Near as I can tell, you've sacrificed a great deal." Dylan had a reasonably fair sense of that much, after living with the two of them for weeks now. "Your future, for one thing."

Marielle scoffed. "Don't be preposterous."

"Do you really think a man will want you *and* your brother? Everyone in town knows you won't marry until Hudson does."

"What? That's outlandish! No one knows any such thing."

"Then you *haven't* turned down a number of marriage proposals?" Dylan shrugged. "Maybe I heard wrong about you."

Maybe he'd overestimated her fascination with his muscles, too. After all, he possessed nothing more than ordinary arms and legs and shoulders. There shouldn't be any fuss about them. But as Dylan disgruntledly tucked in his shirt, he realized that Marielle was still watching him. With interest, she followed the motion of his hand... all the way to the top of his britches. Then a bit... lower. That was bold of her. It was also gratifying.

He *hadn't* been wrong about her. She liked him.

It required all his resolve not to laugh triumphantly.

Rather than deny what he'd heard in town, Marielle hedged.

"We are getting sidetracked." She was caught, and she knew it. Dylan's reconnaissance was irrefutable. He was, after all, a security expert. He knew how to extract information. In this case, he was interested in Marielle, who appeared to be on the verge of kicking him again as she added, "I'm merely saying—"

"I'm still waiting for you to tell me what's wrong with my shaving technique." Dylan grinned. "With bated breath."

"—that it would be very helpful if someone in a position to do so would give Hudson a job. Even a temporary one," Marielle persisted. She stepped closer, then gazed up at him with evident hopefulness shining in her blue eyes. "Say…as acting deputy?"

Even knowing it was coming hadn't prepared Dylan for the impact of having Marielle actually ask him for a special favor.

He'd suspected it would eventually come to this. He had something Marielle needed—and it wasn't what he would have hoped she'd need: namely, him. It was a job. The kind of job that might endear her layabout brother to industrious Corinne Murphy. The wonder of it all was that it had taken her so long to ask.

Because it hadn't taken long for Dylan to realize how things sat in the Miller household. Marielle worked herself to a frazzled state, dancing at Jack Murphy's saloon *and* doing expert seamstress work for the townspeople *and* seeing to all the housekeeping, while her goodhearted lummox of a brother idled by, sporadically doing his bit by "protecting" her at the saloon—in between drinking ales, playing hands of faro and keeping suspiciously friendly company with the Sheridan boys.

If Hudson had been at all malicious, his behavior would have been criminal. As it was, the man was just too mollycoddled by Marielle to know any better. If not for Marielle's injury, Dylan doubted Hudson would ever have stepped up, not even in the limited way he had by cooking, cleaning and mending fences.

Dylan doubted Hudson could be any practical use to him. The man wasn't stupid, but he was careless, impulsive and far too quick to trust people. Those were hardly the qualities necessary in an exemplary sheriff's deputy. Marielle must have known that.

He couldn't be cruel enough to point that out, though. He didn't want to dim the hopeful light in her eyes. Not now or ever. Inanely, he wanted to spark it to an even greater glow. He wanted to be her hero, Dylan knew, as irrational as that was.

"Hmm. I reckon I might be able to see my way toward such an arrangement." Dylan gazed down at her, wondering if her cheeks would feel as soft as they looked—if her mouth would taste as sweet as he imagined. "Only…well, there's a problem."

"A problem?" She whipped her gaze up to his face.

Satisfactorily, that meant she'd been studying

his chest again. It was only too bad that propriety had demanded he get dressed. Otherwise, he'd have tempted her with nakedness for far longer. It seemed that Marielle might be as curious about his more intimate attributes as he was about hers. He'd dreamed of her coming to him, unfastening all the mind-bogglingly myriad buttons on one of her dresses as she did, gradually baring herself to him, smiling in a way that was seductive and loving—

With a start, Dylan ended that tantalizing train of thought. He didn't need *loving*. All he needed was information.

And maybe, as a bonus, one of her smiles. He loved those.

"Yes, a problem," he alleged. "After all, *someone* just said I'm hardly fit to act as sheriff, on account of my raggedy shave job." Musingly, Dylan rubbed his nonexistent beard. "Too bad."

He expected her to backtrack. Instead, she surprised him.

"Oh, that's no trouble." Confidently, Marielle waved her hand. She eyed his jaw with an air of expertise. "I can fix that for you. I'll tell you everything you need to know."

"You will?" Amused, Dylan put his hands on his hips.

"Absolutely." With a serious mien, Marielle examined him.

"You're going to help me not look like a gypsy vagabond?"

A nod. "Not look like one," she specified. "I can't help if you still are one. I'm not packing any miracles, after all."

"I suppose not." Another stifled grin. "I am a hard case."

"What *you* are…" Marielle circled him, looking him up and down as she trod in crutch-assisted loop. "Is in dire need."

"Of?"

"My help, of course."

"Well, go ahead, then." He inhaled. "Or are you bluffing?"

Her smile refuted the very idea. Marielle stopped directly in front of him. Her flowery scent reached out to him. Her warmth did, too. Dylan fancied he could feel her skirts brush his trouser legs. They were that close…then, suddenly, *closer.*

Startled, he almost stepped back. But that would have been madness. If Marielle wanted to stand on his toes to examine his shoddy shaving job, then he was in the perfect mood to let her.

Besides, he didn't want to topple her on her crutch.

She raised her hand and touched his jaw. At that, he *did* jerk. It was just so unexpected to feel her hand on his face.

"I'm sorry," she murmured. "I'm going to have

to touch you if this instruction is to go anywhere. Is that all right?"

If she meant *could he stand it?* then maybe not. Contrarily, he nodded. When it came to her, he wanted to try.

He also wanted to hold her steady. Chivalrously, Dylan brought his hands to her waist. Neither noticing nor strictly requiring his support, Marielle raised her hand again to touch the other side of his face, exhibiting an impressive sense of dancer's balance that he didn't have the wits to contemplate further. Held thus, clasped gently by her, Dylan felt himself go rigid all over. He needed...her. He had all along.

He thought he might die if he didn't kiss her.

Oblivious to that, Marielle stood on tiptoe, the better to study his slapdash workmanship. Her brow furrowed. Her breath feathered over his mouth, lightly enough to set his senses atingle. Then, in a shocking gesture undoubtedly meant to test the closeness of his shave, Marielle pressed her cheek to his.

At the same time, she inadvertently pushed her bosom against him. Their bodies touched, pressed together then held, tremblingly, for the longest thirty seconds of Dylan's life.

"Mmm." She exhaled. "This side seems all right to me."

Dylan began feeling lighthearted. He couldn't

stand this. Being so close to Marielle, yet unable to really touch her…

"You'd better," he said gruffly, "check the other side."

Obligingly and remarkably, Marielle did. She shifted subtly—increasing the pressure and friction of their bodies in the process—then gently put her opposite cheek against the other side of his face. For balance, her hands dropped to his chest.

Brashly, Marielle dug her fingertips into his muscles.

Faintly, Dylan remembered feeling cocky about those muscles of his and the effect they seemed to have on her. Now, though, the joke was on him. He'd never been affected more by anything in his life than he was by Marielle's evaluative touch.

"Hmm." Without moving her body, she leaned her head back. She gazed directly and teasingly into his eyes, reminding him of nothing so much as a woman who wanted kissing. "This side seems all right, too. Perhaps I'm wrong about you. Perhaps—"

"You *are* wrong about me."

Dylan wanted to say more. He wanted to say that he was a drifter by necessity, not by choice. He wanted to say that he already wanted to stay in Morrow Creek and she was the reason. He wanted to say that he would have given anything to believe things could be good and lasting between them. But that was unthinkable. That would only ensure, as it always did, that everything unraveled in the end. So instead, he let his need for her say everything. He let his need for her—so long denied—move his hands to her face, cradle her jaw and pull her nearer.

"You're wrong about everything about me," Dylan said.

She was wrong—because he'd made damn sure she would be.

He'd made sure everyone would be. For so long now.

Marielle hauled in a breath, probably to argue. But by then his mouth was already meeting hers. By then he was kissing her, and her fingers were curling into his chest again and the whole world seemed to light up with pleasure and Dylan didn't care about anything except the next kiss, the next sigh, the next time he would feel Marielle's body close against his this way.

For several long moments, he felt he'd gone to heaven.

She was the first to break away, eyes still closed.

When she opened them, she seemed…bedazzled. But she managed to set herself to sensibleness again with striking quickness.

"I'm afraid *that* experience only proves I'm right about you," Marielle said. "I knew I was. I usually am. You'll see."

Then she swiveled on her crutch and left him behind in the yard without even the pretense of an excuse—or the memory of a shave lesson—to keep him company.

Damnation. Watching the side-to-side sway of her bustle as she left, Dylan realized that he'd done it again. He'd tried not to talk too much or reveal too much. But somehow, had anyway.

Somehow, he'd let slip that most shameful part of him—that unmanly, usually hidden part that was soppy and sentimental, foolish and better excised. Wholly accidentally, he'd let Marielle see past his disreputable-looking outsides to his less than tough insides. Marielle—who'd rattled on and on about masculinity and toughness just moments ago—obviously wanted no part of that. Of him.

He couldn't blame her. A man didn't want to hold a woman closer, cover her with kisses *and* hear her laughter…all in equal measure. A man didn't love sharing a meal with a woman as much as he loved admiring her beauty. A man didn't think about poetry and blue skies, flowers and softness. Dylan knew that.

He'd learned it long ago. He'd tried to stop being so damnably mush-hearted. Evidently, he hadn't yet buried his flaw all the way. Not if Marielle could see—and reject—it so easily.

Her reaction had been the same as every other woman's had been: to leave him by the fastest means possible. Inevitably, Dylan knew, that's what always happened. Sooner or later, his hard facade gave way to the softhearted man beneath... and then everything crumbled. That was why he'd always moved on.

He never wanted to reach that point, not with anyone.

But now he couldn't move on. He'd made a commitment—to himself, to Marielle, to the people of Morrow Creek.

He was stuck. Because he always kept his word.

For however much longer it took to nab the Sheridans, Dylan knew, he would have to rein himself in. He would have to be steely. Closed off. Possessed of a need to neither talk nor be spoken to. Indifferent to being spoilt in a household full of laughter and hugs. He would have to do his utmost to be the man his father had tried and failed to teach him to be, so long ago.

Maybe, with the sting of Marielle's rebuff fresh on his mind, he would succeed this time, Dylan told himself. At the very least, he acknowledged with a rueful grin as he gathered his things, Marielle wouldn't try to tempt him anymore. Not now that she'd glimpsed the real him. Women wanted him as a hard-nosed protector. But as soon as his softer nature appeared...

Well, he'd never been freer of Marielle than he

was at that moment. But he'd never wanted freedom less or resented it more.

Hellfire. He was sunk.

Chapter Six

In the end, Dylan *did* take on Hudson as a provisional deputy. But not, Marielle was forced to concede, because she'd been especially ingenious or persuasive—merely because she had allowed him to kiss her...and thus had influenced him.

Unfairly, as it turned out. Because while she'd imagined herself playing a game—admittedly one with very high stakes—involving securing the upper hand with the new sheriff, from the moment Dylan had kissed her, everything had changed.

One moment, Marielle had been clumsily sneaking around the yard, purposely allowing Dylan to believe he had the advantage so he'd be more malleable later. The next, she'd been dumbstruck by the rippling strength of his muscles, the golden sheen of his skin, the pure and powerful masculinity that hung on his every gesture. One moment, Marielle had been cleverly manipulating the conversation toward Hudson and her wishes to help him make a positive impression on Corinne Murphy. The next, she'd been entirely provoked by Dylan's needling her about how she took on too much when it came to Hudson. She'd revealed much more about her past—and her feckless, unreliable father—than she'd ever intended to tell a soul. One moment, she had been authoritative and enjoying it. The next, she'd been overcome with hesitancy.

She'd planned, Marielle knew, to spur Dylan into kissing her as proof of her ability to make him trust her. Instead, she'd only lulled herself into trusting the new sheriff more than ever. Because Dylan Coyle was unlike anyone she'd ever met.

When she spoke, Dylan listened. When she argued, he took her seriously—and then he stated his own case with equal intensity. When she asked him for something, he made sure he gave it. They'd disagreed about Hudson and the "sacrifices" she was supposedly making for her brother, of course, but the mere fact that they'd discussed it was remarkable. Because if there *was* gossip in town about Marielle refusing to marry until Hudson's future was settled, none of it had ever reached her.

Evidently, no one had ever thought she'd listen.

But Dylan did. He did, and he'd confronted her with what he thought were her mistakes. As much as Marielle hadn't liked hearing that, she respected him for taking an honest stand.

She wished she could respect herself for having followed through completely with her plan. But the truth was, Marielle had quailed. Intolerably so. Because when she'd worked up her courage, when she'd gotten herself smack up against Dylan with her palms against his beating heart and his whole handsome face within reach, she'd decided then and there to kiss him herself.

She'd abandoned her wily plan altogether, overcome with a curiosity so intense and unquenchable that it had demanded more.

She'd almost made it, too, Marielle remembered with a hot, shaky feeling. She'd dared enough to rise and aim her mouth at Dylan's. She'd dared enough to inhale and then make the decision to just…kiss him! Do it! She'd dared enough to want him.

But then, on the way to doing so, she had somehow found herself awkwardly smashing her cheek against his face instead, pretending she was double-checking the closeness of his shave.

Stupid. *Stupid!* Even now, a whole three days later, Marielle didn't know what had gotten into her. Ordinarily, she was courageous—unbowed by troubles, hecklers, stage fright and worry. But somehow, faced with Dylan's nearness, she had been entirely unable to keep her head. Make him kiss her? Be sure to kiss him herself? Do neither of those things? She'd been unable to decide and had thus had the matter decided for her. By him.

Dylan's kisses had been...*stirring*, to say the least. Moving. Surprising and forceful and exactly as passionate as Marielle might have imagined. Despite her determined resolve not to enjoy them—because they were, after all, supposed to have served as proof she could offer to Charley Sheridan in order to be free of him—she did enjoy them. She enjoyed them a great deal.

She spent the next few days savoring them, in fact. When she rested her ankle, she thought of Dylan kissing her. When she climbed into her bed at night, she thought of Dylan kissing her. When she ate supper, when she cleaned her teeth, when she saw a hawk on the wing or a neighbor on the street, she thought of Dylan kissing her...and experienced a powerful urge for more.

Unfortunately, more kissing was not forthcoming.

Because just as Marielle had changed after their kiss, so, too, had Dylan. Directly after she had crutched herself away, uncertain and aflutter and knowing only that she had to get some distance from him to think about her quandary, Dylan had turned more remote than she'd ever seen him. In the place of the jovial, joking man she knew, a stranger arrived—one who was stony and terse, gruff and businesslike, scowling and hard.

Marielle knew that she had caused that change

somehow. Somehow, with her inexpert manipulating and inexperienced kissing, she had turned happy-go-lucky Dylan Coyle into a verifiable misanthrope. He was hard on Hudson and indifferent to her. He even quit joking with the neighborhood children.

Watching from her front porch one afternoon as those youngsters ran around hollering their heads off and quick drawing their imaginary guns, Marielle had laughed at first.

"They're almost just like you," she'd told Dylan, who'd paused to frown at the spectacle. "All that's missing is for them to swear at their toy gun belts before strapping them on."

His frown had deepened. "I don't do that."

"Indeed, you do!" She'd laughed. "Every single time."

"A man protects people. With guns, if need be."

"That's why I don't understand your reticence. After all, most men in the territory carry a firearm. You're not—"

"I'm not most men. I'm deadlier with mine."

Momentarily thwarted by that, Marielle had watched more of the children's shenanigans. Then, "There is one more thing missing in their play. It's lacking real authenticity."

Dylan had only stood by, hands on his hips. He'd grunted.

"They all need to swagger around a great deal more."

Her teasing had only made him look angrier.

"Some men have cause to swagger. I'm one of them."

Marielle hadn't doubted it. She'd told him so. "I know. That's why I'm so grateful to you for taking Hudson under your wing. He's benefitting immeasurably from your good example."

"Humph. If you're trying to start a fight, just say so."

Perplexed, she'd been forced to let the matter drop when Dylan had—unmistakably—swaggered off the front porch and saddled up his horse to make his daily sheriff's rounds. But Marielle hadn't been able to quit thinking about it…or about similar run-ins she and Dylan had had since the day he'd kissed her.

Maybe, she speculated, he'd found her kiss lacking.

After all, she was admittedly inexperienced. Maybe the trouble with the kiss they'd shared owed itself to her lack of familiarity with such intimacies. Or maybe all she needed was more effort. Because it was still inevitable that Charley Sheridan would come back, and Marielle needed to be ready.

I'm sorry. I couldn't make the new sheriff trust me because I'm unfamiliar with kissing was not an excuse she could offer.

Determinedly, she vowed to make another attempt. Surely a well-delivered kiss could cement her position of trust in Dylan's heart—and also help soften his newly churlish mood, too. Because she did not believe for one instant that the grumpy, taciturn man she'd been sharing her household with was the true Dylan Coyle.

Where was the man who'd called her *a damn poet* onstage? Where was the man who'd smiled over her obduracy, laughed over her mocking guess that he might be nearing forty, and willingly served as her cushion when she'd fallen offstage? Where was the man who'd looked at her as if she was precious?

Marielle wanted that man back. If she'd accidentally shooed him away with one kiss, then maybe she could bring him back with another.

So she lay in wait for Dylan, exercising both her patience and her imagination in the meanwhile, and finally was rewarded when Morrow Creek's interim sheriff came home at the end of a rain-filled, springtime day without his new deputy trailing him.

Lately, Dylan had been using Hudson's presence as a nominal chaperone as an excuse not to revisit their kiss. But on that day, Marielle had seen to it that her brother was occupied by seeing to an errand for her friend Jobyna after finishing his peacekeeping duties. Feeling almost unbearably ingenious because of her maneuverings, Marielle was ready when Dylan returned.

At the sound of his boots on the porch, she felt her heart begin to race. At the rattle of his hand on the door, her mouth went dry, too. Full of anticipation and resolve, Marielle made sure her injured ankle was exactly as ruinously bandaged as she'd been capable of. She'd nearly shredded her poor bandages a short while earlier, then poorly rewrapped them in a way she knew Dylan would find irredeemably vexatious. *That* would get his attention, she knew. So would her pose on the front room settee.

She was there when Dylan stepped in, rainwater dripping from his long coat and puddling in the crown of his black hat.

"Dylan!" Marielle couldn't stop the heartfelt smile that raced to her lips when she saw him. "I'm so glad you're home!"

Maybe, it occurred to her, there was more going on here than some simple, well-intentioned plotting on her part.

But by then Dylan had turned to look at her, startled out of whatever reverie had darkened his expression when he'd come into her warm, lantern-lit house. Rather than speak at first, he instead gave her the one thing that she waited all day for.

Just as she'd hoped, Dylan looked at her...and his whole face lit up. His eyes brightened. His lips turned up. A kind of radiance seemed to travel from him to her in a single breath.

Marielle *loved* that moment. For her whole life, she'd thought there could be nothing better than standing onstage amid thunderous applause. But since Dylan had arrived to begin their unusual living arrangement, she'd learned there was something better than wholehearted applause. There was him.

The way Dylan looked at her sometimes…well, it made her feel as if there had never been another woman in the world quite as wonderful as she was. Loving it unreservedly, she sighed.

Hearing her sigh, Dylan frowned anew. He took off his coat, hung it on the peg near the door then followed with his hat. His broad shoulders slumped slightly with the movement. His footsteps were heavy. Clearly, he'd misunderstood the nature of her sigh. She wished she'd had the wherewithal to contain it.

For a moment there, she'd had the old Dylan back. The man she'd come to appreciate as much for his warmth and caring as she did for his intelligence and strength. But now…

"The fire's low," he said. "I'll see to it."

"But it's raining so hard outside! Leave it." Marielle reached for his hand, hoping to draw him near. "It's fine for now. I don't want you to have to go out in the cold again."

But Dylan didn't listen. As though it were his

lot in life to do everything that was unpleasant but necessary, he went to haul in more firewood. Capably, he stoked the fire.

Stoically, he nodded. "What else needs doing?"

"Not a thing," Marielle fibbed. *Kissing me again, so you quit behaving so grumpily*, she couldn't help thinking. She patted the settee cushion beside her. "Come sit by me. Please."

If he did, he would be bound to notice the poor bandaging job on her ankle. It would be impossible for him—as opinionated as he was—not to use his own expertise to fix it. Marielle was in such a sorry state that just the suggestion of Dylan's hands on her, even in a medicinal capacity, made her feel overeager.

For a heartbeat, he seemed tempted. Then he deliberately swept the room with a critical eye. "I'll fix those floorboards. They've been bothering me for weeks. They need seeing to."

"Not right now, they don't!" *Heavens*. He was the most stubbornly oblivious man she'd ever met. Couldn't he tell she wanted to enjoy a cozy tête-à-tête with him? She'd fixed her hair especially for him, in a braided style he'd once remarked upon. She wouldn't have done that for just anyone. "Please."

"A man sees to what needs seeing to," Dylan insisted, closing his hands into fists at his sides. He didn't look at her. "I don't have time to prattle on with you, Marielle."

Stung, she stared at him. "Well, that was just mean."

"Sometimes, men have to be mean."

"Oh, really?" That was news to her. "Hudson isn't mean."

Dylan made a face. "Hudson is an overprotected child of a man, and if you weren't responsible for that, you'd see it."

"What?" Stunned by his harsh tone, Marielle reeled.

"You're making him soft. You should let him grow up."

"Grow up…to be like *you*, I suppose? Hard? Unyielding? As grumpy as the day is long and twice as intolerable?"

Dylan looked away. "That's who I am."

But Marielle doubted that. "If that's true, then why do you sound so sad? There's a catch in your voice, Dylan. I swear, something has happened to you. Whether it's our kiss or—"

"Our kiss?" He laughed. Bitterly. "You'd like to think so."

"I do think so." Now more than ever. "If it's not that—"

"It's not that."

"Then why don't you prove it to me?" Marielle felt her heart gallop away at double its usual speed. This wasn't quite what she'd planned, but now it was too late. "Make me believe."

"Believe what?"

"That I didn't somehow turn you into an ogre by kissing you!"

At that, it was Dylan's turn to look stunned. But he covered his surprise with his now customary frown. "You didn't do anything. I'm fine."

"You're not 'fine'!" As proof, Marielle added, "You haven't said three polite words to me in days. *Days*, Dylan!"

"A man doesn't have to talk to make himself heard."

She gawked at him. "What is that supposed to mean?"

Mulishly, Dylan looked away. "A man doesn't blather on making useless chitchat. A man does things. Just like I'm going to do, when it comes to fixing that damn floorboard."

"Well, good luck finding the tools to do so." Cleverly, she'd anticipated this from him. "I hid them all."

"You didn't."

"Of course I did." Who did he think he was dealing with?

He swore again. "Don't test me, Marielle."

But she'd swear he seemed impressed by her strategy.

"I'll do whatever I like. This is *my* house. You are *my* guest, and I've decided we are going to have this out. Now."

Dylan longingly eyed his hat and coat. "I don't want to."

"I'll bet a man doesn't run from trouble," Marielle pushed, borrowing a page from his book. "I'll bet a man stays."

His answering gaze penetrated her with uncomfortable insight. "You've never believed that. You never will."

He was right. Probably. And sadly. All the same, Marielle wasn't giving up on this. "Something changed after our kiss. Whether you were disgusted by my eagerness or appalled by my inexperience, I can't rightly tell, but one way or the other—"

"Marielle—"

"—I think we ought to confront it, straight on, and have it settled," she went on doggedly, ignoring his aggrieved tone. "Because there's no telling how much longer it might take for things to be safe around here—"

Dylan's expression sharpened. "Safe? Did something happen?" He moved nearer, concern deepening his voice. "Are you all right? You said you were glad I was home. Is that because someone threatened you? Was someone here?"

She couldn't believe that he was being so dense.

Or that she'd nearly blurted out her own concerns about the Sheridans and how long it might take to have them dealt with.

"I'm glad you're home because I like seeing you, you dolt!" It felt crucial that he believe her—

and not just because Hudson's safety depended on it. Charley had threatened them both. "I'm always glad you're home! When you come in the door at night, it feels…" She broke off, considering it. "It feels as though everything is finally going to be all right."

Dylan shifted. He cleared his throat. His gaze moved from her face to the very uninteresting spectacle of the fireplace.

Was he truly…*emotional* about this, between them?

He seemed to be. Marielle devoutly hoped he was.

She could hardly admit it, though. What kind of woman would she be if she outright encouraged tender feelings in Dylan? She couldn't trust him. So she couldn't conscionably admit what she knew to be true: that she cared for him despite her intentions not to. More so all the time. Not in the hope of fooling him, like Charley Sheridan wanted her to do, either. She cared for him just because she couldn't help it.

She thought Dylan was the finest man she'd ever met.

When he wasn't being such a chowderhead, at least.

Proving her point, he squared his shoulders. "Everything is going to be all right. That's why I'm here." He cleared his throat. "That's what a man—a *real* man—makes sure of."

Puzzled by his continual insistence on talking about what "a man" did, Marielle frowned. "I liked the man you were when you arrived," she said. "Before you kissed me. Which means—"

"That never should have happened."

"—we should probably try it again, just to fix things."

Finally hearing her, Dylan went still. Appearing distraught, he ran his hand through his hair. Several damp strands stuck up endearingly. He strode sideways, his handsome face in profile against the lamplight.

"There's no fixing this. Just quit trying."

Marielle laughed. "Me? Quit trying?"

At that, he cracked his first grin of the day. But he sobered quickly. "I'm not kissing you again, Marielle."

"Not even if I want you to? For a good cause?"

For the cause of remaking you into your former jolly self?

"It was wrong to take advantage of you," Dylan said in a daunting tone. "It won't happen again, I promise."

Her spirits sank. But she wasn't licked yet. "All right."

Suspiciously, Dylan darted a glance at her. He nodded.

"In that case, you can come sit next to me and warm up by the fire." She patted the settee. "Perfectly safely."

He looked as if she'd asked him to wrestle snakes.

He did have feelings for her, then. She'd known so! He'd have no other reason to avoid being close to her otherwise.

"Unless," Marielle provoked anew, "you're scared?"

She could have predicted his answer. It was curt and tough.

"Men don't get scared. Not of anything."

He didn't appear entirely convinced of that, but Marielle nodded, all the same. "Certainly not of a small, hobbled woman." Another inviting pat. "I might need your warmth while you're at it. Maybe you could put your arm around me? It's cold in here."

"Cold? I stoked an infernal blaze!" Dylan eyed the fire he'd tended to earlier. "Honestly, Marielle, if you're provoking me—"

She batted her eyelashes. "Yes? What if I am?"

He set his jaw. "Then you'd better stop."

"No, you'd better come over here. Please. Just do it."

"I can't."

"Are you afraid you'll kiss me again?"

A headshake. "I won't. I'm stronger than that."

"I'm strong, too." Putting on her most beguiling expression, Marielle reached for his hand. "Strong enough to say that I want you to kiss me again. Please. Just one more time?"

* * *

It would never stop at *one more time*. Dylan knew it.

Doubtless, Marielle did, too. But the vixen was repeatedly inciting him with the notion of kissing her again, all the same. Didn't she know what she was doing to him? Coming into her warm household, spying her waiting there for him, seeing her smile at him…he'd been shamefully unable to withhold a smile of his own. Worse, he knew it wasn't the first time he'd done that, either.

Seeing her was like seeing the sun after a long, gray winter. Marielle woke him up. She made him feel again.

The trouble was, Dylan didn't want to feel anything. He still wished he could call back that damn telltale unabashed grin and put on some manful indifference instead.

That's what his father would have done. Dylan could count on one hand the number of times he'd seen his father smile. Certainly none of those smiles had been called up by the sight of Dylan's mother—the woman his father had blamed for trapping him in a big city he loathed, doing factory work he despised.

Marielle was preoccupied with men leaving. Understandably so, Dylan knew. But he also knew that sometimes, leaving was better than staying. Better than misery. Heywood Coyle had wanted to go West from Boston—to explore the territories and live as an adventurer. He'd wanted to, but he never had.

In truth, he'd lacked the gumption to do so. As a grown man, Dylan recognized that. He'd tried to fulfill his father's dream in some small way, too, by traveling the world on his own. But as a boy, he'd only felt the weight of his father's blame. He and his mother had been poor anchors, both of them. They'd dredged up Heywood Coyle's discontent and duty without ever securing him to them. Not in any way that had truly mattered.

He hadn't punished them for it. Not directly. But the example of his unhappy life still dragged at Dylan's conscience, even now, when his parents were both long departed.

The least he could do as penance, he knew, was try to be the man his father would have wanted him to be. The man his father had tried to teach him to be. Was that so much to ask?

With Marielle patting the settee cushion, her eyes alight with hopefulness and naive passion… hell, yes, it was. It was a lot to ask of any man to resist her tempting invitation.

I want you to kiss me again. Please. Just one more time?

Her notion that she'd scared him away with her inexperience and her eagerness was laughable. Because Dylan knew that the former would melt away with ease and the latter was nigh irresistible—especially when aimed in his direction.

He loved an enthusiastic woman. Truth be told, he almost loved *her*. More than he'd ever intended to. Far more than was wise. But he couldn't give in. That way lay disappointment—and another rejection from a woman he cared for.

"If you don't believe me," Marielle added cheekily, "all you have to do is come over here and test me. You'll see."

What he wanted to see was why she kept on goading him, Dylan knew. After glimpsing the gentler side of his nature once, during their first kiss, Marielle had walked away. So why did she persist in pretending she wanted more of the same from him?

Trying to reason it out, he darted a glance at her. Hell. She looked as pretty as a picture and as soft as a raindrop.

She plainly expected a response from him, too. Caught, Dylan clenched his hands again. He had to resist her. But when it came to Marielle, he didn't have much fight left in him.

His gaze fell to her ankle. There, he found the diversion he needed. "Those bandages are appalling. Did Doc Finney wrap them while blindfolded? They're doing more harm than good."

Nonchalantly, Marielle glanced at them. She seemed peculiarly pleased by her inept bandaging job. "They're fine." She raised her gaze to his handsome face. "And you're stalling."

He scoffed. "Men don't stall."

"Men are mean. Men fix things," she mimicked cheerfully, putting on a hilariously deep voice to simulate his. "Men don't have time to chat. Men can't ignore the floorboards for even one more day. Men can't ever, *ever* admit they're wrong."

"I'm not wrong."

"See?" Her impish grin touched him…lured him. He mustered the means to remain steady… but those bandages were still vexing him. "You have an awful lot of rules," Marielle observed. "Where did you learn them?" A pause. "Or do men never tell?"

He frowned. "You're mocking me."

She grinned. "It's what a woman does."

"I swear, Marielle, if you knew what you did to me—"

"Tell me," she said pertly, "and I will."

He swerved his gaze to hers again, wishing she didn't seem quite so forthright. Because he wanted to believe. He wanted to believe in her. To trust her. He wanted to let himself soften in her presence, to fold her in his arms, to bask in her warmth and generosity. He wanted to give Marielle things that went beyond kindling and repairs and late-night vigils to watch for the Sheridans—things Marielle didn't know about and never would.

He wanted to relax. Once, and maybe for all. His memories of their kiss told him he could not.

If he did, if she saw him as he really was, full of sentiment and yearning to cherish her...

"You don't want that." *You don't want me.* Dylan frowned, stopping himself before he got carried away. "Stop pretending you do."

To his befuddlement, Marielle seemed confused.

"Have you ever known me not to say what I think?" she asked him. "In the weeks since we met, have you ever had cause to wonder what's on my mind? Not once, I'd say. So at least do me the same favor. Either tell me what's wrong or kiss me!"

Faced with that impossible choice, Dylan detoured instead. If Marielle wanted to know what had made him grow closed off with her and critical with Hudson, what had made him become gruff and businesslike with their neighbors...well, she could just go on wondering. Because he refused to admit that he'd put on those rough-hewn attributes like an ill-fitting suit—that he'd been putting them on across territories and towns for years.

He wasn't tough, Dylan knew. He was just a man—a man who found solace in women only until they spied his inner softness.

Decisively, he knelt in front of Marielle. He caught hold of her injured ankle, then propped it carefully atop his thigh.

"My father taught me what it took to be a

man," he said in his sternest voice. He diligently unwrapped her bandages, then rewrapped them with nimble fingers. He did not look up. He didn't want to see her dismay. Her pity. Her aversion. "To his disappointment, his lessons didn't take. Not with me."

"I can't believe that," Marielle assured him. "Anyone looking at you can see how strong you are. How tough."

But Dylan knew her assurances to be false. How strong and tough could he really be, if he couldn't stop being soft on the inside, no matter how hard he tried?

"You can stop goading me, Marielle," he said stonily. "If you think contrariness will make me sweeten up toward you—"

"I absolutely don't think that!" she said. "Or... do I?"

Her renewed grin as she pretended to be deliberately contrary lightened his heart. But, necessarily, only briefly.

"You're joking now," he said, "but if I kissed you again—"

"We would both feel better. I know it."

"Kissing is not a cure-all."

"How would you know? Have you tried it?"

He delivered her a sardonic look. "Obviously, I have."

"From what I hear, the second time is the charm."

At her persistence, he almost gave in. How could he still want her, even after she'd all but rejected him in the yard?

He was just that much of a fool, Dylan judged.

"But if you'd rather hurt my feelings than kiss me," Marielle mused aloud, making a down-hearted face, "then I guess—"

"I've hurt your feelings?" Inwardly, Dylan swore. "I'm sorry. I never meant to do that." Another swearword. "I—"

"There he is!" Marielle marveled, stunning him. Her eyes sparkled. She smiled broadly. "*That* is the man I'm looking for. That man who is caring, kind and sweet. And foulmouthed, too."

Her direct look clearly indicated him. Joyfully.

Confused, Dylan went still. She *wanted* him to be soft?

He hadn't meant to be, damn it. He'd been so taken aback by her comment about having hurt feelings that he couldn't help it.

She'd tricked him. He'd never seen it coming.

"*You* are the man I'm looking for," Marielle continued, warm-eyed and full of certainty. "Please don't go away again."

Dylan's every instinct told him to close himself off, take himself away, harden himself against her. But he didn't.

"I don't know what you mean," he lied, knowing he did.

Could he risk this again? With her? Did he dare to try?

In the end, it wasn't his choice to make. Because even as Dylan prevaricated over the issue, Marielle did the same thing she always did: she surprised him.

"Just stay with me," she told him, letting her gaze roam over his face. Impulsively, she joined him on the floor. She turned his face to hers. "Get ready for me to kiss you, too."

Her mouth met his, freely and softly. Her hand held his face, gently but firmly. Her kiss was inexperienced, just as she'd noted, but it was also perfect…especially afterward, when Marielle leaned back to gaze into his face, saw all the helpless hopefulness and joy Dylan knew must be evident in it…and smiled.

She'd *seen* him, he realized. She'd seen all of him, softness and hardness combined. She still wanted him.

"You see?" she exulted. "That was better already. I am a prodigy." Her smile broadened. "It helps not running away."

Dylan blinked. "Well, you did run away because of me."

To his amazement, Marielle refused to confirm his worst fears. "I ran away because I was overwhelmed. But now…"

"Now?"

"Now I'm happy." Provocatively, she eyed his

mouth. "Can I kiss you again? Because I think some practice would be good."

Nearly overcome with surprise and relief—and a nearly unwholesome amount of zeal—Dylan nodded. "I think so, too."

She hadn't rejected him, he reminded himself, wishing kissing could supplant conversation altogether. *But she had seen his gentleness… and she'd liked it.* Marielle Miller truly was one woman in a million. But since he couldn't have her believing that he was all softness and no toughness—which wasn't true, either—Dylan decided to take charge. That, he loved to do.

So he met Marielle halfway to their kiss, delved his hand in her hair and made her wait. Drawing out the moment to almost unbearable anticipation, Dylan gazed at her. He imagined himself kissing her lips, parting them, making Marielle feel the depth and extent of his need for her…one hot, wet moment at a time.

Then, expertly and passionately, he did.

The minute their mouths parted, Marielle smiled. "I have a feeling," she said, "that you have a lot to teach me."

"I do." In that moment, dealt a hand of acceptance and adventurousness both at once, Dylan gave over completely. Maybe it was foolish. Maybe it was risky. But it was also necessary.

To him, so was Marielle. So was her smile. And her light.

"I will," he added, gesturing at the awkward position they'd wound up in as she'd fallen to her knees to be kissed. Her skirts spread all around them, hiding her true position. "Just as soon as you stop crushing my foot. You landed on me."

"That's what you think." Her grin matched his. "What I think is that you got in my way again. Just like at the saloon. Just imagine if we'd never met…"

Mentioning that, Marielle seemed suddenly troubled. But she obligingly shifted, just the same. Then she regained her glow.

"Mmm." She flung her arms around his neck. "How's this?"

She looked so pleased. Dylan would have died before mentioning that she'd accidentally knee trod on his other foot.

"Perfect," he said instead, then he put his arms around her waist and got started with their first official kissing lesson.

Chapter Seven

It wasn't long before Marielle found herself unable to concentrate on anything at all, whether she was hemming dresses for her neighbors or listening to Jobyna plan her wedding. Every thought she had, every task she attempted, every moment was interrupted by memories of Dylan's mouth on hers, of his hands on her waist, of his body showing her—in ways large and small—that she was precious to him and growing more so every day.

His dazzling smiles returned upon seeing her at the end of each evening, newly augmented with other smiles that arrived every morning, every afternoon and every possible occasion in between. His happy-go-lucky moods came back, too, bolstered by a new optimism she fancied herself having kindled. His patience with the neighborhood children was redoubled. His forbearance for Hudson's various idiosyncrasies had never been stronger.

She had indeed cured Dylan with their second kiss. And although that triumph was mostly hers, Marielle knew she had to share with Dylan some of the credit. He was the one who had taken a single moment and then transformed it into several.

He was the one who brought her coffee and a secret kiss every morning while Hudson was visiting the outhouse. He was the one who bandaged her injured ankle, tested its strength between wrappings and then improved her tolerance for resting it further by bribing her with a kiss for every hour spent doing so. He was the one who complimented her on her beautiful eyes; who regaled her with tales of his adventuresome life as a detective, security man and railway man; who spent each evening contentedly sprawled beside her on the settee, reading from the *Pioneer Press* or another periodical while she devoured a novel.

Sometimes, Marielle caught Dylan gazing at her during those times in the lamplight as though he couldn't quite believe she was there beside him. That was doubly moving, to her, because she felt the same way. Every morning, she half expected to find his place vacant at his shaving mirror. Every evening, she still doubted Dylan would return from his sheriff's rounds.

It was unfair to him, and all the more unreasonable as time went on. Because he had, after all, made a promise to the people of Morrow Creek.

Marielle believed he'd meant it. But she couldn't shake the feeling that she ought to remain wary.

Of course, her wariness came in different strengths, depending on the situation. When Dylan was sitting across from her at dinnertime, his face lit by the lamplight and his hair askew from a hard day's peacekeeping, Marielle felt satisfied. When he read aloud to her some newsworthy tidbit or patiently taught hapless Hudson how to repair the water pump, she felt contented. But when Dylan questioned her about people in town, when he got that familiar faraway look in his eyes…well, *then* Marielle felt a bottomless fright that never truly left her.

She didn't know what it would take for her to trust Dylan as completely as she wanted to. She suspected that miracle would start with her taking the first step—and telling him what was going on with Charley Sheridan and his outlaw brothers.

Everyone knew that the most skeptical man was a liar himself. Likewise, Marielle reasoned, maybe she could not trust Dylan because she was not trustworthy herself…and knew it. But since she had a good reason for that, and since the danger of Charley's return still abounded, she could not let down her guard. Not altogether. Not the way she wanted to. And when Dylan kissed her… *oh*, how she wanted to.

His mouth was like a drug. His hands were like a gateway to heaven. During every encounter with him, Marielle felt more transfixed. Nothing else mattered except having more of him.

"I think that you've quite mesmerized me," she confessed one afternoon while they were alone in the house, Hudson having providentially gone to call on Corinne Murphy. "When we're together this way, I can't think of anything else in the world."

"Me, either," Dylan confided, stroking her hair back from her face with hands tender enough to safely cradle a baby—or her poor confused heart. Then he cleared his throat. "Aside from all the chores I aim to do, I mean to say," he clarified, "and all the protecting and fixing I'm planning around this place."

Marielle only smiled and let him believe that he'd fooled her. Because as much as Dylan enjoyed sounding mean and hard-nosed, he was as soft as daisies on the inside. She loved that about him. She had, however, distinctly learned not to say so.

"I love how gentle you are," she'd said to him one evening as she lay in his arms, during another of Hudson's convenient outings with Corinne, with his newspaper and her book set aside. "You make me feel safe. For so long, I've had to be the one handling everything. But now, with you here to help—"

"You *are* safe," Dylan had interrupted huskily

before she could finish praising him, "but I'm anything except gentle. Not all the time, at least."

Her skepticism had only incited a round of merciless tickling unlike anything she'd ever experienced. Laughing uproariously, Marielle had finally given back as good as she was getting. Somehow she'd wound up atop him, victorious and proud.

Then she'd seen Dylan's besotted face and known she'd won much more than a respite from being tickled. She'd won...*him*.

Doubtless, she'd appeared equally infatuated. Also, tumbled and disheveled and breathless. But just then, Marielle hadn't cared. Against all reason, she'd found a man she could feel equal to—could feel at home with, even while feeling thrilled by his touch. It was more than she could ever have bargained on.

It was also more than she rightly deserved, she remembered on the afternoon that marked Dylan's first month staying with her and her brother. Because that was when the first crack appeared in her idyllic facade and Marielle recalled the ugliness that lay beneath—the ugliness that was supposed to have been her tricking the new sheriff into unwisely trusting in her.

She was making her way around her yard, in the space that Dylan had cleared and leveled for a dance practice area, when it happened. Afterward, Marielle was only glad Dylan hadn't been there to witness it. She never could have explained it away.

"That was very good, ladies!" Marielle called, beaming at her breathless assembled troupe of dancers. "I think this new dance will be spectacular when you debut it at the saloon."

"We only wish you could be there," Jobyna said loyally.

Beside her, silly Etta only examined her frilly skirts.

But all the other dance hall girls nodded. "It's not the same without you, Marielle!" one of them called out. "You always had the best ideas for new dances. Even Harry is starting to recognize our same old routines after seeing them repeated."

Picturing Jack's old barkeep nodding his head to the steps, Marielle grinned. "Well, that's why we're here today. To learn some new dances! I might not be allowed to dance just yet—"

There was a good-natured round of feminine boos for Doc Finney. He'd decreed that Marielle was "almost, but not quite" ready to dance again. At this point, though, she only required her crutch at the end of the day, when she was getting tired.

"—but I can still help our troupe in other ways!" Marielle finished, bolstered by how well their few practices had gone.

It had been Dylan's idea to invite all "the girls" to her house for their first outdoor practice session. He'd recognized, even before she had, that

Marielle needed to do more than rest her ankle and fritter away her days matchmaking Hudson with Corinne. Her brother had become more independent since becoming Dylan's deputy, anyway. He didn't need her help as much as he once had—which had the direct effect of making Marielle feel especially useless. What she needed, more than ever, was to feel vitalized—and as though her contributions were important.

Thanks to her outdoor dance practices, now she did.

In fact, she enjoyed coming up with dances and teaching them to her fellow dance hall girls as much as she did dancing herself. She did not miss the threat of brawls, the necessity of feathers and rouge or the late nights—or the pervasive aromas of whiskey and cigarillo smoke. Without them, Marielle had fun thinking about dancing again. She was not, frankly, as eager to return to the stage as she'd once expected she would be.

During her convalescence, she'd devised more and better routines than she ever had while squeezing in that task between seamstress work and housekeeping. Marielle would have liked to continue on that way. Unfortunately, no one would ever pay her simply to concoct saloon shows. Not even goodhearted Jack Murphy was that generous. She still needed to be able to support herself and Hudson—more so than ever when Dylan eventually left and quit contributing part of his sheriff's salary to the household. Even if she *had* begun hoping he might stay in Morrow Creek instead...

But those worries would keep. They'd be just as troublesome later, too. Knowing that, Marielle trained her attention on her troupe. "All right, then. Let's go through that one more time!"

She clapped, signaling her friends to line up in their usual positions beneath the towering ponderosa pines and the scrubbier oaks at the edge of her property. Everything at her place had never looked nicer, she realized with pride, thanks to the combined efforts of Dylan and Hudson. Speaking of whom...

Her brother appeared at the edge of her kitchen garden, between the shed where Dylan so scintillatingly shaved each morning and the pathway to the house. He moved slowly...panting?

His next step made his leg buckle. Something was wrong.

With her heart in her throat, Marielle hurried toward him, cursing the still unmended ankle that slowed her down.

"Hudson!" She saw him right himself. He offered a lopsided smile, then kept going. It was evident that there was a hitch to his step. He held his right arm at a funny angle, too. Marielle frowned as she reached him. "Are you all right? Why are you walking?" She looked behind him. "Where's your horse?" It was the middle of the day. He shouldn't have stabled it yet. A new thought struck her. Had he and Dylan been ambushed? "Where is Dylan? Tell me!" She grabbed her brother. "What's going on?"

"If you'd give me a minute," Hudson managed, "I'd tell you." He looked beyond her at the women gathering in her wake, all of them dressed in old practice costumes with headdresses perched incongruously on their heads. "Afternoon, ladies. Sorry to bust up your practice like this. I'll just be going inside."

"Oh, no, you won't!" Marielle stopped him. His clothes were smudged with dust, his shirt was ripped and… "You're bleeding!"

Wincing, Hudson touched the corner of his mouth. "Huh. Yep. I guess I am. I'll have to see to that in a minute."

"'Yep'? Is that all you can say?" Impatiently, Marielle turned to her troupe. "I'm sorry. I'm afraid practice is over with for today, ladies. I have to see to my lunkheaded brother."

Seeing the emergency, everyone began collecting their things. They drifted away with flighty Etta at the lead, headed toward town like a collection of headdress-wearing charwomen.

But Jobyna lingered. "Do you need me to fetch Snub?" She examined Hudson. "He's a good man to have close by in a crisis."

Hudson waved her off. "I just need to clean up,

that's all. I thought I could get in the house without you seeing, Mari—"

"You should know better than that by now. Mama taught me her 'eyes in the back of her head' trick before she passed."

Her brother gave her a weak smile. "I wanted that one. It would have been mighty useful for playing cards."

Marielle snorted. Then a new, more worrying idea occurred to her. "*Were* you playing cards?" *With the Sheridans?* "Why weren't you at work with Dylan? Is he all right? Where is he?"

Hudson gave her a surprisingly patient look as he ambled over to the water pump. "No, I wasn't playing cards," he said as he pumped up some cool water to splash over his grimy, scratched-up forearms. He cupped some water, scrubbed his face with it then grimaced anew. She noticed several cuts on his cheek and forehead, too. "Dylan is fine," Hudson promised. "He's collecting tax money from folks on the east side of town today. He's doing it methodically. 'Bout what you'd expect from him."

Marielle didn't understand. But she did sense that there was something her brother wasn't telling her. Worried, she faced Jobyna again. "Thanks for offering to get Snub. But I think we'll be all right. I'll just take Hudson inside and get him patched up." She managed a smile. "Same time tomorrow?"

"If you're sure." Jobyna studied Hudson. With an air of familiarity, she added, "The way he's moving, looks like a couple of broken ribs to me. Should I ask Doc Finney to come?"

"Broken ribs?" New dread washed over Marielle. "Hudson! If you weren't already hurt, I'd pummel you myself. What happened?"

Pointedly, her brother glanced at Jobyna. "Nothing."

"All right, all right. I can take a hint." Jobyna raised her arms—then she wrapped them around Marielle in a hug. Her concerned gaze met hers. "You know I'm here if you need anything, right? Anything at all. Just yell. I'll come running."

Marielle smiled. "I know you will. Thanks, Jobyna."

"Don't go getting all mushy on me now," her friend warned jokingly. "I'm just worried about having somebody reliable to stand up for me on my wedding day. I'm about going crazy waiting to finally be married to Snub." Jobyna elbowed her, then offered a characteristically feisty wink. "Not everybody has a sweet situation like you do with handsome Sheriff Coyle, you know." A sassy look. "You know we're all pulling for you two, don't you?"

With a guilty flush, Marielle looked away. "I'm sure I don't know what you mean. Come on, Hudson. Let's go inside."

"I'm sure you *do* know what I mean!" Jobyna

hollered as Marielle helped her brother—and the last shreds of her virtuous reputation—inside the house. "Otherwise, why are you so pink?"

"The sun!" Marielle called, almost laughing despite the dire circumstances with Hudson. Jobyna was famously ribald and notoriously freethinking. She was the last person who would judge her—and the first who would tease her. "That's it."

"Mmm-hmm. Tell me another stretcher—like how you don't fancy that tall drink of water whose boots are under your bed."

"Jobyna!" Shocked, Marielle waved away her friend.

Did folks in town really think she was getting *that* familiar with the new sheriff? Dylan had behaved respectfully so far. He'd kissed her, yes, but they'd never crossed the threshold of her bedroom! What if, Marielle wondered, they did?

Would they be swept away? Would their encounter be as pleasurable as kissing him was? Would she get to see even more of Dylan's naked body than his muscular torso and arms? Intrigued by the idea, she bit her lip. It was completely wicked, of course, but—

—but Hudson needed her. What was she doing daydreaming?

The fact that she was woolgathering under such dire circumstances only proved what she'd known from the start: she couldn't get too giddy over

Dylan Coyle. He wasn't there to fall in love with her. Or to create a scandal with her. He was only there to do the job he'd agreed on…and be hoodwinked into letting the Sheridans get away with something devious.

With a fresh surge of remorse, Marielle pushed away that thought. She didn't want to be reminded of her duplicitous—if wholly unwilling—part in the brothers' plan. So far, she hadn't strictly done anything wrong. She hadn't yet spoken to Charley or revealed the influence she had on Dylan. If she never did—or if she instead told Dylan what was going on—maybe she could still be free of this situation without any wrongdoing herself.

Yes, Marielle decided. She would confide in Dylan. It was the only way. With him on her side, they were bound to prevail.

"We'd better get a move on." Hudson looked up with a pained expression on his pale face. He held his midsection, lending veracity to Jobyna's supposition that he'd broken a few ribs. "I hurried as fast as I could to get here, but I reckon Dylan won't be too far behind me. He can't know about this, Mari."

And that, as they said, was that.

"Are you asking me not to tell Dylan you're hurt?"

"I'm telling you if he finds out, it won't go well for him." In her grasp, Hudson panted. He was big, but not impervious to pain. Marielle tried to help. Her brother rolled his eyes at her, as cocky as ever. "Hey, quit it, will you? I won't have you hurting your other ankle on account of me."

"We're just going to have to take that risk." Stepping as ably as she could, Marielle maneuvered to his other side. She put her arm around his massive body. "I'm helping you."

"You've done enough helping me. I'm a grown man."

Wonderful. Now Hudson was committed to sounding tough, just like Dylan was. She guessed all those hours they spent together, sheriff and deputy, had rubbed off on her brother.

"You're a grown man who's going to tell me every detail of what happened to you," Marielle informed him. "Come on."

Thirty minutes later, Hudson was cleaned up, patched up and obviously feeling more obstinate than ever. As he sorted through his trunk of clothes, Marielle cornered him.

"What happened to you?" she asked. It was hard to speak around the lump in her throat. It had been growing ever since she'd seen her brother falter in the road. It had only gotten bigger while she'd tended to the many scrapes, bumps and bruises Hudson now sported. "You can't put me off any longer."

"Try me." Hudson dragged off his dirt-smudged

Henley, then pulled on another clean shirt. "I'm pretty sure I can."

"We're not children anymore, Hud. This is serious!"

"It's taken care of." His face turned unfamiliarly stark. "I took care of it. You don't have to worry about a thing."

"I'm already worried!" Marielle moved closer. "You have broken ribs, a sprained wrist, a lump on your head, scrapes and cuts all over…you can't even move without wincing!"

"I'm fine. I'm tougher than you think."

"Well, I'm heartily sick of 'tough' men." Marielle threw up her arms. "What is wrong with all of you? *I'm* supposed to be content to recuperate all day, being waited on hand and foot, minding doctor's orders and not doing what I want, but *you*—"

"Yes. You are." Hudson looked at his trousers, decided the damage to them was minimal enough not to require a new pair, then veered past her. "Thanks for seeing to me, Mari."

Incredulously, Marielle watched her brother stride across the front room. He tucked his pocket watch in its place, then bent to slip a knife into a holster strapped to his calf.

"You're wearing *a knife* now?" Goggling at him, Marielle trailed her brother. She grabbed his arm, making him stop. "What is going on, Hud? I know it has to do with the Sheridans."

"I'm heading back out. If Dylan asks, tell him

I'm at the jailhouse, seeing to Mr. Jeeter. He's locked up drunk again."

But Marielle didn't want to discuss Hudson's alibi. Deliberately, she moved to block his path. "If you want me to keep secrets from Dylan, you'd better start talking. Now."

Hudson looked exasperated. But he apparently knew when he was beaten. Probably, a lifetime of being a little brother had taught him that much. With a sigh, he relented.

"It was the Sheridans. They cornered me out back of the smithy. I'd just got done collecting McCabe's taxes—"

"Which they stole, I imagine. Those heartless, thieving—"

"—when Peter and Levi jumped me. I guess Charley got in a few licks, too. I was on the ground for most of the time, so I'm not rightly sure. Leastwise, I was until Daniel McCabe broke up the fight." He shook his head. "That man is fearsome."

"Oh, Hudson!" Marielle moved toward him, simultaneously distraught over what he'd been through and grateful for the timely interference of the town's brawny blacksmith. She was no longer concerned with blocking Hud's path out the door. "That's awful. You have to tell Dylan! He'll deal with them. He'll—"

Her brother cut her off with a despairing look.

"Do you really think I can go to the law? Against the Sheridans?"

The grimness of their situation struck her again.

"Then you *are* in cahoots with them?" Marielle asked.

To her immeasurable relief, her brother laughed. It was an acerbic chuckle, but it was better than nothing. "I owe them something. That's all. They're tired of waiting to be paid."

"Did you lose to them gambling?"

Hudson turned away. Slowly. Painfully. Drat it all.

"It's worse than that," he said. "A lot worse. But you don't have to worry about it!" Hudson hastened to add. "That thrashing ought to hold them for a while. Plus, I paid a bit."

"You paid? With what? I know darn well you've spent your deputy's salary on squiring Corinne Murphy around town."

There was a pause. A patently disbelieving one. "You're going to choose now to lecture me about spending money on courting Corinne? Because near as I can tell, you've been nothing but in favor of me and Corinne being together. Or was I wrong thinking you're the one who made Dylan give me that deputy's job in the first place, to impress her?"

Now it was Marielle's turn to be uncomfortable. "I may have *suggested* the idea to him, yes.

But that's not the point. I—" She broke off, suddenly reaching a new insight. "Your horse. You gave them your horse! That's why you were walking home."

"It's also why I've got to leave right away."

"Oh, Hudson. That horse was the most valuable thing you owned. It was the only thing that was solely yours." He'd been proud of it. He'd saved during his off-and-on jobs. Then he'd used his irrefutable charm to finagle a good deal. "Without it—"

"Without it, it's going to take some time for me to walk back to the jailhouse," her brother continued. "If Dylan knows—"

"Maybe he can help. If we tell him what's been going on—"

"He can't help." Hudson's voice was bleak. Certain. "Unless you count on him throwing me in the clink for associating with Charley and his brothers, I guess. Then interrogating me until he finds out where their hideout is. *That* he might do." He cast her a wry look. "Even you thought I was in cahoots with them."

"You didn't give me much choice."

"You're supposed to know me better than that!"

Sadly, Marielle thought, knowing Hudson as well as she did was *why* she'd thought he might have gotten mixed up with the Sheridan boys.

Even though she didn't say so, her brother could tell.

Fierce and tight-lipped, he looked away. "If that's what you think of me, I might as well tell you the rest." He put his hands on his hips and then heaved in a breath, reminding her too much of the little boy he'd once been…who'd been afraid of the dark and had needed his big sister's comforting. "I'm the one who got Deputy Winston hauled off to Yuma Prison. I'm the reason Sheriff Caffey ran off the way he did. It was because of me."

Caught off guard, Marielle frowned. "How could it be?"

"Because I'm the one who got drunk, played cards with an undercover federal marshal and jawed all about what's been going on in Morrow Creek." Finally, Hudson faced her. "I'm the one who accidentally told that marshal about seeing Deputy Winston cubbyholing away some money at the jailhouse."

"When were *you* at the jailhouse?"

Her brother looked sheepish. "Remember that night I told you I picked up a short-term job working at the railway depot?"

"You *lied* to me?"

"It made you so happy!" Hudson protested, throwing his arms in the air. "That's all I ever wanted. All of it. But nothing I ever do is good enough. I can't stick with any jobs, on account of worrying over you dancing at the saloon. I can't court anybody, because of not wanting to leave you here on your own. I can't head West to a bigger city, and I can't go back to the States, not without making you think I'm just like—"

Our father. But Marielle stopped him before he could say it. She didn't want to hear any more. She especially didn't want to think that she might have accidentally been keeping Hudson from living his life the way he wanted. Not when she'd desired nothing but the best for him all along. It was too painful.

Instead, she asked, "How much money did Deputy Winston hide?"

Hudson shrugged. "I don't know. Heaps of it. All the greenbacks were bundled up. I couldn't tell for sure. Deputy Winston thought I was plumb passed out drunk, or he'd have never chanced moving the money when he did. I thought it was funny. I was just making a joke to that marshal. I said I knew where I could get a good loan to keep on playing cards with him."

Marielle could well imagine the scene. Her brother was always quick with a quip. Once started gambling, he was loath to quit, too. Even as a boy, he'd refused to give up on games and puzzles and contests until they were finished. The two of them had always been alike in that way. Stubborn and idealistic.

They both had always thought they could win. Somehow, Marielle still did. Even in these awful circumstances.

"I can't remember it too well, to tell the truth," Hudson admitted. "I guess that marshal must have wheedled out some more information from me—enough to put him on Winston's trail."

"Once Deputy Winston was fingered, Sheriff Caffey must have reckoned they'd be after him next," Marielle surmised. "So he took whatever money he could from that cache and skedaddled."

"It's worse than that," Hudson informed her. "Somehow, Caffey got wind of who the marshal was beforehand. He knew he was onto him. He could have warned Deputy Winston. Instead, he deliberately left Winston to take the blame—and to keep the marshal busy with arresting him and whatnot, too."

"Leaving himself more time to get away with that money," Marielle guessed. She shook her head. "I guess Sheriff Caffey really was as crooked as everyone said." She paused, feeling sorry that he was unlikely to ever be brought to justice. Then, "But what's all this got to do with the Sheridan brothers?"

Hudson cost me something, Charley had told her menacingly on her porch that night. *So far, he ain't been able to pay.*

"That money I saw Deputy Winston putting away? It was the town's tax money," Hudson said. "It was overdue because it hadn't ever been paid. Sheriff Caffey was squirreling it all away, doling out little bits of it to keep Deputy Winston quiet, counting on nobody at the territorial level to notice it."

"And the Sheridans?"

"They got a piece of it, too. They've been collecting protection money from the sheriff all this time."

"That was why Sheriff Caffey never ran them out of town." Marielle marveled at the audacity of it all. Their scheme was as out-and-out devious as anything she'd ever heard of. She'd guessed as much when she'd wondered if Charley had the sheriff in his pocket, but she hadn't counted on the overall venality involved in their payoffs. "So long as nobody ever found out about their arrangement, all of them were sitting pretty."

"Well, the folks in town aren't. Not anymore." Hudson shook his head. "The territorial government *did* notice that missing tax money, or they wouldn't have sent any marshals to investigate. Most likely, Deputy Winston told them plenty while trying to save his own skin. Yuma Prison is a damn scary place."

"If all the money hasn't been recovered," Marielle mused, because it was reasonable to assume Sheriff Caffey had gotten away with much of it, "and the taxes aren't ever properly paid—"

"Well, they aren't going to be forgiven, that's for sure."

"—then everyone in Morrow Creek is going to be defaulting on their taxes, without even meaning to. Nobody can afford to pay twice. Not even if they want to."

With her heart sinking, Marielle realized what that meant. *She* paid taxes on her house and land. All of her neighbors did, too. From the smallest family to the most prosperous business, everyone she knew was indebted to the territorial government for the right to inhabit their properties. If they didn't pay, they'd lose those rights. They'd all be homeless. Eventually.

Probably, the marshals were keeping the particulars of Caffey's crime a secret until they caught him. But once they did—or if they gave up trying—they'd be back to settle up.

Morrow Creek was on the brink of being in deep trouble.

"So…" Hudson broke in, gracing her with a tentative, bruised-up smile. "You still want to tell Dylan about all this?"

Marielle sighed. She shook her head. "He's an outsider. He won't be here long enough to deal with the difficulties this will cause. Plus, he's as upright as the day is long. He won't understand your part in this, Hud." *Not to mention mine.*

She looked away, feeling all the more trapped. If she helped Charley Sheridan, Dylan would never understand. Or forgive. If she didn't, Hudson might pay an ever bigger price next time. Next time, Daniel McCabe might not come to the rescue. Next time, the Sheridans might not settle for a horse.

Next time, they might hurt Hudson worse… or even kill him.

Until now, Marielle knew, she'd been feeling as though she knew better than her notoriously credulous brother. But was she really any smarter than Hudson? After all, she'd gotten herself wedged into a promise to help the Sheridans herself.

"For all we know, Dylan's already offered the Sheridans more protection money," Hudson argued. "He's a drifter. He's not *that* upright. He's experienced. He's probably corruptible."

But Marielle knew he wasn't. Charley Sheridan had told her so. *He can't be bought*, the outlaw had grumbled on the night he'd threatened her. *What kinda lawman can't be bought?*

"Dylan isn't corruptible," she disagreed. *But he is capable—and malleable, too. At least he is when it comes to me.* She drew in a fortifying breath, then faced her brother. "I think the Sheridans are planning to let Dylan lead them to Sheriff Caffey. When he does, I bet they're planning to steal all that money."

She also bet they planned to use *her* to keep Dylan out of the way while they did it. That had to be the reason Charley had pressured Marielle into "cozying up" to the new sheriff. With her as a decoy, Dylan wouldn't suspect anything was amiss.

All this time, she'd thought the Sheridans were waiting for her to give them a signal. She'd been trying to avoid the whole situation by not giving them one. But this meant that Charley Sheridan could call on her at any moment—as soon as he thought Dylan had found where Sheriff Caffey and the money were.

"Everything he got away with?" Hudson whistled with apparent awe. "I heard that Deputy Winston didn't have much on him, on account of being caught by surprise by the marshals. But if somebody catches up to Caffey, it'll be a gold mine."

It would be Dylan's job and reputation, too, Marielle realized, if he let anyone else track down the runaway sheriff in his stead. In the townspeople's minds, the obligation to find Sheriff Caffey came second only to forcing outlaws out of town.

Most likely, Dylan was already gathering leads…and inadvertently playing into Charley's hands in the process. All the Sheridans had to do was sit back and wait for Dylan to do the work for them, then sweep in and take the stolen tax money.

For all she knew, Dylan already had found out where Sheriff Caffey had gone but was waiting until he could catch the miscreant lawman with the money in his possession. How else could Caffey be prosecuted? Dylan *had* to apprehend him with that tax money.

Considering all the details, Marielle felt more fraught than ever. *How* had they ever gotten mixed up in all this?

"Dylan might be able to do it. He might be able to catch Caffey." Looking encouraged, Hudson nodded. "He's tight-lipped, but I know he's got some leads after nosing around town the past month. The way that man can make people talk… it's something to behold. Plus, there was some of the tax money left. I know because I checked. Sheriff Caffey had more than one hidey-hole. I guess he couldn't clean out all of them before he left."

That meant Caffey probably was lingering nearby, Marielle knew, waiting for a chance to do so. "How much money is left?"

A shrug. "Not enough to get Morrow Creek out of hock."

"Enough to pay off the Sheridans with?"

Her brother seemed inspired. It occurred to Marielle that it might have been a good idea for the two of them to put their heads together on this issue before now. Sadly enough, she hadn't even trusted her own brother with this problem.

"Maybe. I know they're not happy about losing that money from Sheriff Caffey, but they're none too patient," Hudson said. "They might have decided to settle on getting whatever they can, then leaving town for someplace more amenable to their kind."

"Someplace with a more bribable sheriff?"

"Maybe." Hudson's nod of agreement made her feel no better.

But now that she had an understanding of what Charley and his brothers must be planning, Marielle felt better about trying to handle it herself. "It won't be easy for the Sheridans to stay in Morrow Creek. Not with Dylan on the job." *For however long he lasts.* "They'll be wanting to move on soon."

"That might be why they jumped me today," Hudson agreed. "I know Charley. Peter and Levi, too. They get bored easily. Really easily. They used to have free rein of this town. But now that Dylan is on the job, they've had to hole up in their hideout most of the time. They're probably antsy."

"Probably." She gave her brother a disconcerted look. "Do you really know where their hideout is? Have you been there?"

Hudson grinned. "Are you asking me to confess all my sins in a single afternoon? Leave a man some dignity, Mari."

"Then you *do* know."

He nodded and told her. She knew the place—a prospector's shack in the mountainous foothills that bordered Morrow Creek. She didn't know where she found the restraint not to lecture Hudson from now till next Wednesday over his mistakes, though.

"You can't tell Dylan about it," Hudson said,

turning serious again. "If he knows I told you, putting you in danger—"

"Pish posh. What am I going to do? Ride in there with my crutch for a weapon? Be reasonable, Hud." She had her own reasons for not telling Dylan everything she knew—including, increasingly, not wanting him to know the missteps she'd made. Thinking of them all, Marielle moaned. A moment of dread gripped her. "I wish I didn't know about any of this to tell!"

"You're strong," Hudson told her. "We'll manage. Heck, I've successfully kept the same job for weeks straight now. That's impressive!" With new liveliness, her brother hugged her. He winced as their bodies made contact, then laughed. As always, he was irrepressible. "Things are going well with Corinne, thanks to my deputy job and Dylan's help. I don't want to lose all that now, just when I'm making progress. I kinda like being deputy."

Marielle swore, in that moment, that she'd make sure Hudson could continue progressing happily. She didn't want to be responsible, even inadvertently, for him postponing his future.

Before she could say so, though, there was a knock at the front door. Startled, Marielle glanced toward it. So did Hudson.

In a flash, he'd drawn the knife from his leg sheath. At his aggressive, ready stance, trepidation raced through her.

"Put that away," she admonished, making her way to the door. "It's probably just Doc Finney. You'll scare the poor man half to death, brandishing a blade like that one."

Uncertainly, Hudson glanced at his knife. At the same time, Marielle put on a sociable smile. She opened the door.

Charley Sheridan lounged there, clenching a cigar in his teeth. He squinted at her through smug eyes, inciting chills.

"Why, howdy there, Miss Miller!" He strolled inside, his boots clunking on the floorboards. He eyed Hudson, giving him an insincere tsk-tsk over his obvious wounds. Then he turned back to Marielle. "I see you're familiar with what happens when a body crosses me," Charley said. "That's good. 'Cause I got me a brand new job for you. I want you to do your best at it."

Chapter Eight

"I'm surprised you wanted to come out with me today." Dylan slowed his horse to better keep pace with Marielle's borrowed mare from Cooper's livery stable. "I have to warn you, though—it's like I said before: most of the time, making sheriff's rounds is about as exciting as waiting for flowers to grow."

"I don't care." Catching up to him, Marielle delivered him a vivid smile. Her roan mare tossed its head with eagerness. "I want to see what you do all day when you're away from me."

Her sweet tone almost deceived him. But Dylan Coyle was no sap. Not even for her. "You don't fool me. You're just itching to get out of the house, and the only outing Doc Finney would approve for you is a ride. So you're tagging along with me."

"I happen to like the way you ride." Not taking the bait, she swept him with an admiring look.

"That horse acts as though she wants to take you wherever you want to go."

"The secret is apples. Lots and lots of apples."

Marielle laughed. Her cheeks pinked. This time, Dylan *did* soften toward her. He just couldn't help it.

"If I could," he said, "I'd enchant you as ably as I do this horse." He leaned across his saddle, the better to soak up the view he had of her pretty profile. "Do you like apples?"

"More and more all the time."

"Then I'll be sure to lay in a few bushels."

"I'll be sure to arrive home hungry."

"When it comes to you…" Dylan glanced sideways again, enjoying the capable way she rode. Not to mention the hint of slender calf she'd revealed below her skirts. Sidesaddle riding had practically been invented for such scandalous glimpses. "I'm always hungry. All the time. Everywhere."

Her sassy look caught him off guard. "Everywhere?"

"Everywhere," he confirmed.

"I see." She smiled anew. "But not for apples?"

"If you think I'm talking about pie," he said as they rode onward toward the mountains, "I've given you too much credit."

"If you think I won't give you some of those 'apples' you're hankering for, Sheriff, you're sorely mistaken."

Her sparkling eyes fascinated him. Her tantalizing talk teased him. But he knew Marielle better than that. "That's easy for you to say, six feet away on a moving horse. I've seen you ride, remember? You rode up to the jailhouse like your skirts were on fire and I had the only bucket of water in town."

"Yes, sir. That's how I think of you, all right. Just like a big ole bucket of water." She slanted him a sideways glance. "Just ready to quench my thirst, whenever I want you to."

Damnation. Inwardly, Dylan groaned. Lately, Marielle had stepped up her flirtatious way of talking to him. There'd been no denying that she'd been behaving more boldly than ever toward him. Unfortunately, Marielle's newfound brashness had coincided with Hudson's unfortunate "fall" off his horse—and that selfsame horse's inexplicable decision to "run clean away!" Dylan was far too experienced to consider those coinciding events accidental.

He was sure that Marielle and her brother were hiding something. His attempts to find out what had so far delivered nothing. But that didn't mean Dylan intended to give up trying.

"Oh?" He quirked his eyebrow. "Are you thirsty now?"

"I might be." She went on riding nonetheless.

"I'm not sure I believe you."

"I'm not sure I can prove it to you while on

a moving horse." Marielle smiled at him. "Too bad your schedule is so very demanding." She glanced ahead, studying the isolated road leading to the Morrow Creek adjunct telegraph station that was operated by Savannah Corwin with help from Mose and her husband, Adam. "Some of these tax-collecting stops are remote, aren't they? Aren't you scared somebody might jump you?"

Dylan felt his interest rise. "Depends on who it is."

"It could be somebody dangerous."

She was dangerous—to his sense of duty and his ability to do his job alike. He shouldn't be flirting with her—not when there were outlaws afoot, a reprobate sheriff to catch and a whole lot of missing tax money to recover. So far, Dylan hadn't made as much progress as he'd have liked toward those aims.

He couldn't help feeling he'd been set up to fail. No one had told him about that tax money having gone missing. He'd only learned about it, bit by bit, as he'd seen it was in arrears and had begun going door to door to collect it as the territorial government demanded—only to be told, time and again, that each townsperson had already paid their taxes…to Sheriff Caffey.

The scoundrel had obviously absconded with the lot of it, leaving the innocent folks of Morrow Creek to be potentially evicted from their homes and businesses as a consequence.

"I'm not worried," Dylan told Marielle. "I have a plan."

"So do I." She smiled to herself. "It's a doozy."

At her enigmatic expression, his imagination went wild. He hoped, as unlikely as it was, that her "plan" involved him, her and a whole passel of kissing. He'd never done so much kissing in his whole life as he had since meeting Marielle. His lips ought to be chapped. For certain, his manhood was up-and-up baffled by recent events. Because ordinarily, he'd never have needed to withstand such seductive torture as he had with her. But Dylan had too much respect for Marielle to push for more.

Not when he couldn't promise her a future.

Not that that meant he didn't *think* about more. Hell, he thought about having *more* with Marielle night and day. While sitting beside her on her settee, while seeing to her almost healed ankle, while washing up, while riding his rounds…

"You're not going to tell me what your plan is?" he asked.

She shook her head. "You'll find out."

"Does it have something to do with recovering Hudson's 'missing' horse?" Dylan pushed. He had to consider that as a potential motivation for her interest in coming on his rounds with him. It would be just like Marielle to want to solve that particular problem for her brother. It wasn't unreasonable for her to hope she might spot his "lost" pony while out and about.

Just as he'd expected, Marielle looked guilty as sin. But she didn't come clean. "Why would I do that? The silly thing just up and ran away. Hudson's probably better off without it."

"That 'silly thing' is worth a lot of money."

She shrugged. "Hud's looking for it himself. Remember?"

Dylan did. Privately, he suspected that charade was going nowhere. He figured Hudson had lost his horse while gambling and hadn't wanted to admit as much to his overprotective sister.

But he still couldn't credit her overall lack of interest in the situation. When it came to Hudson, Marielle typically left no shirts unmended and no advice ungiven. But she'd been curiously indifferent about her brother's missing mount. There'd been no lectures about carelessness, no advice that Hudson should work harder to save for a new horse...nothing of the kind.

It was as if she'd forgotten her own take-charge nature.

Or as if she knew what had *really* happened with that horse.

"Anyway," Marielle went on with a suddenly overly bright smile, "why are we going on about Hudson's horse at all? You have much bigger fish to fry than one lost horse, don't you?"

The sheriff. And the tax money. Dylan knew

that must be what she meant. Now that several weeks had gone by, the people of Morrow Creek were growing disenchanted with his inability to nab that knuck and set things to right again. He felt the weight of their expectations keenly. He'd never failed a job before.

He didn't intend to fail this one now.

"That's right." Squinting at the sunlight, Dylan urged on his horse. "These taxes aren't going to collect themselves." He patted his saddlebag. "Besides, I have some mail here from the post office to deliver. We'll save the Corwins a trip to town."

Marielle wasn't interested in discussing the mail. Her eyes widened as she looked at his saddle. "You keep *all* the tax money in your saddlebags? Is that safe? What if you're robbed?"

He chuckled. "Nobody's going to rob the sheriff."

"They might not see your badge."

Her naïveté was sweet. "I mean they're not going to rob *me*. You know my past. I'm a man of the world, Marielle."

Her gaze remained fixed on his saddlebag. "Is there money in there right this minute? How much money?"

"What if I told you there were heaps of it?"

"I'd tell you to take it out and put it someplace safer!"

"Such as?" The place Hudson had stashed his horse?

If he hadn't lost it gambling, he'd assuredly lost it in some other way, Dylan reckoned. Maybe by wandering into trouble.

During their time working together, he'd gotten to know Hudson better. The man was well-intentioned. He was willing to work hard—much harder than Dylan had expected, given his history of failed jobs. Hudson had simply been afraid of letting any harm befall his sister—up to and including loneliness—so he'd stuck by Marielle's side as much as possible. For years now.

Surprisingly, Dylan had learned, Hudson had had his share of courtship opportunities, all of which he'd only minimally indulged in on account of feeling responsible for Marielle. Both Hudson and his sister had been postponing their lives, each while waiting for the other to be settled. If their mutual self-sacrifice hadn't been so tragic, it would have been comical.

As it was, Dylan had made it his duty to put an end to such goodhearted nonsense. He'd done what he could to see that Hudson and Corinne Murphy were well and truly matched. He'd even done the unthinkable and let Hudson leave work early on several occasions to call on her—more recently in the past week. Dylan wanted Marielle's brother to be content—for her sake and his.

Not that it should have mattered to him, Dylan

reminded himself. He still ought to leave Marielle in peace, he knew, and go on to Sacramento after he finished his work in Morrow Creek.

More and more, though, he didn't want to leave. More and more, he wondered if he could be happy staying put—continuing his work as sheriff, loving Marielle, fixing up her house…

"Mmm, I don't know. You're the expert," she was saying as Dylan had that astonishing thought about loving her. "You would know best where to hide a whole lot of money, wouldn't you?"

Her leading look baffled him. Was she worried about her own taxes being paid? He didn't know. It felt as though Marielle were nettling him—just the way he expected the townspeople to do, once they all figured out the truth of their situation.

"Why do you care about the tax money?" he asked.

"I don't care!" She tossed her head with unconvincing nonchalance. Another sideways glance at his saddlebags. "Only, if you're riding around with all of it in your saddlebags—"

He grinned. "I'm not." Did she think he was that green? Damnation. He needed to impress her more. "I was joking."

"Oh." She furrowed her brow. "Then where is it?"

"Where is what?"

"The tax money!"

"I'm starting to think you'd rather cuddle up

with a bunch of greenbacks than with me," Dylan joked.

Marielle bit her lip, still riding. "Some people say Sheriff Caffey ran off with all the tax money he collected." Her blasé tone seemed less than convincing. Was she trying to finagle information from him? "Some people say our taxes won't ever get paid." She glanced at him. "Are we really in arrears?"

They were…but Dylan didn't want to admit it. Once he found Sheriff Caffey and recovered the money, it wouldn't matter anyway. But he wasn't happy to hear rumors were circulating.

"You can tell anyone who asks that things are fine."

"That's not an answer to my question."

"It's all the answer you're getting for today." Smiling at her, Dylan tipped his hat with finality. He nodded at the fork in the road they'd reached. One road led to the Corwins' adjunct telegraph station; the other led to the small neighboring town of Avalanche. "Shall we collect the Corwins' taxes another day and have ourselves a frolic in Avalanche instead?"

Marielle looked tempted. But only for an instant.

"Do you think Sheriff Caffey will come back?" she asked.

"Do you *want* that thieving, backstabbing crook to come back?" Settling into his saddle,

Dylan stopped his horse to examine her. "Sounds to me as though you miss the man."

She gave an unsteady laugh. "I do fancy a scoundrel. You know that. Just look at my fondness for you!" Then, with her usual unwillingness to back down, Marielle added, "If Sheriff Caffey did come back, where exactly do you think he would go?"

Dylan tightened his lips. "I can't rightly say."

"But if you had to make a guess," she pressed. "Where?"

That was it. Pushed to his limit by her questioning, Dylan decided to end Marielle's prodding once and for all so they could enjoy their outing. If she wouldn't quit interrogating him— and she wouldn't quit—he'd just have to give her something.

"If I had to guess," Dylan lied, "I'd say Caffey would hole up someplace at the edge of town, near the creek bridge."

Marielle nodded. "I know the place you mean."

He bet she did. Unhappy with her unusual interest, Dylan added ammunition to his deliberate misdirection, just to make sure things were perfectly clear in her mind. "There's a traveling medicine show camped near there right now. Maybe you know the people who run it. Will Gavigan and his wife, Rose?"

"I do!" Marielle confirmed. "Their show is a highlight every time they come through. People all over town use their elixir. The only remedy more popular is Milky White Complexion Beautifier and Youthful Enhancement Tonic, and that's only because Olivia Turner's likeness is lithographed onto every bottle. She's the most beautiful woman in town, you know."

"I'm afraid I'll have to disagree with that claim."

"You can't. Everyone's already decided it. She's famous!"

And he was a fool, Dylan knew as he took in Marielle's earnest expression and frank tone. How could he mistrust her? Likely, she'd only been making conversation earlier. He should never have purposely given her false information about Caffey.

But, curiously and unhappily, as soon as he did, Marielle quit interrogating him altogether. Instead, she squared her shoulders, looked at the forested landscape around them then exhaled deeply. Her lively look met his. "So…shall we stop?"

Only if you promise not to hate me for deliberately leading you astray, Dylan couldn't help thinking. He guessed that, after a lifetime of suspecting people of the worst, he couldn't put his wilier instincts behind him altogether. He'd been stymied in his search for the sheriff and was thus feeling prickly about the situation, that's all. None of that was Marielle's fault.

Right then and there, he vowed to make it up to her.

"We can do whatever you like," Dylan promised sincerely. "If you want to ride farther, we can. If you want to hie off to Avalanche, we can. If you want to go swimming in the creek, have a picnic, catch a wild rabbit and tame it for a pet… anything."

Marielle laughed. "You can't really tame a wild rabbit."

"I've done trickier things." *Like loving you.*

Hell. He really *did* love her. How had that happened?

"Well…" She pretended to consider all those options. "We'll have to ride to the adjunct station eventually, I guess. I'd hate to abuse Owen Cooper's trust by taking his borrowed horse all the way to Avalanche without permission. I *did* bring a picnic for us. I don't really have space for a pet rabbit. But—"

"But…?"

"But I *do* fancy the idea of swimming in the creek." Marielle's impudent gaze moved directly to meet his. "With you."

In a heartbeat, Dylan forgot about Marielle's inexplicable curiosity about his work as sheriff. Instead, all he could think about was…*her*. Naked.

No. That was outlandish. She was a good

woman. She wouldn't be naked. Not in a creek. With him. Just minutes from now.

Oh, how he wanted her to be. But he wanted to be a good man, too. For her. Despite the yearning pulling at him.

In the end, he wasn't all that good. Because in the end, all Dylan could say was, "Won't you get your dress all wet?"

She shrugged. But she also blushed. "Not if I take it off, I won't. I'm wearing about a dozen layers underneath."

But all of them were sheer, Dylan suspected. Lacy. Frilly. Prone to showing off certain parts of her and covering others.

Just then, he wanted to see…*everything*. All of Marielle.

More strikingly, she apparently wanted to show him.

At the realization, he could have sworn his heart stopped.

But he managed a nonchalant shrug of his own, all the same. "That sounds reasonable," Dylan said, trying not to betray his own suddenly hammering heartbeat. Or his shaky hands. "The only trouble is, I'm not wearing much under my own duds."

"Well, I've already seen you without your shirt," Marielle pointed out. Her blue eyes danced at him. "I liked that, so…"

"I wasn't worried about whether you'd like it

or not." He wasn't being arrogant when he added, "I'm pretty sure you will."

Marielle swallowed. Hard. She reined her restless mount.

"You must have on underdrawers, though. Right?" she asked, eyeing his coat and britches. "Couldn't you swim in those?"

Her tremulous tone made him feel twice as tender toward her. Apparently, Marielle was only capable of teasing to a point. That point was where he made himself wholly naked to her.

"I could. I'm wearing very modest underdrawers," he assured her, blessing the time she'd spent living with Hudson, taking on seamstress work and becoming comfortable with men's clothing. "I'm practically wearing two pairs of britches." Dylan calmed his own fidgety horse, everything else forgotten. "You won't see a thing that's improper, if that's what you're asking."

He could have sworn she seemed…*disappointed?* by that.

Had Marielle Miller come out today to *seduce* him? Dylan wondered. That would explain all her chitchat. Maybe it had been nothing but nervous chatter, with no greater significance.

Maybe he'd been suspicious of Marielle for nothing.

Overrun with regret—not to mention warmth and affection for her—Dylan smiled. "Unless you want to see more, that is."

He was a rogue for even offering. But Marielle didn't seem to mind his scandalous suggestion. Maybe she did want him.

"If I do want to see more," she told him pertly, "I'll be sure to let you know—just as directly as I possibly can."

Then she cantered off the road and headed for the creek.

Riding into the undergrowth, following the burbling sound of Morrow Creek's namesake waterway farther into the pines, Marielle knew that her heart was about to burst with daring.

She'd only come out with Dylan today to try to complete the latest odious mission that Charley Sheridan had given her: to find out what Dylan knew about Sheriff Caffey and the tax money.

She'd been charged with learning, if she could, where the money might be hidden and whether the sheriff might come back to claim it—and to report her findings later to the Sheridans.

She hadn't wanted to. But Charley had made it plain that Hudson's well-being was at stake. She'd *had* to spy on Dylan.

In doing so, though, she'd actually succeeded. Marielle still couldn't believe it. She felt awash with relief. She'd been so worried that she would fail at spying and Hudson would be hurt again— this time, because of her own shortcomings.

It had taken some effort, but she'd finally managed to wrangle some useful information from Dylan. If she absolutely had to, she knew, she could tell Charley about Sheriff Caffey's supposed hiding place near the Morrow Creek bridge, where the Tillson medicine show was camped. Then she and Hudson would be free. She knew Dylan would have preferred to catch the runaway sheriff himself. But if letting the Sheridans do it hastened their departure from town, wouldn't that be a good thing?

The way Marielle saw it, Dylan couldn't argue with having those outlaws gone. Nobody truly expected him to catch up to Sheriff Caffey and make him pay for his misdeeds. Even Thomas Walsh, the rabble-rousing editor of the *Pioneer Press*, had quit running weekly editorials lambasting the former sheriff. If Mr. Walsh was content to let their deceitful prior lawman go free, then they should probably all be willing to let him go free.

Even if it did rankle her to know the risk that Caffey had put everyone to by running off with all their tax money. If she'd had her way, the man would have been brought to justice.

But there was nothing Marielle could do about that—and everything she could do about the man who was currently riding in her wake, snapping twigs and pushing through the bushes in his haste to keep up with her. When he'd offered to go for a swim with her, Marielle figured he hadn't expected her to agree. But just then, suffused with relief and filled with her own reckless bravado at having tried at all, she'd been in the mood to let go—to stop being afraid of little things and just *live*.

If there was anything positive that had come out of the whole mess with Charley Sheridan and his brothers, it was that after being threatened by them, Marielle found all other dangers to be almost laughable. She'd been seized in the arms of a killer at midnight. She'd bandaged her brother after that same outlaw had almost beaten him to death. She'd withstood more threats on that same afternoon, when Charley had shown up on her doorstep, arrogant with the full knowledge that he owned her.

After all that, being thought of as improper for taking an impromptu afternoon swim in the creek didn't scare her. She didn't care what people thought. Heck, in her current state of mind, Marielle reckoned as she reached the creek and stopped her horse beneath some trees, she felt as if she could do anything.

Even swim in her skivvies with the handsome new sheriff.

At the notion, a new frisson of excitement raced through her. She'd always been talented and independent, but she'd never been quite this brazen before. She was about to let a man see her practically in the altogether. It was wicked and it was irresponsible, but just then, Marielle didn't care. Because it was also what she *wanted*—to feel the cool creek water on her skin, to let the currents ripple across her body, to pull Dylan closer in their watery idyll and let him kiss her again.

Nearby, the creek flowed past in its usual sun-dappled glory, bordered by grassy banks and protected by trees. Here, the scrub oaks grew low but sheltering; the pines stood like tall sentinels, lending a peaceful windswept sound to coordinate with the birdsong. There had never been any-place more lovely.

To her, there had never been any man more fascinating, either. Marielle knew she was taking a risky step, but Dylan was worth it. She felt awfully guilty about having successfully fooled him. She wanted another memory of this day to tide her over—another keepsake aside from the smug grin Charley Sheridan would give her when she revealed what she'd learned from Dylan.

Shoving those dreadful realities from her mind, Marielle waited as Dylan came over to help her from her horse. As she stood nearby, her ankle now strong enough to support her but not to withstand the antics of vigorous saloon dancing, Dylan was getting their mounts properly seen to and tied off, also. It was so like him to take on whatever responsibility was looming.

It was like him, as well, to turn to her after

those tasks were done, then dispel almost all of her nervousness with a smile.

She loved the way Dylan smiled at her. In fact, she loved almost everything about him. If he hadn't been the sheriff—if she hadn't been pressured into bamboozling him—then things would have been perfect. They could have called on one another, grown gradually closer, had an engagement like Jobyna and Snub…

But Marielle couldn't think about what wouldn't be. Because even as she did, Dylan took off his broad, flat-brimmed black hat. He hung it on a branch. He kicked off his boots. He took off his coat—with its shiny-starred badge pinned prominently to its front—lowered his braces, then grabbed his shirt's collar.

By the time he peeled off that garment and flung it toward a waiting creek-side rock, Marielle knew her mouth was watering.

There had never been a man more appealing, more genuine or more fascinating than her resident drifter. Just looking at his broad shoulders, sculpted chest and muscular arms made her long to touch him in all those places—to make him feel, if she could, as good as she felt whenever he was touching her. Because although Marielle was inexperienced, she was not insensible to the effect she sometimes had on Dylan. When she touched him, he often sucked in his breath and moaned.

When she kissed him, he clutched her to him as though he needed her as much as air.

She wanted to be everything to him. Maybe only for an afternoon. Maybe for longer. Because the more time Marielle spent with him, the more she wanted to keep spending time with him. She had never felt more smitten with anyone—nor was she ever likely to feel this way again. Right now, today, was her best chance at being loved… no matter what the future held.

Confidentially, she believed that Dylan was coming to like Morrow Creek. She believed, more and more, that he wanted to stay. It seemed inevitable that he would. Then, after a while, they might become engaged, like Jobyna and Snub. If her friend's assurances were correct and the whole town really was pulling for them, she and Dylan would enjoy a tremendous party when they got married, too. Everyone would come. Hudson, the Murphys, all her friends, from Corinne to Rosamond to Violet to Adeline…

It could happen that way, Marielle assured herself as she soaked in the sight of Dylan's bare skin and the outrageously masculine chest hairs that meandered down to his britches. It could only happen that way. Because she loved him. She did.

Proving it, she said, "I love…the way you look."

Dylan arched his brow with surprise. And pleasure, too.

Drat it, though! She'd meant to tell him more. Much more.

"I love the way you look, too." With supreme confidence, he gestured toward her ensemble. "That's a lot of clothes to go swimming in. You should probably at least shuck your shoes."

She was being so silly. She'd been so busy day-dreaming and planning and savoring the sight of him that she'd forgotten what they'd come there for. Biting her lip, Marielle glanced over her shoulder at the creek. Its burble had never sounded more inviting. Riding was dusty work. So was interrogating someone.

She'd earned the right to relax for the rest of her day.

"Aren't you even going to turn around like a gentleman?"

"While you take off your shoes?" He shook his head. "I've been fixing your ankle for weeks. I've seen your bare feet."

He had her there. They had reached a certain level of familiarity with one another. Marielle smiled. "For the rest?"

"Nope."

"What?" But he *had* to. It was only courteous.

She didn't think there was a large enough quantity of brazenness in the whole territory to do what he was asking.

Except…Dylan crossed his arms. "I don't think

you're going to do it. I don't think you *will* go for a swim with me."

"Of course I will!"

"Nope. You're all talk, Miss Miller."

"Well." Indignantly, Marielle unlaced her shoes. She kicked them aside, where they came to rest near his boots. "See?"

"Humph. That's a start. A meager one. I suppose."

Dylan's teasing, doubtful tone goaded her. Lifting her chin, Marielle started unbuttoning her dress. "How about now?"

His gaze arrowed to the slender triangle of skin she'd exposed so far. He swallowed hard. "Mmm. You're bluffing."

She couldn't believe he doubted her nerve. She stopped.

He uncrossed his arms. "I knew it!"

But Marielle was too busy tromping to a nearby boulder and then getting situated comfortably atop it to pay much mind to Dylan's triumphant remark. Keeping her back to him, she fussed beneath her skirts. She unfastened her garters, one at a time, then rolled down her dark stockings. She threw one at him.

"I can't very well swim in stockings, now, can I?"

His astonished expression as he caught her stocking almost made her laugh. "I don't know," he said. "I've never tried."

"Well, I can't." Marielle tossed him her other stocking.

Dylan caught it with a look that lay somewhere between thrilled and disbelieving. Did he really think she was a coward?

Proving him wrong, Marielle brought her hands to her dress bodice again. She didn't want to be unusually aware of her bare legs beneath her dress and petticoats, but she was. It felt so…*free* to be standing outside with the sunshine warming her and the breeze tossing her hair, herself the whole focus of a man's attention. It was, in a way, just like a performance onstage.

Summoning up that part of herself, Marielle winked.

Dylan put his hand to his heart and mimed being bowled over. He staggered sideways as though she'd done him in.

She couldn't help laughing. "If you think *that's* good…"

She finished unbuttoning, knowing that her chemise and corset were probably peeping from between the halves of her dress's bodice. Feeling voluptuous and daring, she lifted her skirts and performed a single kick. She had to use her good leg for balance and kick the mending one, but the trouble she took was worth it when she noticed Dylan appreciating her private show. He looked as though he'd waited *years* for it. For her.

Given all his time wandering alone, maybe he had.

"…wait till you see more," she teased further.

Full of tenderness for him, Marielle managed still more bravery. She unbuttoned her sleeves, then gave a shimmy. She toyed with her dress's unfastened bodice, then allowed him a more provocative glimpse of her lacy chemise. She felt womanly and wanted, wanton and protected, desirous and irksomely naive, and if there was any justice in the world at all, Dylan would—

—come to her on the grassy creek bank, pull her into his arms and kiss her as though he wanted to never stop. Again and again his mouth touched hers, warm and soft and insistent. Again and again, Marielle yielded, giving him what they both wanted.

It felt as though she *needed* Dylan somehow. But she wasn't sure why. Breathless and unsteady, Marielle clung to him.

"My heart is racing!" she exclaimed.

"I guess you're really excited about that swim."

"I guess I am," she agreed, letting herself touch his bare chest. "Yet here you are, distracting me with kissing."

"I aim to keep doing that, too. I *love* kissing you."

For a moment, Marielle had the impression that Dylan had done the same thing she'd done earlier—gotten just to the edge of declaring his feelings, only to retreat at the last instant.

She hoped he had. That made everything even better.

"Then you want to kiss me some more?" she asked.

His dark eyes flared. "That…and a lot more, besides."

The mysterious notion of *a lot more* intrigued her. It scared her a little, too. But Marielle was nothing if not brave.

"Well, good. But you'll have to catch me first!"

Then she wiggled out of her dress, left it in a calico puddle on the grass and ran all the way to the creek with her underdrawers on full display to the squirrels and everyone else.

If Dylan didn't follow her just as eagerly as he'd seemed to want to, Marielle just knew that she'd expire on the spot.

Chapter Nine

Dylan did more than follow her. Much more.

In her nervousness over getting herself ready to swim, Marielle had forgotten that Dylan would have to do the same thing to himself. So after she splashed her way into the dancing creek water, after she sucked in a breath at the refreshing coolness of it all, after she felt her myriad lacy underclothes instantly get soaked and swirl all around her…well, after all that, Marielle dashed the water drops from her eyes and glanced again to the creek bank—only to get the surprise of her life.

Because Dylan had been wrong. He'd said he was *practically wearing two pairs of britches* earlier. But the overall effect, as he stepped out of his trousers and dropped them to mingle, scandalously, with her own discarded dress, was much more remarkable and revealing than his description had implied.

Dylan was built much differently from her,

Marielle realized anew as he headed toward her. He had a muscular torso, of course. He was also lightly hairy where she was not. He moved with a certain prowess that could never be applied to her, too.

There was more to it than that, though. Because she'd never seen anything quite as provocative as the way his dark cotton drawers clung to his hip bones and then scandalously dipped just a bit lower than was strictly proper, making her realize that the chest hair he sported really did swirl all the way down.

All the way down…to that most compelling and personal part of him—that part that she'd never directly seen but had certainly wondered a great deal about while they'd been kissing.

Transfixed by the sight of him, Marielle ducked shoulder-deep into the water and then went right on looking. Dylan came closer to the creek's edge, not hurrying so much as parading for her benefit, and she would have smiled if not for the rousing effect his near nudity had on her. She couldn't believe how hard he looked, how strong, how utterly capable and undeniably good. His legs were long and lean, his hips spare, his pelvis—

Shocked, Marielle swerved away her gaze. She had no business looking at him there. Did she? They'd kissed, yes. But that didn't mean she was at liberty to scrutinize the buttons on his drawers, to wonder about the bulk of him beneath, to almost squeal over the way that certain parts of him seemed almost to sway in a very mesmerizing fashion as he got closer. Did it?

She could have sworn she caught a glimpse of that most scandalous part of him, outlined clearly beneath his drawers. Her heart hammered at the immensity of what she was doing.

They were both almost naked. And he'd almost reached her.

When he did, though, Marielle's concerns vanished like eddies of creek water moving happily downstream. Because in the moment between reaching the creek and reaching her, Dylan became more than the sum of manliness and muscles and imposing strength. He became, once again, the man she knew and cared so much for. When he smiled, his strength was again the strength that had protected and helped her. When he touched her, his near nakedness was natural and expected. When he kissed her again…

… Marielle jerked backward, startled. "You're all wet!"

"Of course I'm wet." Dylan's smile touched her again. "So are you." He looked toward the creek bank, probably to assure himself their horses and possessions were still safe, then dunked underwater. When he came up, he swore. "You should have warned me it was so cold! I haven't swum in a creek for ages."

Startled anew by the change in him—because

she hadn't seen him with his hair completely wet and his near nudity on display—Marielle gawked. She couldn't believe they were there.

Somehow, Dylan knew how she felt. He brought his drippy hand to her face, then cradled her cheek. Water droplets teased her neck. "It's still me," he assured her. "If we're going to be together, we're going to see *all* sides of each other."

Marielle hoped that didn't mean he'd see the side of her that was supposed to deceive him. Shoving away that thought, she followed his example and dunked herself—but only to her neck.

Dylan laughed. "You can't do this halfway!" He shook his head, still smiling at her. "Are you going to swim or not?"

"I'm going to swim while keeping my hair dry," Marielle returned primly—at least as primly as she could while being pulled into his naked arms, wearing a sopping chemise that offered no real protection against nudity. "I can dry my things by hanging them up, or wear them damp if I have to, but I can't dry and redress my hair entirely. Not before sunup, at least."

"Then let's stay until sunup."

She almost wanted to. That way, no one would bother them. They'd have no responsibilities, no troubles…only hopefulness.

"Hudson will wonder where I am."

Dylan dismissed that. "He'll be with Corinne. You know it."

She did. "I still can't get my hair wet."

"Why not?"

"Because…" She hesitated. "Everyone will know what we did."

"Swimming isn't a sin."

Marielle looked up at him. "I don't aim to *only* swim."

She was certain his whole body tensed against hers. But Dylan only gave her a quizzical look. "What do you aim to do?"

"Things I've been wanting to do. For a while now."

And that's when it struck her: if she was saying something so brash, she really *did* trust him. Finally and irrevocably.

Otherwise, why would she be there with him at all?

He grew still, even as the water eddied around them. His breath touched her neck, warming her. "Things? Like what?"

At his question, she felt excessively brave. As long as she was here, Marielle reasoned, she might as well commit entirely.

After all, he was right. She couldn't do this halfway.

"Things like *this*," she murmured…then she put her hand on his chest, trailed it down his abdomen, and delved even lower.

* * *

Certain he must be dreaming, Dylan tensed as Marielle touched him. Her fingers grazed his belly, making him suck in a ragged breath. Then she leaned nearer in the busy water…and slipped her hand to the top of his drawers. As the creek water whirled around them, splashing over rocks in the distance and meandering around a bend closer by, as the birdsong twittered and the sun beat down on them with impossible springtime warmth, Marielle traced the waistband of his drawers. She learned their shape, their sodden fabric, their drawstring fastening…their utter inability to contain his eagerness for her.

Another few inches, and she'd encounter *all* of him.

Dylan had never wanted anything more. Imagining Marielle's hands on him had been wondrous enough. Actually *feeling* that miracle take place existed on a different level altogether.

He ached for her to touch him. Full of yearning, Dylan battled to remember why he was resisting at all. Dimly, he remembered that Marielle was innocent. That they'd never been this intimate before. That, for her sake, he had to take things slowly at the least and not at all at the most. He oughtn't take her outside at the creek, no matter how beautiful the spot was.

Marielle deserved soft sheets and feathery pillows. She deserved candlelight and promises. She deserved a wedding ring.

Instead, her ringless fingers played over the buttons of his drawers, dancing over each one, moving lower. Lower. Damnation. All he wanted was to let her continue. *Yes…*

"Stop." His own harsh voice surprised him. Incredibly, Dylan felt himself wrap his hand around Marielle's. "You can't."

Her wide-eyed gaze met his. "But I seem to be already."

She was. Why wasn't she more scared? Weren't unmarried women supposed to be frightened by such things? He knew Marielle was guileless. The only explanation for her bravado was…*him*.

She must truly, completely, trust him.

Humbled by the realization, Dylan curled his hand more gently around Marielle's. "I don't expect you to touch me."

"Why wouldn't I? You touch me."

He did. As often as he could. "We could just swim."

"That's true." She glanced around at their peaceful forested surroundings. "But we're not likely to have this much privacy again. Not without raising Hudson's suspicions."

"I don't care about Hudson's suspicions."

"I do. And I want you. So, in order to manage both—"

"We have to be here now. Like this?"

Her nod all but inflamed him.

"It just occurred to me," Marielle said, "while we were riding." She glanced to the clear blue sky, pantomiming having a moment of inspiration. "I was thinking about kissing you—"

"You think about kissing me?"

He'd thought he was the only one.

"All the time," she confessed. "I think about other things, too." Her gaze traveled downward, taking in his water-dappled chest, his shoulders, his arms and his middle and…more. "I think about the places where you're hard and I'm soft, where you're strong and I'm…less strong, where you're here…and so am I."

At her typical refusal to admit any weakness, Dylan grinned. He felt besieged with love for her—and concern, too.

"I'm powerfully curious," Marielle said. "Please. Let me."

She wriggled her hand, making her intentions plain but not yet acting. For the space of an uneven breath, she waited for his response. Dylan felt wholly unable to give it. Because while he knew he should say no, every single part of him screamed yes. Yes, yes, yes. He needed Marielle's hands on him the same way he needed sunlight. He needed to know that she *did* want him.

When he didn't answer, she slipped her hand from his. She drew in a breath. She lowered her gaze to watch the progress of her hand as it slipped lower under the water…then over to him.

Caught, Dylan jolted. He gave an involuntary shudder, torn between need and responsibility. He ought to…ought to…do *something* besides clench Marielle's shoulder and bite his lip.

She caressed him, tentatively. A low groan escaped him.

"Oh! Does that hurt?" Marielle stopped. "I'm sorry."

"It…doesn't hurt," Dylan assured her huskily. "Only in the way that not having you hurts. Or the way not kissing hurts."

"Ah." Her gaze suggested she knew what that was like. Again, he couldn't help marveling that she desired him, too. "The best remedy for that is to keep going. Wouldn't you say?"

Dylan couldn't say a thing. Not as Marielle's curious hand found him again—not as she stroked him from root to tip.

"My goodness!" she breathed. "I've never felt anything like this before." Her gaze flew to his. "You need bigger drawers."

He almost laughed. "That's not permanent. It's only because—" *I want to lay you down on the creek bank and ravish you. I want to pull off your underthings and taste you. I want to lose myself in your warmth and femininity and sweetness…* "It's a natural consequence of me wanting you," Dylan managed.

"All this is because of me?" Marielle seemed delighted.

"It's all because of you," he confirmed. "But—"

His words ended on another strangled groan as Marielle seized him afresh. She stroked him more boldly, then kissed him.

For long moments they shared kisses, sweet and hot. Their secluded spot near the creek fell away, vanishing beneath more stroking, more caressing, more eddies of water that swirled around their movements as they dropped, as one, to their knees in the water. As they did, Marielle laughed with new gladness.

For his part, Dylan did, too. Because he was with Marielle. Because she wanted him, and he wanted her. Because there was no reason now not to peel away the wet fabric clinging to her skin, not to lower his mouth to her damp shoulder and kiss her there, not to bring his hands to her breasts and explore his fill.

As her nipples budded against his palms, revealing that she felt as passionate as he did, Dylan felt a fierce mingling of joy and protectiveness well inside him. In that moment, there at the creek together, Marielle was his. But it wasn't enough.

It couldn't be. He wanted her forever.

"I need you, Marielle," Dylan breathed, bringing his hands to her waist. He couldn't tear away his gaze from the stirring sight of her breasts, almost fully revealed to him by her soaked chemise. "Please say you'll be mine forever. I'll be so happy if you will. I could never ask for more. Not more than you."

He wanted to say more, but he didn't have the words. Not even at his floweriest and most poetic did Dylan have the ability to express how much she meant to him. But somehow, Marielle understood. She kissed him before he even tried again.

"Yes." She nodded. "Of course I'll be yours!" Her exhilarated gaze merged with his. Her expression softened as she stroked his cheek. "Why do you think I'm here otherwise?"

Flooded with awe and gratitude, Dylan grinned. "Because you enjoy kneeling on a rocky creek bed more than you enjoy riding?"

Marielle made a comical face. "It is a little uncomfortable." Then her gaze arrowed lower. "But it has its compensations." She drew in a breath. "I find you…fascinating."

He shrugged. "I'm not so mysterious."

"You are to me." Another indrawn breath. "For now."

He knew what she was implying. "And you, to me."

"But since…well, given what you've just told me—"

"That I want you to be mine?"

Marielle beamed as though he'd suggested they troop to Reverend Benson's distant church in Morrow Creek and have done with a wedding right then and there. She was transparent to him.

"—we don't have to remain mysterious to each other, do we?" she finished. "My underthings will need time to dry, and we'll need to do *something* during that time, now that we've swum—"

He arched a brow. "Is that what we're calling it?"

"—and if you would just quit arguing and kiss me—"

Gladly, Dylan did. Stirringly and at length, besides.

With that done but not finished, he smiled at her. "Miss Miller, are you suggesting what I think you're suggesting?"

"That depends. What do you think I'm suggesting?"

He couldn't believe Marielle had chosen now to be coy.

"I think," Dylan said as he stroked her arm, then skimmed his hand along her curvaceous waist, "that you want to find out exactly how good you can feel while letting your underthings dry." He kissed her again, then gazed into her eyes. "I think that you lured me out here with the express intention of finding that out." He raised his hand to her wet breast, caressed her, then felt her shiver against him. "I think I'm just the man you need, and I think that if I have to wait a second longer—"

"You don't have to wait any time at all. Not if you follow me." Marielle coquettishly pushed away. Giving him a look of clear invitation, she floated away along the creek water. Then she gracefully got up and headed for the grassy bank.

Dylan doubted she realized the picture she made with her wet, mostly transparent underthings clinging to her body. Or the effect such an image had on him. But he didn't need Marielle to realize what she did to him to know that they belonged together, now and…well, if not forever, then for a long time to come.

Dylan had no doubts. Not then, with Marielle. Between them, the future would take care of itself. It simply had to.

So he rose from the creek himself, sluicing water from his body as he did, and followed Marielle to the soft grass beyond.

It turned out, Marielle realized as she reached the creek bank and noticed a blanket providentially spread on the grass—right beside her cast-off clothes and Dylan's equally strewn about duds and boots—that Dylan was every bit as thoughtful with her as he was handsome and intelligent. Because he'd had the foresight to grab that blanket from his saddle roll, unbeknownst to her, and leave it for them to share in just such a circumstance as this.

Not wanting to soak it by lowering her wet self

onto its surface, Marielle hesitated. Her former daring at the notion of being naked while letting her underthings dry started to wane.

What if she was being foolish? What if she was making a mistake? She'd loved everything about their swimming session so far—including all the ways Dylan had touched her...and all the bold ways she'd touched *him*. But she wasn't married, and this wasn't a wedding bed she was looking at. It was an ordinary blanket, woven of wool and not her girlish hopes and dreams.

On the other hand, Dylan *had* just pledged himself to her.

I need you, Marielle. Please say you'll be mine forever.

If that wasn't nigh on a verifiable proposal of marriage, Marielle didn't know what was. For certain, it was a promise—a promise she could rely on and take into her future with her.

So, newly emboldened, Marielle turned. She saw Dylan stride out of the creek, his drawers soaked and his manhood arrestingly proud, and got herself ready to make good on her own pledge.

Of course I'll be yours, she'd said. She'd meant it, too.

She loved Dylan with every single part of her. So when he spied her waiting and smiled at her, her heart melted. When he shook his head and sent water droplets pinging everywhere onto the trees surrounding them, her belly tightened.

When he leaped nimbly onto the creek bank and just kept coming, his body tall and strong and promised to her, her whole being lightened.

This was it. She was going to love Dylan Coyle.

He reached her with a kiss and a quizzical smile. "You look as though it's Christmas morning and you got all the oranges."

"I feel as though I got all the oranges," Marielle said.

They were the best part. Everyone knew that. She and Hudson had always gotten one apiece in their stockings, but her brother had always given his to her. It occurred to her that he'd always been watching over her, in his way, ever since they were little.

But that was a reminiscence for another time. Because now Dylan was in front of her, and now the sun was shining down on them both and now she wasn't cold at all—because she was loved.

How long had it been since she'd felt so loved?

Marielle wasn't sure. But she was sure that she couldn't help smiling even more broadly as she looked up at Dylan. "How can I make you feel like it's Christmas, too? Because that's all I want. I want to please you, in every way."

"You don't have to do anything. Not anything at all."

"But I want to! There must be something."

His grin flashed at her. "If you're going to be stubborn—"

"We can probably take that as a given."

"Then just be yourself." Dylan took in her swim-soaked form, seeming to love every inch of her. "And let me do *this* while you're at it."

He moved nearer as he said so, then examined her corset's hooks. Above that garment's edge, her breasts heaved. Dylan ran his fingers along those many hooks. Deftly, he unfastened one, then another. Her corset gapped slowly, inch by torturous inch.

It finally fell to the grass, leaving her one step closer to naked. But Marielle didn't mind. Because Dylan kissed her as he did it. He made her head swim with wonder as his lips plied hers, teasing them apart and then delving sweetly inside, making her tremble and yearn and clutch at him. She needed...

When she popped open her eyes again, trying to discern what she needed, her petticoats were on the grass. They'd joined her abandoned corset, having been hastily spread to dry in the sunshine, besides. Dylan must have reached behind her, Marielle realized, and untied them all without her even noticing.

"You're sneaky," she marveled, dressed only in her chemise. A breeze fluttered its hem, making her twice as aware of her near nudity. "I suspect you have experience with such things?"

"No. Nothing in my life has ever come close to you," Dylan swore before kissing her again, making her swoon. His fingers plucked at her wet chemise, hiking up its delicate fabric. It rose a few inches, then a few more. His hands followed that motion, warming her with every stroke of her calves, of her knees and scandalously of her thighs. "You're a wonder to me."

"I'm a wonder to myself sometimes," Marielle joked, hardly able to believe that she was really there, with him, this way.

"You're the best person I've ever known," Dylan declared.

His words held a ring of truth that Marielle couldn't deny. Not that she could truly think clearly on the matter—not with his palms brushing along her thighs, making her squirm.

"If I could," Dylan said, "I would stay with you forever."

Moved by him, she felt happy tears sting her eyes. With effort, Marielle swallowed past the rising lump in her throat.

"Don't you know?" she asked. "You *can* stay."

She wanted to give him a home, to give him her heart, to make him know that he was wanted and needed and welcomed. But since all she had was herself and an afternoon to do it in, Marielle settled for pulling him closer. Then she kissed him.

"There's no way I'm leaving now," Dylan joked huskily. His hands found her bottom, still nestled in her wet underdrawers. He squeezed her there. "Not when I've just found *all* of you."

Glad to give him that and more, Marielle pushed herself closer. Her clothes—what remained of them—were disheveled, her hair was coming undone and her heart was likely to beat out of her chest with excitement, but she didn't care a whit. All she'd ever needed was someone to love. Now she had him. Dylan.

Besides, hadn't he just promised himself to her? Hadn't she just heard him say outright that he'd stay with her forever?

She had. That meant, Marielle knew, that it was all right to let Dylan remove her drawers, pull her chemise higher, lay her on the blanket he'd left and then kiss her passionately—and entirely nakedly—in the sunshine. It was all right to grasp his head and kiss him back, to writhe beneath his increasingly maddening touches, to moan as he lowered his mouth to her breast and kissed her there, too. It was all right to *need*…and she did.

She needed Dylan to go on touching her, shockingly, right between her thighs. She needed to understand what lay beyond the ache that was building, sweetly and compellingly, in her most private places. She needed to pull him to her, to kiss him, to—

"Oh, my word!" Marielle exclaimed as she felt Dylan move away. She opened her eyes to discern what was wrong, propped herself up on her elbows and glimpsed him stripping off his wet skivvies. "Oh, my word! You're so—"

"Eager?" he offered with a mischievous look.

"—*big*," she contradicted, eyes wide. She couldn't tear her gaze away from him. How did he get all that girth into his britches each day? The seams ought to split clean apart, she knew, given the stress on them. "I honestly had no idea."

Frankly, she was a little concerned. She had some hazy notion of what was meant to happen between them. But Dylan—

"You can't tell me you've never sneaked a peek at me."

She couldn't. "Of course I have." Marielle felt her face heat as a rosy blush likely overtook her cheeks. "But that wasn't the same. You were never quite so…imposing as all that."

"I was. You just didn't know." He knelt beside her, then stretched out with his body touching hers. He played his fingers along her hip, then skimmed them to her ribs. She desperately wanted him to touch her peaked nipples again. She wriggled to encourage him. "All those times we were kissing… I was like this," Dylan confessed. "All those times I touched you—"

"Like *this*?" Disbelieving, she dared to glance downward. His manhood wasn't quite touching her hip, but she still felt heat and power radiating from him. "That's impossible."

"To the contrary. Feeling this way and not acting…*that's* what's nigh impossible." Dylan smiled, then caressed her face. His gaze remained on her, steady and warm. "I wanted to protect you. To watch over you. To cherish you. Not to ruin you."

"I don't care about ruination." To prove it, Marielle flopped flat onto her back. She put her arms to her sides, then stared straight up at the clear territorial skies. "Go ahead."

Dylan didn't move. "Go ahead?"

Why did he sound so bemused? "Yes." She gestured. "I'm ready. I know what's supposed to happen, and I want it to, so—"

"You don't know what's supposed to happen," he argued with certainty. "Otherwise, you wouldn't be lying there like that."

"All right." Obligingly, Marielle squeezed shut her eyes. The action made her feel cranky about missing the enthralling sight of Dylan's nudity, but she did it, all the same. She'd heard this was sometimes a recommended step. "How about now?"

"Nope." Now he sounded amused. "Not yet."

Frustrated and feeling wiggly, Marielle squirmed. "What then? Jobyna told me *everything* about her upcoming wedding night. She spoke to her landlady, Mrs. Viola Sunley, about the matter and came away very well informed. So…go ahead!"

"I think I may need to have a word with Snub," Dylan told her. "Because he might wind up pretty alarmed otherwise."

On the verge of giving up, Marielle frowned at him.

"I don't know why you think you have all the answers."

"Because I do," Dylan said matter-of-factly. "About this."

"You don't seem as though you do." Newly suspicious, Marielle levered up on her elbow. "Is this your first time?"

His smile was dashing. "It's *our* first time. You're not going to enjoy it if you decide to close your eyes and bear it."

"Then you don't know what to do! Well, that's all right," she hastened to assure him. "We'll learn together. We will."

She didn't know why that made him smile so broadly.

Or why it made him say, "You're a treasure, Marielle."

All she knew was that a moment later, Dylan resumed stroking her again. Without even requiring her to change positions or close her eyes, he kissed her…and loved her, too.

Within moments, she thought she might die if Dylan didn't hurry up and do…something important. Moaning in his arms, she writhed and clutched him, begging for more. More touching. More kissing. More of the very wicked kissing in very special places that Dylan seemed so skilled at giving. Just more. Of him.

"Oh, Dylan!" Marielle grabbed him, panting. "I feel—"

She couldn't describe it. It was necessary, yet wondrous.

"You feel amazing," he breathed, reassuring her. He stroked her and kissed her, caressed her and held her close, and just when she knew nothing could feel any more indescribably good...

"Oh!" Another moan escaped her as Dylan moved atop her. He had the strength to balance himself above her, but that didn't seem to matter to Marielle. She needed to be even closer. She arched her hips to accomplish that, and was rewarded with a new and better acquaintance with Dylan's audacious member. "Oh, my!"

"Yes," he murmured. "Just hold me, Marielle. Go on..."

She could do nothing else. Not even as he parted her thighs wider, situated himself between them and moved inside her.

The sensation was unlike anything else. Gasping and wide-eyed, Marielle went still. She felt filled, yet incomplete. But a heartbeat later, as Dylan started slowly moving, she realized this was why they were made so differently...and why they fit together so beautifully, too. Awed by the incredibleness of it all, Marielle moaned and held him closer. Doing so seemed to transport him. Eyes closed, Dylan thrust his hips faster.

Their panting breaths met and joined, then

feathered away. Their bodies strained, reached then came together in the sunlight. Quaking with pleasure, Marielle clutched him harder.

Something was happening to her. Something unbelievable.

But Dylan seemed to expect it. Opening his eyes, cradling her face, he encouraged her. "It's all right, Marielle. Just let it come." Muscles flexing, he thrust again. She'd never witnessed a more thrilling sight in her life than she did in that moment, with him moving against her. "If you will, I will."

Aha. He was being chivalrous. Nodding, Marielle groaned.

"I…I'll try," she gasped, wanting to do her part.

But in the end, there was no trying necessary. Because as Dylan next cradled her close, as he whispered sweet things about her beauty—and scandalous things about what she did to him— Marielle suddenly felt herself come undone, entirely without trying. Her body contracted thrillingly around him. At the same time, Dylan gave a hoarse shout. Gazing into her eyes, he thrust again. Then, exquisitely, again. Wearing a grin, he lowered his face to her neck, then nuzzled her there. She could feel his heart pounding against hers. She could hear his raspy breath.

"Aw, Marielle," he murmured. "You're everything to me."

Feeling bedazzled, Marielle looked sideways.

She couldn't believe she was there, with him, having done that. Especially so pleasurably. She'd been misled into believing that relations between them would be arduous—not that they would leave her tingly and happy, ears ringing, with a wall-to-wall grin on her face. She felt hot and relieved, bold and sweaty. She was truly a woman now—and Dylan Coyle was the reason. He was… miraculous.

"You're everything and more to me," she replied.

For whatever reason, her response made him laugh.

There had never been a sweeter sound. Not ever.

"You always have to beat me, don't you?" Dylan asked.

"Not always."

"Always."

"Maybe ninety-nine percent of the time."

"Always," he insisted with a kiss.

"From here on, everything's going to change," Marielle told him, loving his weight and his gentleness and his care. "It might as well start now. So…you're correct. I'm always right."

He laughed again. "That's not what I meant."

"Doesn't matter." Gleefully, Marielle hugged him to her. She wasn't concerned, just then, with tomorrow or the day after. This was enough, with Dylan. "We both know it's true."

"I know that the secret to bliss is agreeing. So, yes."

"You're humoring me now?"

"Isn't that what you want me to do?"

"No!" Indignantly, she wiggled. "Of course not."

"Then I'm absolutely not doing that."

His mock serious face made her fall in love with him all over again. "Sometimes," Marielle said, knowing she hadn't done this halfway, "I think you'd do anything in the world for me."

At that, his pretense fell away. "I would," Dylan told her solemnly. "I'm a fool for you, Marielle. I'm glad to be one."

But she wasn't entirely content. "Do you think this will change things between us? Do you think marriage wrecks it all?" she wondered. "Because according to Jobyna and Mrs. Sunley—"

"According to *me*, it's time for another swim." Dylan stood, then held out his hand to her. "I'll help you wash up."

"I'll help *you* wash up." She stood to do so.

"There you go again."

"Yes, and you love it." Feeling unfamiliarly achy, Marielle clung to his hand. She squeezed. "Just like I love you."

Then she pulled him harder and led them both to the creek.

Chapter Ten

Marielle loved him. Even days after first hearing her say so, Dylan couldn't get those words—or their significance—out of his mind. Marielle had confessed her feelings casually while on her way to the creek, it was true, but that didn't mean those words didn't still hold consequences for them both. They did.

Yes, and you love it, she'd said. *Just like I love you.*

He hadn't meant to make her love him, Dylan knew. In the tender aftermath of their loving, he'd been dazed and content. Stripped bare. Without defense. Marielle had found the one best way of forcing him to admit his feelings for her—at least to himself—and now there was no turning back from that.

As unlikely as it was, his longtime drifting days might be over with, squashed beneath an onslaught of love and domesticity that no ordinary man could have withstood. He wanted a future with Marielle, Dylan acknowledged as he stood outside Reverend Benson's small Morrow Creek church, waiting for Snub and his new bride, Jobyna, to emerge. But he couldn't rightly take that future. Not yet. Not until he made sure he caught Caffey.

The town expected that of him. They had a right to. If he wanted to continue as their provisional sheriff—if he wanted, even better, to be elected as Morrow Creek's sheriff on a more lasting basis—then he had to prove himself. He had to keep his word. He had to clear out the last known outlaws—the Sheridan brothers—find Sheriff Caffey and recover that tax money.

If he couldn't do those things, what did he have to offer Marielle? Nothing, save himself. That wasn't nearly enough.

So as Dylan stood there, dressed in his hat and sheriff's togs with his coat and newly ironed britches all spiffed up, watching the other guests at Jobyna and Snub's wedding mill around outside the church to greet the happy couple, he made a promise to himself. He would find Caffey, oust the Sheridans and pay the town's taxes—and then he would propose to Marielle.

She would be *so* surprised to find herself on the receiving end of a proper proposal of marriage, Dylan knew. As near as he could tell, Marielle nearly believed they'd gotten engaged that day at the creek—and the intervening days hadn't done much to dispel that notion, either. Because he and Marielle had spent every possible moment alone together since that afternoon. They'd slipped away in the moonlight. They'd met late at night in her bedroom. They'd stolen daytime moments when Hudson was gone, reveling in more touching, more kissing, more loving.

Through all of it, scandalous as it was, Marielle was glorious. Her enthusiasm was endearing, her generosity breathtaking. She gave as much as she received, glorying in their mutual nakedness and newly discovered closeness. Dylan reckoned he'd never been happier. Hell, even today, when he was stuck attending a froufrou wedding, he felt mighty content.

Full of affection and overwhelming protectiveness for her, he glanced from the opposite side of the walkway to the church steps. Marielle stood in a pretty yellow dress, her hair piled up in a becoming fashion, chatting with her friends. After all his time in town, Dylan recognized the women. He knew Grace Murphy, of course, the saloonkeeper's suffragist wife, who was currently expecting a new little suffragist to be born in a few months' time. He knew Sarah McCabe, the schoolmarm who'd wed the blacksmith Daniel McCabe, and Molly Copeland, who ran the town's best bakery shop and had married lumberman Marcus Copeland.

All of them clustered around a glowing Marielle, laughing and chatting. The supposed prettiest woman in town, Olivia Turner—recently married to Boston business magnate Griffin Turner—said something to Marielle, making both of them grin. Privately, with that clear comparison laid before him, Dylan still believed Marielle to be the prettiest…not that he intended to say so with Olivia's glowering, redoubtable husband in the vicinity. Some distance away, famous cookery book author Daisy Cooper, wife of stableman Owen Cooper, kissed her husband.

Lowering his gaze, Dylan noticed Daisy's pigtailed stepdaughter Élodie, who jigged impatiently with her hand in Daisy's. Cheerfully and deftly, Daisy nonetheless managed to keep a firm hold on the bundle in her arms—her baby boy.

"Yep. I saw that, too. It's pretty terrifying, isn't it?" Adam Corwin stepped up beside Dylan, having arrived at the wedding about as stealthily as he did everything else. The former detective eyed the Coopers' tranquil family. "To think I'm going to have one of those myself pretty soon." He swore, shaking his head with apparent wonderment. "The baby can't come soon enough for Savannah. She's getting a mite ornery nowadays."

Corwin aimed his chin at his telegraph operator wife. In contrast to Corwin's description, Dylan found that Savannah gave off a regal appearance as she sailed through the waiting crowd in a billowy flowered dress with her hair braided atop her head. She was the picture of femininity. No one looking at her would have guessed her prowess with complicated telegraphy equipment.

"I reckon I'd be ornery, too, if I had to tote around the equivalent of a sack of potatoes under my shirt night and day."

Corwin laughed. "Well, you might find your patience tried, once it's your wife." He gestured toward Marielle. "I'm not sure Miss Miller is the settling down type, though. From what I hear, she's had plenty of offers—and didn't ever take a single one."

"She just needed the right man." Dylan kept his gaze roving over the crowd, unable to help himself from keeping watch. He was still sheriff—and a security man—whether he was officially on duty or not. He spied his former employer, Rosamond McGrath Dancy, and her beau, Miles Callaway, talking with the town's best-known gambler, Cade Foster. He gave them all an amiable nod, then moved his attention to Hudson. Fortunately, that sometime miscreant was busy with some tomfoolery with Corinne Murphy. It was a good thing Dylan had helped them get paired off. "And the right situation. Now that she's got both—"

"You'll be getting yourself fitted for a wedding

lasso any day now." Corwin nodded, still grinning. "I didn't think I'd ever do it. But all that mush has a way of wearing down a man."

Dylan agreed. He wondered what was keeping Jobyna and Snub. He saw Violet Foster part from her husband and head inside the church where her father, Reverend Benson, still remained. Like most women in Morrow Creek, Violet seemed certain she knew how to manage the delay and get the wedding frolic back on track.

"It has a way of distracting a man, too," Corwin said in a more serious, quieter voice. His gaze also tracked the crowd—but this time, he wasn't savoring the sight of his wife. "Have you had any new leads on Caffey? Mose is still sure he saw him—"

"Near the old lumber camp downstream from your telegraph station. I remember." Dylan nodded, keeping his voice low, too. "I checked it out. There were signs Caffey had been there."

Unfortunately, there'd been no indication of the man himself—only a cold, charred fire pit, a few tin cans and the torn-up pine trees that suggested he'd tied up a makeshift tent.

"But he'd already gone." Corwin swore again. "I wish I could be out there looking for that thieving bastard myself."

"I'll get him," Dylan promised. "Don't worry about that."

Around them, an expectant murmur moved

through the crowd. Ahead, the church doors opened. A flushed and smiling Violet Foster hurried down the stairs. "They're coming, everyone!"

Inside the church, Widow Harrison played a tune. To its accompaniment filtering through the open doors, Jobyna and Snub appeared. She held a bouquet of wildflowers; he stood tall.

Both of them grinned broadly as they nearly danced down the church steps to greet their families, friends and neighbors.

Feeling unexpectedly heartwarmed at the spectacle of it all, Dylan swallowed hard. Someday, he knew, this could be him and Marielle skipping out of a church in their best finery. It could be the two of them getting set to embark on a life together— a life that might well have children to offer.

Beset, he cleared his throat. Beside him, Corwin did, too.

"Bunch of sentimental nonsense, isn't it?" Adam asked.

"Damn right," Dylan replied. "Women like it, though."

"I like it, too." Someone stepped between them, dressed all in black with an intimidating manner. It could only be…

"Griffin Turner." Dylan tugged his hat at the man, owner of the Lorndorff Hotel and many other properties in Morrow Creek. In some ways, Turner was landlord to half the town. "Howdy."

Corwin did the same. "Afternoon, Turner." He

craned his neck to look up at the man's face—which was impressive, given that Adam was reasonably tall himself. "I see you decided against getting all gussied up with a hat for this occasion."

Turner quirked his mouth. "I've worn enough hats in my life to suit me for another hundred years." His tone was gruff, his manner autocratic, his presence faintly foreboding. "Besides, my wife prefers me bareheaded," he added with a fond sideways glance to Olivia. "She doesn't care how improper it might be."

Dylan eyed him. "I don't think you care, either."

"You've got me there." That earned a full-fledged grin from the man. "I found myself some peace here in Morrow Creek. I fully aim to keep it. That means—" he broke off to deliver a formidable look at Dylan "—*not* losing my properties to taxes."

So he knew about that, then. Damnation. Fearlessly, Dylan met his gaze, all the same. "That's not going to happen."

"I don't mean to pay those taxes twice, either," Turner went on with no less formidableness. "I might have plenty of money, but I didn't compile my fortune by making foolhardy decisions." He turned to Adam. "What do you reckon, Corwin? Does this drifting man have what it takes to be sheriff?"

Dylan bristled, even as the crowd pushed closer to the walkway to watch Snub and Jobyna make

their joyful procession through it. "Watch yourself, Turner," he said. "I might be an amiable man,
but I don't take to insults. What you just said—"

But Adam Corwin nodded. "Yep. If it can't
be me—"

"What makes you think you could do better?"
Dylan argued.

"—then it might as well be Coyle, here. He's
a good man."

Speculatively, Turner aimed his full attention on Dylan again. He nodded. "That's what I
thought. That's why I used up a piece of my fortune offering a bounty for Caffey's whereabouts."
With an air of authority, Griffin examined the
crowd. "Turns out, a few hundred dollars goes a
long way toward encouraging folks to tell what
they know about a runaway sheriff."

"What did you find?" Dylan asked, instantly
alert.

"I found I was damn put out by having to learn
about those taxes on my own," Turner grumbled.
"Do you know how much I have at stake in this
town? I might not have been here much lately—"

Dylan knew that Griffin Turner and his wife
had been occupied until recently, traveling the
world on their wedding trip. Now that they were
back, he apparently meant business.

"—but I aim to be here for the long term,"
Turner finished. "So we might as well get a few
things straight. Starting with—"

"What you know about Sheriff Caffey?" Dylan prodded. The leads he'd rustled up had led nowhere. He hadn't been able to afford a bounty for information, especially not without rousing undue suspicion—or letting the townspeople think he was failing.

Turner glowered. "I want to partner with you, Sheriff. Not fight with you. You've got the wrong idea about me."

"I hear that's a problem with you." Dylan didn't intend to back down. "They must call you the Boston Beast for a reason."

"They don't call me that anymore." For a moment, Turner looked haunted. Then he brightened. "Leastwise, not to my face."

"I'm pretty sure I just did."

Corwin stepped up. He shook his head. "Come on now, you two," he cajoled. "This is a happy occasion. A wedding!"

They both scowled at him, Dylan and Griffin alike.

Realizing it, they both started. Then they grinned.

Hellfire, Dylan realized. He and the Tycoon Terror were both the same kind of man. Both too proud and stubborn to quit.

For everyone's sake, today they had to. One way or another.

Determined to be the better man, Dylan offered his hand. He kept his tone sociable—but not at all lacking in toughness. "All right. I'm indebted to you, Turner. What do you have for me?"

Unfortunately, Griffin Turner was quick on the draw, too.

He held out his hand at the same time, then talked right atop him. "You're a good sheriff, Coyle," he said roughly, "and I know you'll make Caffey pay for running off the way he did."

Beside them both, Corwin chortled. "I've seen competitive bare knuckle fighters square off with more honest civility."

They glared at him again. Gallingly, in unison.

"You're just mad," Dylan diagnosed, "because you can't be leading the chase for Caffey and the ousting of the Sheridans."

Turner agreed. "Don't worry, Corwin," he said with a faintly menacing grin. "Someday your babies will be all grown up. Then you can take your gray-haired, wrinkly, weak old self out on the detective trail again, just like you want to."

"Ha. I'll have the last laugh." Corwin grinned, not bothered by Turner's mockery. He nodded toward the women nearby, who all squealed as Jobyna passed. "Or is that *not* your missus right over there, cooing over that little baby she's holding?"

Turner looked. He gawked. He frowned. "Uh-oh."

Dylan and Adam poked the imposing hotelier. "Good luck."

"I might need it." Turner appeared concerned. Maybe a bit mush-hearted, too. He squared his shoulders, giving every suggestion of denying both emotions. "In the meantime, I'll tell you what I know—so we can protect all these exasperating, confusing, indispensable women and safeguard our damn town."

Just when Marielle thought that Jobyna and Snub's wedding couldn't get any nicer, she looked up from her conversation with the women gathered around, spied Dylan among the menfolk on the opposite side of the church walkway…and noticed him smiling over Daisy Cooper's baby boy, who was presently being cradled in Olivia Turner's cuddly arms. Did Dylan like babies?

Enchanted by the notion, Marielle watched him more closely.

Yes, she determined, Dylan certainly seemed to like babies. Because even though he had been engaged in what had seemed to be a very serious conversation with Griffin Turner and Adam Corwin, he had stopped that dialogue to gaze intently at little Jamie Cooper. She'd never seen Dylan's face look quite so captivated.

If anything, Dylan's softheartedness toward babies only made her love him more. They hadn't discussed having a family yet, but Marielle felt heartened to know that Dylan would not cast aside the idea altogether. She'd been afraid he might, on account of the drifting life he'd lived so far. It was probable he hadn't had much experience with babies—unlike the gambler Cade Foster, who next took a turn with the infant and had Daisy's baby boy gurgling with delight within moments.

Mr. Foster's familiarity with sleight of hand had some handy nongambling uses after all, Marielle reasoned as she watched the big, hard-looking gambler and his tall brother, Judah, take turns gently tickling the baby. Nearby Cade, all the women oohed over his gentle way with the child.

There was nothing like a man with a baby to make a woman swoon. Proving it, Sarah McCabe gave Cade Foster a poke.

"Psst! Give Daniel a turn!" she instructed in a low voice, gesturing toward her husband. "Let him hold the baby, too."

Cade glanced at the blacksmith. He shrugged.

"McCabe!" he yelled. "I've got something for you."

Cade had the bundled-up baby boy in McCabe's brawny arms before the big man could even blink. But blink he did, the moment he glimpsed what he was holding. His eyes widened.

Then they widened still further. "Coochy-coo!" he said.

Sarah burst out laughing, startling everyone. "Oh, thank heavens!" she declared. "I was worried you didn't like babies."

Her husband angled his head quizzically at her. "Who doesn't like babies?" Then, to tiny Jamie, "Nobody, that's who!"

A dozen nearby bachelors took a skittish step backward.

Sarah shook her head at the lot of them. "Settle down, all of you. It's not catching, you know."

But she rested her hand on her abdomen as she said so—which made the gaze of every woman present arrow in on that telling gesture. As one, Marielle and her friends went still.

Obliviously, Daniel McCabe went on playing with the baby.

Finally, Grace Murphy broke the silence. "Sarah Crabtree McCabe, you just *had* to do it, didn't you?" Wearing a disgruntled frown, she put her hands on her hips. She faced her younger sister. "You just *had* to steal my thunder, didn't you?"

"Steal her thunder?" Next to Marielle, her friend Adeline Davis gave her a puzzled look. "What does Grace mean?"

"Grace is expecting," Marielle explained, smiling at her boss's wife. "Evidently, so is Sarah. Since Molly had little Clara first, I guess Grace and Sarah were competing to be next." She shook her head. "The Crabtrees will be so pleased."

And to think—at one time, no one had thought the Crabtree sisters would ever be married…least of all, have children.

After a pause, the sisters' conversation reached Daniel. He went still. He gawked at Sarah. Then he stared at the baby.

"Are we...*really* going to have one of these?" he hollered.

The whole assemblage turned to face him—all except Grace Murphy, who snorted and marched over to congratulate Jobyna.

"Yes." Sarah moved closer to her husband. "We really are."

Their affection and delight were plain for everyone to see. So was the blacksmith's sudden urge to hug his wife...except he still had an armful of swaddled baby boy to deal with.

"Uh, help!" Daniel thundered. "Where's Daisy gone off to?"

Everyone could see that Mrs. Cooper was busy with Élodie in the nearby field, leading her and some of the other children in a game to entertain them. Everyone could see...including Dylan.

He stepped up, arms outstretched. "I'll take that."

His gruff-voiced offer seemed to startle everyone.

Everyone except Daniel. "Thank you kindly, Sheriff!"

As Dylan wrapped his hands carefully around the baby, letting Daniel transfer the child to him before hurrying to embrace Sarah, Marielle watched...and positively melted. There had never been anything sweeter or more touching than the sight of the man she loved cradling a baby—except the sight of that same man making goofy faces at that baby, to the infant's delight.

There was no way, Marielle knew, she'd be able to let Dylan leave Morrow Creek now. Not when she knew he was so nurturing.

A few others in town, though, seemed surprised. A buzz swept the crowd, neighbors nudging each other and pointing. To them, Marielle realized, Dylan was only their fearsome sheriff.

They would never have guessed he had a softer side at all.

Hearing that hum, Dylan looked up. He frowned at his friends and neighbors. "What's the matter? You've never seen a man with a baby before? I'm not going to drop him, you know."

"Don't crush him, either!" Clayton Davis advised.

"Don't toss him in the air too high," lumberman Marcus Copeland added, giving Molly a knowing look. "It's bad."

"Don't try to name him Mortimer!" Adam Corwin put in. "Not even if it's a good family name. Even for a little girl."

But all the women were mute, content to simply watch.

Hudson arrived, saw the cause of all the hullabaloo and frowned. He shouldered his way closer. "I want a turn."

"Well, you can't have one," Dylan singsonged to the baby.

"Don't be that way, Dylan!" Hudson spied Corinne in the crowd. He lowered his voice. "Give over. Corinne likes babies, too! Don't hog up all the means of impressing the ladies."

But Dylan only shook his head. "This child," he said in a steady voice, "is not bait to snare a woman with, Hudson."

Marielle watched her brother stamp his foot. "I want to ask her to marry me, now that you and Marielle are all settled. If she sees me with that baby, then she's bound to say yes."

But Marielle's attention wandered after Hudson's remark about her and Dylan being all settled. Was it possible that her brother had spent all this time waiting for *her* to be happy?

In retrospect, it made sense. She wished she'd known.

But there was nothing for Marielle to do about it then. Because just as she had that revelation, a man she didn't recognize tapped her on the shoulder. One of Snub's relations?

"Sorry, ma'am." He clutched his hat in his hands, working its brim over and over with evident concern. "I'm powerful sorry to disturb you, but…are you Miss Miller? Miss Marielle Miller?"

Marielle turned toward him. "Yes, I am. Is something—"

"You've got to come with me, Miss Miller. Right now!"

His strident tone and hasty backward glance made his air of concern catching. Marielle felt her heartbeat kick up a notch.

"What's wrong?" she asked, moving away from the crowd. "The sheriff's right over there, so if something's happened—"

"It has. But ain't nothin' the sheriff can do about it."

She furrowed her brow, glancing in the direction he'd indicated—toward the church, she saw. Inside, the music had quit, but the doors were still open. "Is something wrong with Reverend Benson?" Marielle asked. "I believe I saw Doc Finney—"

"It's Savannah Corwin!" the stranger blurted. "She's having pains. Bad ones. I think her baby's coming! She asked for you."

Trepidation raced through Marielle. "Me? Here? *Now?*"

It was possible, she supposed, given how unwieldy and uncomfortable Savannah had gotten—how ready for her baby to be born. Most likely, Marielle knew, Savannah had sent this man to fetch her so that she wouldn't spoil Jobyna and Snub's wedding.

"You don't want me to tell her you won't come, do you?" Urgently, he waved his hat. "I'm supposed to find the doc, too, but I saw you first."

He showed her his teeth in a nervous smile. Well, she'd be nervous, too, if a baby was about to be born and she was in charge of gathering support. "Go on inside!"

"I'm on my way." Marielle picked up her skirts and ran for the church doors, all the way up the steps and into the gloom.

Behind her, the wedding party continued in all its frivolity, but Marielle had larger concerns to deal with. She wished she'd reminded the stranger to seek out Adam Corwin, too, she dithered. Savannah would want her husband by her side. She would want Doc Finney or a midwife or somebody knowledgeable—more knowledgeable than Marielle, as well, that was for certain.

The two of them had been friends for a long time, drawn together by their similar backgrounds as dancers. In her time of need, Marielle decided, she might have wanted an ally nearby—someone who was friendly and a mite less judgmental than, say, Doc Finney's wife. That woman was famously pious. She'd had at least one unpleasant run-in with Savannah in the past, too.

"Savannah?" Peering into the darkened church, Marielle stepped between the pews. She could still hear children playing outside, and Daisy Cooper encouraging them. "Savannah?"

There was only silence…then a low, feminine groan.

"Savannah!" *Of course!* Marielle realized. She

must be in Reverend Benson's office, tucked away beside the chancel.

Forgetting all about the wedding party outside, Marielle hurried in that direction. She heard another groan, then a murmur.

Determinedly, she ran the rest of the way through the nave, past the empty pews where Snub and Jobyna's guests had wished them well earlier. She ascended the steps toward the chancel.

The reverend's office door stood open. Marielle burst in.

Savannah was there in the arms of a hat-wearing man. She stood panting and defiant, both hands protectively cradling her abdomen. Her blond hair clung to her cheeks in damp tendrils.

"Go get Adam and Dylan!" she yelled. "Don't—"

The man hit her.

She gave a grunt. Her breath left her in a whoosh.

"I warned you to be quiet, you dumb cow," the man said.

Charley Sheridan. Marielle jolted at the sight of him. She wanted to help her friend—and the eldest Sheridan brother knew it. He shook his head. His firearm gleamed as he pointed it at Savannah. In a flash, Marielle realized what was happening.

The Sheridan brothers had set a trap for her. They'd always liked to think of themselves as cunning. Today, they were.

Savannah wasn't having her baby at all. They'd lied to her.

Even as she understood that, the stranger from outside ambled into the office and shut the door behind him. He'd obviously not gone to fetch anyone except her. He'd put back on his hat. He tipped it to her in a derisively cordial gesture.

Marielle didn't have time to think about how they'd fooled her. Not now, with Savannah in danger. She cast her friend a worried glance. She appeared all right—just shaken and scared.

That made two of them. "Don't hurt her!" Marielle held out her palms pleadingly. "*Please* don't hurt her. Please."

Charley rolled his eyes at her. "If you were so all-out concerned, you should'a come quicker. I sent Peter a while ago."

"I couldn't find her! It's crowded out there," his brother whined, obviously taking Charley's comment as a criticism. He aimed his head toward the safety that lay just outside. "It's packed tight with rough men, too. Coyle, Turner, Corwin... not to mention that blacksmith who cracked my arm a while back."

"You deserved that for being so stupid," Charley said.

"Just let Savannah go," Marielle pleaded, out of patience with their bickering. "Please. Take me instead. Let her leave!"

Charley gave her a despicable look. He seemed

unbothered by the fact that he was holding an expectant woman at gunpoint—and pleased that he'd duped Marielle, besides. He grinned at Peter, then glanced back at Marielle. "Now why would I go and do that?"

"Because I've got something you want. Let her go."

"What is it?" He eyed her skirts. "Or is it… private?"

Marielle tried not to shudder. "Let her go. I'll tell you."

Surely Charley would want to know about Sheriff Caffey's secret hiding place—the one Dylan had told her about, near the Tillsons' medicine show campsite at the Morrow Creek bridge.

She never should have put off telling Charley that she had Dylan suitably distracted. Now, because of her, Savannah was in danger.

"Well, now…I don't rightly believe you. You've been pretty contrary all along, Miss Miller." Charley lowered his gun to Savannah's abdomen. She went rigid. "Seems to me, if I give up this here advantage I've got, I won't have nothing."

"If you don't let her go, you'll have even less. I swear."

He seemed unconcerned. Marielle was resolute.

They were deadlocked. And she was terrified.

"Aaah!" Savannah suddenly squealed, stag-

gering sideways as she clutched her belly harder. "The baby! It's really coming!"

At that, Charley's and Peter's eyes both bugged.

Marielle wondered, briefly and crazily, where their other brother, Levi, was. Had he left town? She looked at Savannah—just as her friend gave another agonized, bloodcurdling scream.

"Shut your mouth!" Charley hissed, looking suddenly less certain. "If you're trying to make somebody hear you—"

"I can't help it! *Oww!*" She swayed. "It hurts. So much."

Peter swore, looking flustered. "We can't take us a screeching lady on the road, Charley! That'll wreck our getaway plans." His gaze skittered to Marielle. "'Sides, she's expecting. Hurtin' her has gotta be some kinda big ole sin."

"Like *you're* worried about sin," Charley shot back, looking increasingly agitated, "given all the things you've done."

Peter seemed disgustingly pleased with himself. "Well, I guess you're right about that much." He straightened. "But maybe I wanna be nice to this here knocked-up lady." His expression took on a cruel gleam as he walked around Savannah. He leered while she panted in pain. "This one wouldn't even git me in no trouble afterward, neither, on account of her already having a baby in her. Yessir. I like that idea. I like it a whole lot."

Adam Corwin, Marielle knew, would have

killed any man he saw looking at his wife that way. She started to shake.

"No, idiot," Charley bit out. "You *ain't* doin' *that* again. We don't got time for any of your perverted carryings on."

Marielle took advantage of their unease. "Just let her go and you won't have to worry about it. You'll still have me."

"She ain't as good," Peter complained. "Not to me. You know why. We can get away without her help, anyhow. Just ask Levi."

Charley tightened his mouth, looking powerfully riled.

Apparently, there was some dissention among the brothers.

"Aaah!" Savannah clutched her belly. "The baby! *Ooh!*"

A torrent of swearwords came from Charley. With sudden decisiveness, he moved his gun—straight to Marielle.

"Have it your way," he said, smug and scary. "I'm gonna leave the screecher here, just like you want. But you—you're comin' with us. Right here and now."

Chapter Eleven

The first sign Dylan had that anything was wrong was an awful feminine scream.

It came from the peaceful white-steepled church a few yards away, where Snub and Jobyna had pledged their troth just an hour or so ago. Having already surrendered tiny Jamie Cooper to his father, Owen, Dylan turned his head toward that sound.

Instantly alert, he started moving in that direction.

"That was Savannah." Adam Corwin strode right beside him.

His face was white. His steps quickened to a run.

In unison, trailed by Cade Foster and some others, the two of them reached the church steps. Dylan grabbed for the door.

Savannah burst through it at the same time, moving at a dead run. He staggered backward, trying to avoid being walloped by the church door's fifty-odd pounds of hung and polished oak.

"They've got Marielle!" Savannah yelled, her hair tumbling and her breath coming too fast. Urgently, she gestured at Adam. "The Sheridans. They went out Reverend Benson's back door."

Her husband was at her side before she'd finished saying those terrible words. "What about you? Are you all right?"

"I'm fine. Just scared." Savannah aimed a surprising smile at Adam. "I pretended the baby was coming. I really played it up good, too! You should have seen those boys panic. They didn't know which way was up once all the squalling started."

He held her close. "*Is* the baby coming?"

She shook her head. "Not yet, drat it all." She hauled in a huge breath, then gave a shaky curtsy. "They didn't know who they were dealing with! Ask the folks I performed for! Ask your old partner, Mariana! Ask any of the Bedell brothers! Ask—"

"Me," Adam finished for her, stroking her hair. "Just take another breath and settle down. You're getting overexcited."

Dylan agreed. He hadn't been in town during the Bedell brothers' time—whoever they were—but he recognized the signs of shock as well as anyone. "Which way did they ride?"

Startled, Savannah looked up at him. "I didn't

see. I wanted to run right out here and get Adam. And you, Sheriff."

"How could you not see where they rode?" Dylan bit out, pacing across the church steps. "Reverend Benson's office has windows, doesn't it? You had the presence of mind to pretend—"

"Hold on there, Coyle. She said she didn't see." Adam gave him a warning look. Everyone else appeared stunned by Dylan's forceful reaction— but he couldn't imagine why. *Marielle had just been taken.* Adam gazed past the curious onlookers surrounding them, toward the church's side yard. "They can't have more than a few minutes' head start on us. We'll get them."

"Oh, no, you won't!" Savannah cried. She clutched her husband. "Please, Adam. *Please* let the sheriff do this himself."

Adam hesitated. But Dylan was already on his way to Cooper's livery stable. He'd left his horse there for the day, reasoning that he wouldn't need it at a peaceable wedding.

He'd never needed anything more than to find Marielle.

Beset by thoughts of her in those outlaws' grasp, he moved faster, churning up the ground beneath his boots. He set his jaw and kept going, pushing past gawking Morrow Creek residents.

"Do you need a posse, Sheriff?" someone called.

"I'm in." Marcus Copeland fell in behind him.

"Me, too," Jack Murphy agreed, doing the same.

From all sides, volunteers chimed in. But Dylan didn't stop. He couldn't. Somewhere nearby, Marielle was frightened. She needed him. He didn't care what it took to save her.

Improbably, someone caught up to him. "I'm going with you."

Griffin Turner. The big man was probably beyond useful in a confrontation. Tersely, Dylan nodded. "I'm obliged."

"Neither of you is going anyplace without me," Cade Foster said in a rough voice, hurrying to catch up.

"Or me," Miles Callaway added, wearing a fierce look.

Caught unprepared, Dylan glanced at the impromptu posse that was assembling itself in his wake. He scowled.

"This isn't a damn town picnic," he blurted, grimly striding onward. "Do any of you even have weapons?"

Almost as one, the men of Morrow Creek moved aside shirts, coats and other hiding places. They were all well armed.

Maybe Marielle had been right, Dylan realized. Maybe he'd been worrying too much about his own deadly acuity with a firearm. At that moment, he had to admit as he reached the street, his own gun belt had never felt more welcome.

He wasn't a sought-after security man for nothing.

Tersely, he nodded. "Fine," he declared.

Then, clearing his throat against the dust— because surely it was that and not an unwelcome burst of gratitude that made him feel so damn overcome—Dylan went to track down Marielle.

Stuck awkwardly on a horse in front of Charley Sheridan, Marielle watched as the town's outskirts faded and the forest encroached on their path. The road narrowed precipitously. In the distance, the mountains rose above the pine tops, but that beautiful, familiar sight gave her none of the enjoyment it usually did. Not today. Not now that she had, unbelievably, been kidnapped—for a purpose she couldn't yet discern.

At least Savannah was safe, she told herself, rigid with dislike and fear in Charley's encircling arms. He held her too tightly, as though he had no real sense of her as a living, breathing person. To him, she probably wasn't. She was just a decoy, to be used in whatever way that he eventually saw fit.

Jostled by their rough ride, fraught with the need to keep track of which direction they were traveling in, Marielle looked around her. Every landmark suddenly held new menace. Every rustle or flutter in the dense undergrowth made her start.

She both hoped that Dylan would find her and that he wouldn't. She longed to see him again—to be held in his secure arms instead of Charley Sheridan's. But Marielle didn't want Dylan to be hurt. If he came, he would come packing weapons.

Since Charley—and Peter, she'd noticed—were similarly armed, only terrible things could happen. Peter, especially, was foolish with his pistol. Beside them on his own horse, he fiddled with his gun as they rode, pretending to shoot birds.

"Bang!" he muttered, waving his gun. "Gotcha, cussed bird."

"Put that thing away, you pisspot, before you up and shoot *me*," Charley complained, slowing his horse. "We're here."

Marielle looked around again. "This isn't the bridge."

That was half a mile away…as distant as her fading hope.

"We've got other business to attend to first," Charley told her. His groping hand veered toward her dress's bodice.

Moving awkwardly away, Marielle managed to protect herself. For the moment. "You're not going to find Sheriff Caffey here," she insisted as steadily as she could. "I told you before, the sheriff said Caffey would hide out near the bridge, over—"

"We'll git there." Charley caught her trying

to wriggle out of his reach. He tightened his grip, making her breath whoosh away. Her ribs squished together painfully. "Just sit tight."

His foul breath hit the back of her neck, redolent of last night's dinner, whiskey and stale tobacco. Marielle winced.

Compared with him, Murphy's saloon smelled like roses.

At her wriggling, Peter chuckled. "I don't reckon she likes you, Charley. Maybe you'd better let her ride with me."

"Shut up. Soon as Levi gets here, we won't need her anyway. So don't you start getting all het up about romance. You hear?"

Glumly, Peter nodded. But Marielle froze.

If they wouldn't need her any longer…what would they do to her? The Sheridans were ruthless. They were known killers.

"Come on now, Mr. Sheridan," Marielle coaxed, doing her utmost not to show her revulsion and fear. "I've done my best to help you, all along. I got the sheriff to trust me, didn't I?"

He laughed. "That ain't what I wanted." Mercifully, he quit fondling her. "Did you really think I just fancied you and Coyle gettin' all cozy together, like I'm some kinda mushy *girl*?"

Confused, Marielle frowned. "That's what you said."

"Well, it weren't what I meant." Sounding as smug as he usually did, Charley went on. Evidently, they had time to waste. "All I wanted was for that sheriff to take an even bigger shine to you—so he'd be guaranteed to follow after we nabbed you."

Taking her had been part of their plan all along.

"But what good does that do you?" Marielle persisted, still trying to figure out their strategy. "You don't *want* Sheriff Coyle to chase you, do you? That's how people get caught."

Dear heaven, she hoped they got caught.

Another laugh. "Sure, I do—just so long as he's chasin' us in the wrong direction," Charley boasted. Behind her, he spit a wad of tobacco juice. She cringed at his nearness. "That's what dumb ole Caffey did wrong. He didn't have a good enough getaway plan. But me and my brothers—*we* do. We did it up right."

"Sheriff Caffey *did* get away," Marielle informed him, wishing it wasn't true. "Nobody's caught him yet."

Peter snickered. "That's what *you* think," he crowed.

"Shut the hell up!" Charley bellowed. "Or are you just aching to wind up hanging from a goddamn noose someplace?"

As Peter subsided, Charley impatiently reined in his horse. She could feel tension radiating from him to her, transmitted by his belligerent posture and his ever-tightening hold on her.

"If all you had to do was make the sheriff follow you the wrong way," Marielle tried, "then you've already done that. You don't need me anymore. Why not let me go right here?"

Charley grunted. "I might *never* let you go, sunshine."

Ugh. Terrified and nauseated by the note of lechery in his voice, Marielle clenched her jaw. If she couldn't make them let her go—and then run back to town to warn Dylan and the others—what was she supposed to do now? She had to get away somehow.

"Ha. Now who's actin' all lovey-dovey?" Peter gibed.

"If I have to git off this horse and beat you, I will."

"I'd like to see you try."

"No, you sure as hell wouldn't like that. I'll see to it."

"Them's big words. But I ain't a'feared of you."

"You ought'a be. Or did you forget the last time?"

The sound of an oncoming rider interrupted their squabbling. As those hoofbeats grew louder, Marielle tensed anew. She twisted, trying to see who the new arrival was.

Surely, if it were Dylan, he'd have come in brandishing guns? But maybe not, with her being held by Charley. Oh, *why* had she had to fall for their ruse about Savannah at all?

To her disappointment, it wasn't Dylan. It was

Levi. The third Sheridan brother rode up to the other side of their group.

Charley didn't sound pleased to see him. "Did you get it?"

Levi grimaced. "I'm gonna have it. He's bringing it."

"He'd better, if he knows what's good for him." Charley spat again. "You know I ain't leavin' town without everything."

Confused by their cryptic conversation, Marielle strained to hear more. She was startled by Charley giving her a shove.

"Hear everything you wanted to, nosy pants?" he sneered.

Alarmed, she grabbed the horse's sweaty neck, trying not to fall off. Her heartbeat thundered with fright. She wouldn't put it past these bandits to throw her off the horse and then tromp their own mounts all over her injured body just for amusement.

"I'm telling you," Marielle urged, "the campsite is—"

"Is where we're going next," Charley interrupted, sounding mean. "Who knows?" he added to his brothers. "Maybe this hussy is right. Maybe Caffey *did* hide away even more money there."

"We ain't got all of it. We know that," Levi said.

"I say we just ride straight outta town, now that Levi's here," Peter put in. He sounded agitated.

"Maybe we're gettin' too greedy! After all, that's what Caffey done, and he's—"

"Shut up!" both of his brothers roared.

Then Charley spurred his horse, wheeled around and headed down the road at a break-neck pace, leaving Marielle clinging to that poor sweaty beast for dear life—hoping that what Dylan had told her about the runaway sheriff was true. Because if Caffey and the money *weren't* there...she'd be paying the price for it.

Their best lead didn't pan out. At least it didn't in the way Dylan wanted it to. Because Marielle wasn't there.

Crushed and momentarily stymied, he holstered his gun.

"It's all clear," he yelled numbly to the men outside.

He'd instructed his makeshift posse to wait for him. It had been the only thing to do. Alone and resolute, Dylan had circled the cabin where he'd learned Caffey had been spotted. He'd gone to the door, opened it silently then taken a look in the darkened interior. Nothing had moved. So he'd advanced inward.

That's when he'd found the body on the floor.

Sprawled ignobly faceup, the dead man stared sightlessly at the cabin's knotty ceiling. In his hand, he held a useless firearm. Nearby, an empty satchel lay overturned at his knee.

The place looked ransacked. It was obvious that someone had arrived before Dylan and his posse. They'd had more than rescuing on their minds. They'd had killing in mind, too.

It was a pitiful way to die. Dylan almost felt sorry.

Adam Corwin was the first in. "That's Sheriff Caffey."

Cade Foster followed. "Yep. I guess he got what was coming to him after all." He glanced at Dylan. "Marielle?"

"Not here." Stonily, Dylan marched to the window.

Near the trees, Griffin Turner was talking to a stranger. A woman. Curious and looking for a lead, Dylan stomped outside.

"…and I could tell they weren't no lawmen," the woman was saying, sounding proud of her astuteness, "so I skedaddled round to the foothills for a spell, till I saw they were gone."

Turner nodded. "That was smart of you."

"So…" She bit her lip, seeming suddenly anxious. Her gaze searched Turner's imposing face. "Are you the one who's supposed to give me my money? For that tip I gave you? There's a bounty."

Nearby, Marcus Copeland frowned. "Isn't this your place?" He gestured at it. "If Caffey's been holing up here with you—"

Then she'd turned in her man herself. For money.

Belatedly realizing the truth, Copeland looked away.

"He has been staying here." Jack Murphy joined them. He eyed the woman with unexpected contempt—and a great quantity of weariness, too. "That's how she knew to tell Griffin about it."

"Yeah. It's like *he* said." With faint hostility, the woman put her hands on her hips. "If you found him, I want paid."

Dylan shouldered forward. "We found him," he said coldly. He nodded toward the cabin. "Pay her, Turner, and let's go."

"Marielle?" Somberly, Griffin glanced to the cabin.

Dylan shook his head. At the man's sympathetic look, Dylan nearly broke down. How did Turner know that finding Marielle meant so much to him? Was his anguish that evident on his face?

He should have been ashamed, he knew. A man didn't let himself get *this* caught up in something so flimsy as *feelings*.

Just then, Dylan felt he could have torn apart the whole territory, if it meant finding Marielle safe and sound.

At the prospect of being paid, the woman brightened. "I got a look at them desperados, too!" she exclaimed, glancing from one man to the next. "What'll you all give me to describe them?"

"Advice," Turner said pitilessly as he pressed

some greenbacks into her hand. "Since it looks as if criminals might be your type, don't be fool enough to take up with any of them."

Even as the woman began sputtering with indignation, Dylan headed for his horse. He felt fed up. Disconsolate. Hopeless.

He hadn't caught Caffey—not alive, at least. He hadn't recovered the tax money. Now he'd lost Marielle, too.

Miles Callaway reached him at a run. "We're not giving up yet, Coyle," he promised with all the grit that had made him travel thousands of miles to pursue a missing woman a few weeks earlier. "We've got that other lead from Turner. We can go—"

"We're not going there." Dylan untied his horse. Jaw tight, he led his borrowed mare into the clearing. "This isn't about Caffey anymore. It's about Marielle. And the Sheridans."

"But we don't even know how to find the Sheridans."

"I do." Grimly, Dylan swung into his saddle. He signaled for the other men to join him. "It all starts with Hudson Miller. I've been too soft on Marielle's brother for too long. It's about time I made sure that boy grew up, right quick."

Soon enough, Marielle recognized the direction they were riding. They really were going to the Morrow Creek bridge.

The closer they came, the more her trepidation grew.

She'd come to trust Dylan—but did he trust her? After all, Marielle knew, his investigation into Sheriff Caffey's disappearance was sheriff's business. He oughtn't have shared the information he had with her. Then, too, there was the troublesome matter of her own inexperience, compared with his.

Dylan Coyle was a capable security man. He was a longtime detective, a renowned protector and a legitimately feared gunman. He'd drifted all over. He knew things. Undoubtedly, he knew how to keep a secret. Yet he'd allowed her, everyday Marielle Miller, to wheedle out crucial information from him?

The closer they came to the bridge, the less likely that possibility seemed. She wanted to believe in Dylan, but—

A sharp yank at the back of her dress startled her.

The fabric ripped, then came away in Charley's grasp.

She clutched her collar, twisting around to see the damage.

Charley held up a hank of yellow gingham. "My, my, my. That ripped a whole lot easier than I thought it would." His hold on her waist tightened brutally. "Imagine how easy this entire dress of yours would come off you, if I only ripped harder."

His insinuating tone and waggling eyebrows disgusted her. When would she ever see the back of him? She was trapped.

She reached for that fabric scrap. Charley guffawed.

"That ain't for you. It's for me to set another trap."

Peter's triumphant cackle reminded Marielle of the trap she'd fallen for with Savannah. Hoping to avert another mistake, she made another grab. But Charley was too fast for her.

He tossed that eye-catching yellow gingham toward a ponderosa pine. It landed on a green bough, bright as sunshine.

"Sheriff Coyle's gonna see that for certain. But just to make sure…" Charley waited until they'd ridden another half mile or so. Then he ripped off another hank. Tossed it. "There's only two roads that lead outta Morrow Creek. With them dress scraps pointin' the way we *ain't* leavin' by, things should be fine."

"If you think the sheriff's going to be misled—"

"I'm counting on it, Miss Miller." Charley's self-assured tone sent shivers down her spine. "Him being misled is what's gonna let us get away…unlike that ole cuss Sheriff Caffey."

Marielle hoped not. But as the sound of the

burbling creek grew nearer—as they reached the bridge and rode across it—her heart sank. The clearing Dylan had spoken about was evident.

It was also empty. There was no sign of Caffey ever having been there. Even the Tillsons' medicine show had moved on. That was something to be thankful for, Marielle thought crazily. At least Will Gavigan and his wife, Rose, wouldn't be hurt.

"Hmm." Charley's speculative rumble came from behind her. He reined his horse to a stop. "Don't look like no hidey-hole to me." He paused. Looked harder. "Nope. You lied, sweetheart."

Swaying from their sudden stop, Marielle grabbed at whatever was within reach to steady her. The closest thing turned out to be Charley Sheridan's arms. Inadvertently, she hugged him closer to her in a desperate bid to stay upright.

The horse danced around, sensing her floundering motions.

Levi chuckled. "Peter tole me wrong. She *does* like you."

"Look at her grabbin' you, Charley!" Peter crowed. "I guess them dance hall girls really are a bunch of juicy cherries."

Ignoring that vulgar slang, Marielle released her hold. With as much dignity as she could manage, she straightened.

"Nope. I don't believe it for a red-hot minute," Charley drawled. His breath blasted her neck again. "I think this one's broken or some such. Because that gal Etta was a *lot* nicer."

Etta. Had she really been so foolish as to entertain the likes of Charley Sheridan and his brothers? Marielle felt sick.

"I reckon this is where you git off, ma'am," Charley said.

Before she could react, he shoved her. Hard.

Marielle slid sideways. Scrambling for purchase, she almost caught hold of Charley. She got a face full of his jittery horse's sodden, hairy neck instead. She heard the Sheridans laughing at her. She felt her arms flailing in the air.

Then she felt…nothing at all.

Hunkering on a hillside outside an old prospector's shack a few miles outside of Morrow Creek, Dylan aimed his steely gaze at one of the place's two windows. Inside, nothing moved.

"I can't stand it!" Hudson blurted beside him amid the undergrowth. He made a motion to get up. "I'm going in."

Dylan flattened him to the earth without glancing sideways.

"You're not going anyplace until I know Marielle is safe."

"We've been here for fifteen minutes! She's not there."

She had to be there. The alternative was too horrible to think about. They'd seen the Sheridan brothers ride up. They'd seen them dismount, tie off their horses and head inside while jawing to each other about nonsense. If they'd left the church with Marielle and then arrived at their hideout—for that's what it was, its location discovered courtesy of a fast acquiescing Hudson, once he'd seen Dylan's face—*without her*, that meant...

Dylan couldn't think about what that meant. Not with the memory of bloodied and dead-eyed Sheriff Caffey in his mind.

"If you have the patience to check what time it is," Dylan said coldly, "then you have the patience to wait for my signal."

To his credit, Hudson quieted down. Diligently, he watched.

An instant later... "It's only that I'm so worried! What if—"

"She's not here," Dylan interrupted. "You're going in."

Stealthily, he angled his head upward—just enough to signal the other men waiting in the tree-covered foothills. Thankfully, the countryside offered plenty of coverage. The Sheridans hadn't been smart enough to hole up someplace more defensible.

The other Morrow Creek men each nodded in turn. They all wore decisive, determined looks. To a man, they were ready to back up Dylan—to catch the Sheridans and locate Marielle. Again,

Dylan felt a swell of gratitude. Ruthlessly, he pushed it down.

He wasn't here to feel grateful. He was here to establish order in the town he hoped to settle down in. With Marielle.

"Be on the lookout for sacks, satchels, anything they could have stashed the tax money in," Dylan instructed. "Collecting all of it is why there're here—why they haven't left already."

"Maybe we should have gone for Marielle instead," Hudson fretted. "There were signs on the other road out of town." He eyed the shack with trepidation. "Maybe we should have gone that way."

"If she's not with them, it's probably too late already."

Hudson boggled at him. "So you're just giving up?" he cried in an appalled undertone. "I thought you loved her!"

His outburst made even more *feelings* well up inside Dylan. He'd never welcomed them less. Deliberately, he ignored them.

Situations like this required more than soft-heartedness.

Besides, he'd thought Marielle *would* be there. The fact that she wasn't was an unaccounted for puzzle—one Dylan would require facts and insight and determination to solve. *Later*.

"They wouldn't have gone into town with all their haul," he told Hudson evenly, considering the barefaced way they'd taken Marielle from the church. "They wouldn't have brought it with them to Caffey's place, either. They were there to get what they thought they were owed—not to have their own loot filched. Or to wind up facedown if Caffey turned out to be a faster draw."

Remembering the former sheriff's gruesome fate, Dylan double-checked his gun belt. For once, he was glad to have it.

But Hudson was still gawking at him. Dylan frowned.

"Pay attention," he snapped. "For better or worse, you're the linchpin here. If you don't do this exactly right, people will get killed. Your friends. Your neighbors. Maybe you."

Hud nodded. He clenched the bag of money he'd brought.

Dylan still couldn't credit him having that bag. Guided by a tip from Corinne Murphy, he'd tracked Hudson to the jailhouse earlier. He'd found him shakily extracting money from one of Caffey's unknown hiding places, determined to hand it over to Levi Sheridan. When Dylan had confronted him, Hudson had spilled all. How he'd blabbed to the federal marshal and incurred the Sheridans' wrath. How they'd pressured him, beaten him and taken his horse. How, worst of all, they'd threatened Marielle.

Hudson hadn't been able to stand that, he'd confessed on the verge of bawling. So he'd taken advantage of all the times Dylan had let him leave his deputy's work early—not to meet with Corinne Murphy but to set up an exchange with the Sheridans.

Hudson hadn't even known how far in over his head he was.

But for that, curiously, Dylan could forgive him. Because *his* judgment would have been clouded, too...if he'd let it be. And Hudson had, in all fairness, done what he could to protect his sister. Because when Dylan had turned up to claim their quarters as his sheriff's lodging, Hudson had all but tied him to a damn chair to make him stay. Now Dylan knew why. To protect Marielle.

Unexpectedly softening toward Hudson, Dylan put his hand on the younger man's forearm. He looked directly into his eyes. "You can do this," he told Hudson calmly. "Just stay steady."

Hudson's expression eased. He swallowed. "I can do this."

Dylan waited while Hudson nodded. A breeze whooshed by.

"Do it right now," he amended coolly. "Go on."

"Right." Hudson glanced behind himself, then belly crawled down the ridge they'd been hiding on. He made his way through the trees, still carrying his money bag. He reached the road.

"Careful," Dylan murmured. He withdrew his firearm.

Around him, all the other men waited in position, shielded by the trees. He was glad they were there, but *he* was the leader. If he moved, they would, too. If he made a mistake—

Unable to complete that thought, Dylan watched as Hudson hollered out to the house. Sheepishly, Hud held up his palms.

The door opened. Charley Sheridan sauntered out with a cigar in his mouth and a bag in his hand. "Why, lookee here!" he called to his brothers. "If it ain't that slutty Marielle Miller's little brother, come to pay us a call. Levi! Peter!"

Something inside Dylan snapped. If that bastard thought he could talk about Marielle that way... He was wrong. Maybe dead wrong. Flooded with incoherent rage, Dylan clutched his firearm harder. Then he ran downhill, shouting all the way.

The moment he moved, everything fell to pieces.

Confusedly, Marielle awakened with the sun on her face and the taste of dirt in her mouth. Her back hurt. Also, she smelled...*horse*? On her hands? Baffled and scared, she looked up.

The same old territorial sky looked down on her, blue and scattered with fluffy clouds. But why did her head ache so?

She tried to move and found out why. Wincing, Marielle reached to the back of her head. The lump there hurt like the dickens. So did her hip and—when she tried to stand—her ankle.

Crying out, she buckled to the ground. Falling made her remember what had happened. Charley. The Sheridans. The church and Savannah and the empty bridge-side campground. Falling off Charley Sheridan's horse. Recalling it, Marielle shook her head. She must have landed on her injured ankle. Again.

Woozy and hurting, she decided to rest a minute. She could see no sign of the Sheridans. Clearly, those outlaws had left her there—probably as bait to lure Dylan, as he followed those scraps of her dress...her poor, shredded, falling-off dress.

Clutching its bodice to her, Marielle looked around. She didn't know if she should let Dylan find her—and fall into those outlaws' trap—or if she shouldn't. It was only clear that she couldn't stay there. So she hauled in a breath, got up again and started limping toward the road. Bit by painful bit.

That's when she heard gunshots ring out nearby.

Dylan slowed as he topped the ridge, but the damage was already done. A heartbeat too soon, all the men in his posse followed his lead. They swarmed from the trees. Guns drawn, they bore down on the prospector's shack from all directions.

The Sheridans reacted predictably enough.

Charley raised his arms in surrender, looking surprised. Hudson dropped to the dirt to avoid bullets, then grabbed Charley's leg. He hauled him down alongside him, even as a gunshot whizzed past them both.

Dylan looked down, startled. That had been *his* shot, he realized too late, calculating its probable trajectory. He'd fired without meaning to at the man who'd taken Marielle.

He'd missed. But he'd almost shot Hudson.

That realization snapped him out of feeling and into doing. Just as he had so many times, Dylan let his intellect and instincts take over. He reached the clearing where the shack stood. He spied movement at the shack's door. He fired.

In the opening, Peter Sheridan ducked, his gun drawn.

Nearby, Turner and McCabe and all the rest just kept coming. Following Dylan's plan, they reached the shack's perimeter. Levi Sheridan cussed from inside, then shot at them.

Dylan ran toward Charley, intending on nabbing the bastard himself. For the moment, Hudson seemed to have him handled. With a growl of pent-up fury and grief, Marielle's enormous brother rolled Charley into the dirt. He started pummeling him.

That settled, Dylan moved toward the house. More gunshots sounded—including his—but he knew his men were reliable. He needed to find the tax money. Without it, the Sheridans couldn't be prosecuted. With another gunshot for cover, Dylan veered toward a side window. At the open front door, Peter grunted. He staggered backward, fired another shot in the air, then slumped.

If Dylan didn't miss his guess, that was one outlaw down.

Now, he had to find the money. He nodded at Copeland behind him, then waited as Marcus fired. Inside, Levi yelled for Charley. He ran to the front door to check on his brother.

Taking his best chance, Dylan looked in the window. Its glass was mostly missing; what remained was broken. Through its dirty remnants, he spied piles of cash on a table inside.

With it were several logbooks—Sheriff Caffey's tax records. Dylan recognized them. He'd been using an identical means to track his own tax collecting activities. With the cash and logbooks in their possession, the Sheridans were guilty.

But there was no sign of Marielle inside. Dylan realized he'd been hoping they'd stashed her there in the prospector's shack sometime after killing Caffey and leaving the church. His hopes were dashed.

Dimly, distantly, Charley pleaded with Hudson to let him go. Reflexively, Dylan moved to the shack's front door. He checked his gun, rounded the corner then took aim at Levi.

The middle Sheridan brother took a palms-up stance. Caught standing over Peter's slumped body, Levi Sheridan held up his arms to Dylan in submission. "Don't shoot, Sheriff!"

Dylan looked into the eyes of one of the men who may have hurt or killed Marielle. For a long moment, he deliberated.

In the end, Levi got lucky. Dylan holstered his gun.

He tossed some iron shackles to Turner. Griffin nodded.

As the big man restrained Levi—and Copeland and Murphy saw to Peter, who definitely hadn't survived being shot—Dylan headed toward Hudson. He had things to settle with Charley Sheridan.

The outlaw was bloodied. His face was already starting to swell. When not outnumbered, Marielle's brother could inflict serious damage. But Hudson let up when he saw Dylan coming.

"Get up." Dirty and huge, Hud hauled Charley to his feet.

Dylan had the honor of affixing the manacles himself. But there wasn't much satisfaction in clanking those bonds shut.

With that done, he looked into Charley's face. "Marielle?"

"Yeah. Real fine lady you got there." The outlaw gave him an arrogant, taunting look. "I liked her plenty. I surely did."

He wasn't good enough to say her name.

"What did you do with her?" Dylan asked.

Holding Charley, Hudson looked on with evident concern.

"*Hmmph.* It ain't what *I* did with her, so much as what *she* did with *you*. That's what nearly made all the difference."

"Stop talking nonsense. Where is she?"

At Charley's eye-rolling response, Dylan felt murderous.

With a mighty effort, he tamped down that feeling. Already today, he'd nearly botched their approach to the Sheridans' hideout. He'd heard Charley slandering Marielle and had lost his damn mind in response. He'd gotten caught up in his softer emotions again. That momentary lapse could have been disastrous.

"She's right where you told her to be," Charley said.

Then she was alive. Or...not. Dylan swallowed. "Alive?"

He could scarcely believe he was capable of saying it aloud. He refused to glance at Hudson's face. One look and he'd—

"Eh. Not that *you'd* care." Charley examined his shackles without concern, even as Dylan's posse emerged from the shack with the evidence needed to imprison him for good. "Are you really that tore up about a woman who double-crossed you?"

"Marielle never double-crossed me." But even

as he said it, Dylan accidentally let his gaze slip to Hudson's face—his stricken, all too knowing face. What the hell…? "She's alive?"

"I reckon. Unless a fall off a horse can kill a body."

Dylan clenched his fists, again feeling lethal.

"How do you s'pose I got her away from that wedding so easy?" Charley went on. "Huh? It was 'cause she *wanted* to come."

"She never did," Dylan said…but, damnably, he began to wonder. Marielle should have been too smart to be grabbed.

Savannah hadn't explained to him and Adam how Marielle's involvement had come to happen. There hadn't been time.

"How do you think me an' my brothers almost got away?" Charley pressed. "We almost did, you know." Without a trace of regret, he glanced over to where Peter lay motionless. "I guess when Miss Miller tole me she had the new sheriff locked up good and tight so's you'd pursue *her* 'stead of *me*, she was wrong."

Marielle had talked about him…to this *outlaw*? She'd bragged—to Charley—about having gotten close to him?

The idea gutted him. Dylan shook his head. "No."

Charley raised his brows. "No, you never liked her?"

"No, she never said that. She never—" Dylan

broke off. He clenched his jaw, then paced a few steps away. He couldn't help seeing Hudson's anxious expression as he did, though…and it confirmed everything Charley was saying. *"Where is she?"*

"Aw, that's real sweet. You still want her anyway."

Coldly, Dylan withdrew his gun. He held it at Charley's temple. "It's still possible," he told him in a restrained tone as he cocked it, "that you got killed in the shootout today. There's not a man for miles who wouldn't back me up on that."

Nervously, Charley wet his lips. He glanced at Hudson, but there was no help from that quarter. Marielle's brother looked almost as ferocious as Dylan felt. He still looked…*guilty*, too.

Because he knew the truth about Marielle's deception?

"It's like I said—you'll find her at the place she tole me *you* told her about," Charley stammered. "Over at the campsite—"

"Near the Morrow Creek bridge," Dylan finished.

Near the bridge…where he'd fibbed and told Marielle that Sheriff Caffey might be hiding. She *had* been trying to wheedle information out of him at the creek that day. She'd succeeded.

Then she'd given over that information to Charley Sheridan.

Marielle had betrayed him, Dylan realized too late.

Worst of all, he'd let her do it. He'd let her get to his softhearted feelings, bring out every last damn one of them…and then she'd taken advantage of his softness in the most callous way possible. Marielle had never cared for him. Not ever.

He was the fool who'd cared for her…and had almost allowed a heinous crime to happen because of it. With the truth in the open now, so many things made sense. Marielle's sudden turnabout toward him once he'd moved into her household. Her midnight meeting with Charley. Her questioning Dylan about his past, his investigating methods and his skills as a gunfighter. Her downright interrogating him, persistently, about the tax money.

She hadn't wanted to love him at the creek that day, he knew with awful belated certainty. She'd wanted to trap him, Dylan realized. He'd been a gullible target, too. He'd given her…*everything*. Now that Marielle had sweet-talked out what she'd needed from him, she wouldn't want to see him anymore.

But he sure as hell wanted to see her. Right that minute.

Chapter Twelve

When Marielle first heard hoofbeats plodding down the road, her heart leaped straight to her throat. *Was it Charley again?*

It was possible he'd come back to finish her off. He had to have known that she'd be hurt from falling off his horse. It would have been like that sadistic outlaw to let her worry and wonder over her fate—to let her try and fail to limp away before giving up in pain—before coming back to shoot her for good.

Terrified, Marielle ducked behind the boulder where she'd taken shelter after the gunshots had started. She clenched its gritty, cool surface with shaking fingers, listening hard.

All she heard were those hoofbeats, slowly coming nearer.

If it *was* Charley, he was in no hurry to commit murder.

That didn't sound like him. Paradoxically reassured, Marielle lifted her head a few inches. She couldn't yet identify the rider approaching, but she did catch a blur of movement as the horse crossed the Morrow Creek bridge with steady steps.

She was going to expire from suspense, plain and simple. Already, she'd spent more time than she could identify hiding behind that boulder. She was in no condition to run away, on account of her ankle and other injuries. She would do no good fighting someone, either. She'd failed abysmally to keep Charley off her earlier. Without her wits, she had no chance.

Looking around for a weapon, Marielle spied a fallen tree branch. She dragged it nearer, cringing at the sound it made as its smaller branches and dead leaves bumped over the rocky ground. With a final yank, she pulled it all the way to her.

With that secured, she took another look. The rider had almost reached the clearing. She glimpsed a brown horse. Then, through the trees, a hat-wearing man with broad shoulders.

Dylan. Almost sobbing, Marielle wobbled to her feet.

He saw her the moment she stood. In his hand, he grasped the scraps of yellow fabric that Charley had torn from her dress and left fluttering in the trees. Dylan must have plucked each one from the pine boughs, wondering every time where she was.

He'd come for her. Marielle watched him ride

closer, feeling suffused with relief—and weak with departing tension.

He wasn't shot. He wasn't hurt. He wasn't... hurrying to her.

Why wasn't he hurrying to her? Wasn't he glad to see her?

Maybe he hadn't seen her? "Dylan!" she called. "Dylan!"

At the sound of her voice, he flinched as though shot. Puzzled, she watched as his face drew tighter and more closed.

He had never appeared stonier, nor more fearsome.

He rode into the clearing, surprisingly not accompanied by Hudson or Jack Murphy or anyone else in town who would have ordinarily come on a rescue mission. He dismounted. With taut movements, Dylan tied off his horse. He pulled down his hat, clutched those pieces of yellow gingham then strode to her.

She had never been happier to see anyone in her life.

Until Dylan shoved that gingham at her. "You'll probably want these," he said in a hard voice, "for a trophy."

"A trophy?" Befuddled, Marielle stared at them—then at him. She took a painful step forward, mindlessly dragging her branch.

"You won't need that." Dylan nodded at it. "A woman like you can hurt a man more with a smile than an outright cudgel."

Dazedly, she looked at her defensive branch. Awkwardly, she dropped it, then brushed off her hands. Her head ached, her ankle throbbed and her hip felt increasingly bruised. Her mouth was dry, her mind awhirl and her ribs sore. But none of those things wounded her more than the bleak way Dylan looked at her.

"I thought you might be Charley," Marielle explained.

"You'd like that, wouldn't you?" His gaze swerved to her hair, which was doubtless a calamity. Then to her dress. Too late, it occurred to Marielle that she probably looked a fright. "But I'm afraid your Mr. Sheridan is already at the jailhouse, getting ready to be transported to Yuma Prison along with Levi."

She couldn't help wondering… "And Peter?"

Dylan's expression grew even more grave. "Dead."

"Oh." At that sobering news, Marielle inhaled. She looked away, feeling newly chilled by the pine shadows. Here in the mountainous foothills, sunset arrived early…very early today.

It occurred to her what Dylan had said. "He's not 'my' Mr. Sheridan. I don't want any 'trophies' of what happened to me today, either." She grabbed those fluttering pieces of gingham Dylan was still offering her. She balled them up and hurled them away as far as she could, wishing she could discard her memories of being held at gunpoint as easily. "It was awful. *Awful!*"

Unbelievably, Dylan shrugged. "When you consort with criminals, sometimes it's unpleasant. All of life isn't a stage, Miss Miller. Some of it is real. Some of it hurts. I don't know if you missed all the excitement of performing or if you just wanted adventure, but either way—" He stopped, seeming to momentarily break down. He cleared his throat, looked away then went on. "I'm here to take you back to town. It's my duty."

"Your *duty*?" Marielle stepped nearer, forgetting her ankle. It offered a painful reminder, bringing her up short. "Miss Miller? You haven't called me that for *weeks*!" Feeling increasingly scared, she studied Dylan's face. "What's happened? What's wrong? I know you must have been worried about me—"

"You'd be surprised how little I think about you."

Stunned, she nearly staggered backward. With her hand to her heart, Marielle persevered. "—but I'm all right! I am." Maybe Dylan was in shock. He must have been involved in the gun battle she'd heard a while ago. With effort, she softened her voice. "It's all right to be upset, you know. We've been through a lot today, you and me. I know that I was sure scared, so you—"

"There isn't any 'you and me.' Not anymore."

He wasn't even making sense. Hoping to reach

him, Marielle smiled. "Of course there is." Maybe Dylan had closed himself off to their love, out of fear that she'd been hurt. Or killed. That was comprehensible. "It's understandable if you feel—"

"I don't feel anything. Not anymore."

Looking at him, Marielle almost believed it. But she knew Dylan better than that. She *knew* she did. "That's not true."

"It is." Contrarily, his eyes gleamed. Was it possible that the events of the day had brought tough, take-charge Dylan Coyle to his knees? Because those looked like…tears. "It has to be."

"No, it doesn't. Please, Dylan. Listen to me."

Despite her gentle tone, he moved away. Marielle watched him pace across the clearing and realized what must have happened. After all the turmoil of the day, he'd retreated to his usual manly ways, determined to be strong and impervious.

"You don't have to be strong, you know. Not with me."

His bitter chuckle made her assurance feel hollow.

Nonetheless, Marielle went on. She wasn't a woman who buckled when times got hard. She was better than that. She was.

Even if, just then, she was hard pressed not to feel hurt. Why wasn't Dylan concerned about *her* feelings, *her* injuries, *her* terror and tumult and worrying incapacitation? *Drat her ankle.*

After this, it would be a miracle if she ever danced again.

"I love you no matter what," Marielle went on, hearing her voice break under the strain. "Even if you are done in by the events of today. Especially if you're done in! Dylan, I love it that you're kind, that you're gentle, that you're loving and—"

"Gullible?"

Taken aback, she stopped. "Of course not gullible."

"Of course gullible," Dylan insisted harshly. "Or did you forget your brother, the one hitch in your plan? Because there's a reason Hudson never wins at gambling. He has no ability to keep the truth hidden—whether it's about cards or dice… or his sister's playing the new sheriff for a fool."

Oh, no. He knew. Dylan knew the truth about what she'd done for the Sheridans. Then an even greater terror struck her: the gun battle.

Fearfully, Marielle swallowed hard. "Hudson. Is he…?"

"Alive."

She sagged with relief. "Thank heavens."

Dylan only stared at her. She'd never seen him appear less vulnerable or more controlled. That realization terrified her.

She had to do something to fix all this. Somehow.

"I never thought it would come to this," Marielle began, knowing she owed him an explanation for her actions. "I never—"

His derisive snort did not comfort her. "No doubt you thought you'd be far away with the Sheridans by now."

Far away with the... *"What?"*

"Why did you do it?" Dylan's hard-eyed gaze shifted back to her face. "If you didn't collude with Charley for the adventure, it must have been for the money." He looked back at her. "Or for the thrill. Tell me—how tough was Charley? Because compared to me, he must have seemed hard as nails."

What? Why was he going on this way? "You don't understand." Marielle shook her head, growing frustrated. "I never—"

She'd scarcely begun when Dylan held up his hand to stop her. "On second thought, don't tell me. I don't want to know."

Disbelieving, she gaped at him. "You think I consorted with a gang of outlaws, and you don't want to know about it?"

He laughed. Dismally. "You're right. You want to gloat? I guess that's your right. You won, after all. You beat me."

"I didn't win anything," Marielle tried, but it was no use.

"Tell me everything. Go on. Tell me all the gritty details." Dylan swung on her, cold and furious. "Tell me how *he* didn't think about poetry and flowers…only beating your brother and stealing horses and getting away with cold-blooded murder."

She wanted to explain, but… "Murder?"

He tossed her an impatient look. "Caffey is dead."

Oh, dear Lord. This day was growing worse and worse.

"I'm sorry it's come to that," Marielle said, unable to stop a bit of frostiness from creeping into her own voice. "But you've got this all wrong, Dylan. I didn't collude with Charley. I *certainly* wasn't enamored of him. He threatened me! He scared me. He saw you and me talking at the saloon on the night we met. He thought he could take advantage of that."

"He was right. He could." Dylan frowned. "He did."

"Not in the way you think!" Exasperated and upset, Marielle stared. "Are you truly accusing me of helping those outlaws on purpose?" She'd done all she could to postpone the Sheridans' plans. "I never would have thought you could be so cruel."

"You should have. That's what I'm hired for."

She gave him a long look. "You're not hired to be cruel."

"I'm hired to be hard-hearted when other people can't be."

"Well, you're excellent at it!" Marielle rounded

on him, suddenly fed up. All the fear, all the uncertainty and now Dylan's seeming attack combined to overwhelm her. "No wonder you never stay in one place," she declared heatedly. "Given your expertise, I'm sure no one can stand to be around you for long."

Dylan gave her a cynical smile. "Once the job is done, everyone is ready for me to leave. That's generally true."

"And you're happy to go."

That's what was happening, Marielle realized. Dylan had completed his mission here as provisional sheriff. Now he wanted no more ties in Morrow Creek. No more obligations. No more duties—once he'd seen her safely back to town, that is. He was ready to move on. He was tearing himself away from her to do it.

He was abandoning her, just as she'd feared he would.

She shook her head. "I knew I shouldn't have counted on you."

"Good thing you never did. You never could."

The trouble was…*she had*. Despite her efforts not to, she had. She couldn't believe Dylan would deride her for having trouble trusting him—trusting anyone. Especially now.

"That's right," Marielle lied. "How could I? How could I count on a man who never stays—a man who's *proud* of not staying?" She'd always known it would come down to this. "How could

I count on someone like you? Someone who will scarcely crack open his thoughts and feelings for a single minute—"

His heated gaze struck her. "It was more than a minute."

"—and let me inside him? How can I *love* someone who—"

"We found a way inside one another," Dylan told her. His eyes gleamed at her again. His throat worked with suppressed emotion. Tight-jawed, he added, "I know you didn't forget."

How could she? Those had been some of the most magical times she'd ever spent. Stunned into silence, Marielle looked away. She couldn't believe he was taunting her about that.

But Dylan wasn't finished. "I don't want to hear about you 'loving' the man you thought I was," he said in a rough voice. "Because we both know that's a lie. All I have to do is look around, here at this clearing, to know that's true."

Marielle did look at the clearing—where she'd purposely brought the Sheridans on the strength of the information Dylan had given her—and was struck, unwillingly, with the truth.

"You lied to me," she said.

It was Dylan's turn to seem taken aback. "I never did."

"About this place, you did," she insisted, feeling on the verge of tears. Dylan *hadn't* ever trusted her. The proof of it was in the ground beneath their feet—in the ground where, contrary to what Dylan had told her, Sheriff Caffey had never been hiding. Not ever. "At the creek that day, you told me this was a likely hideout. That's why I told the Sheridans—"

"Yes, *you* told the Sheridans!" Dylan accused at a near yell. "You told them while you were conspiring with them."

"I told them to try to save my skin. To try to bargain for Savannah to be released. It was all I had." Marielle shook her head. "But Caffey was never here, was he?" She swept her gaze over the abandoned clearing. "Go ahead," she pushed. "Tell me it was all a mistake. Tell me you were wrong. Or tell me you lied."

"I'm not wrong about you," Dylan insisted, hands clenched in fists at his sides. "I'm not wrong about you using me."

His counteraccusation was as good as an admission. Marielle had to accept that. Hurt but unbowed, she dashed the brimming tears from her eyes. "If I'd wanted to use you," she informed him tartly, "I could have done it. I could have done it a long time ago. You wanted me from the first night we met."

Dylan stared at the trees, silenced by that.

She knew she had him. But not the way she wanted to.

"I know what it looks like when a man wants

me," Marielle went on. "I saw it every night on-stage. You were no different."

Dylan swallowed hard. He closed his eyes.

She was too hurt to stop. "That's the trouble with you, Sheriff. You've underestimated me, right from the start. I told you I could handle that cowboy, and I could have. I told you I could take care of myself, and I can." *Even if I don't want to do it all alone.* With her heart aching, Marielle said, "I guess you're not underestimating me anymore, are you?"

Dylan's stricken look met hers. "You're admitting it?"

She was doing no such thing. But there was a stark satisfaction in having defended herself—in having hurt him, too.

The only thing worse than being left behind, alone, was knowing that she was pitied for her loneliness. Marielle refused to allow that to happen. Not while she still could change it.

She raised her chin. "I'd be obliged if you'd take me back to town now. My head hurts and my injuries need seeing to."

For the first time, Dylan seemed shocked into realizing that she'd been hurt. He studied her uneven posture, her torn-up dress, her bruised arm and tousled hair. Under it, the lump on her skull throbbed like the dickens. Her heart pained her more.

It was well and truly breaking, right there and then.

"I'll take you to Doc Finney's," Dylan offered. "He'll patch you up while I go home and pack up my things to move on."

He wasn't even going to pretend to want to stay.

Drawing in a breath at the astonishing pain that caused, Marielle nodded. She watched as Dylan held out his hand.

The notion of him being chivalrous—now— was laughable.

"No, thank you," she said. "I can manage."

Gritting her teeth, she hobbled her way to his hitched-up horse. It took a long time. Seeing stars, Marielle turned.

She thought for certain she would keel over, fallen into a dead faint. But providence was not that kind to her. Not then.

Dizzily, she raised her head. "I don't have all day."

For whatever reason, Dylan lingered. Then, "Me, either."

He strode to her position, swung her onto his waiting horse in a parody of caring then mounted behind her and rode away.

Whatever magic there was in the sheltered clearing near the Morrow Creek bridge—and Marielle had, indeed, heard whispers that there'd been a few magical occurrences near there—it was not on offer for her and Dylan on that day. Between them, everything was suddenly all too real…and not magical at all.

He hadn't expected to leave the clearing with Marielle on these terms, Dylan realized as he reined in his horse at Doc Finney's house. He'd expected somehow, foolishly and naively, that Marielle would explain everything and all would be fine.

Instead, he was about to leave the woman he loved in the care of a crotchety sawbones who'd as soon berate her as bandage her—and a cantankerous Mrs. Sawbones who would disapprove of a woman being brought battered and partly undressed to her house.

Reminded of Marielle's ruinous condition, Dylan examined her torn dress. She was more devious than he'd reckoned, if she'd allow herself to be seen in public in such a state. It looked as though she'd been set upon, beaten and rolled in the dirt—surely not things any woman wanted from the man she'd taken up with…no matter how compellingly tough he might have seemed.

Charley Sheridan. No wonder the bastard had been so damn arrogant earlier, even while locked in irons. He'd known that he had Marielle on his side. With backing like that, Dylan knew, it was probably easy to feel on top of the world—even with a stay in a dank, famously inescapable territorial prison looming.

Charley had had what Dylan had always wanted: a woman who would do anything for him. He'd had that because he'd earned it. By being tough. By being strong. By being—almost—the winner.

If not for Dylan's decision to pursue the Sheridans the way he had, he assumed, they *would* have gotten away. He'd have reached Marielle sooner—and would have been oblivious to her part in their scheme, besides—but that wouldn't have mattered.

He'd have failed as a sheriff. He'd have failed as a man.

At least this way, he consoled himself, he would know he'd done all the difficult things… including leaving Marielle behind.

Proudly, she sat upright in front of him, scarcely allowing him to support her on his horse. Her injuries made him ache. Her confessions almost broke him. Why had she told him at all? With Charley gone, Dylan mused, Marielle had had no other prospects except him. Given her prowess at scheming, she should have tried to cajole him and charm him, flatter him and keep him. She should have tried to insinuate herself in his heart even further, to the point where he'd never consider getting off his horse, tying it off, then holding up his arms to help her get away from him forever. But that's just what he was doing.

Because she hadn't tried to keep him. Not even a little.

Stubbornly ignoring his outstretched arms, Marielle gazed straight ahead. "I'm not ready yet," she informed him.

"Well, you'd better get ready. Because I'm leaving."

Even if I don't want to. Damnation. His heart felt black.

Was he really going to never see her smile at him? Never hear her laughter or feel her body next to his? It was…mean.

It was as mean as he'd need to be, to survive having his heart stomped on. Trying to summon up some manly rage, Dylan scowled up at Marielle's flagpole posture. All he saw was loss.

He needed her. How could everything have gone so wrong?

"I need to ask you a question first," Marielle said.

When she turned to face him, he saw that she was crying.

Everything in him wanted to pull her into his arms, to wipe away her tears, to kiss away the fear that she seemed to be feeling and make everything better for her. But wasn't that softness what had gotten him into this mess to begin with?

Dylan frowned harder. He had to learn to refuse her. Starting right now. Instead, gruffly, he said, "Go ahead."

She drew in a trembling breath. He saw her hand shaking and couldn't fathom why. Wasn't she the one critically wounding him?

"When you rode up across the creek bridge to the clearing," Marielle began, "you were going so slowly." She wiped away her tears with the heel of her hand, like a child who didn't know that tears should always be stifled. No matter how hard it was. "Why were you going so slowly? Didn't you want to find me?"

Of course he had. Beset, Dylan stared at his boots.

"Will you go see Doc Finney if I tell you?" he asked.

"Is that the only way you'll tell me?"

He let his silence answer for him.

"Fine." Her shoulders drooped. Just for a moment. Marielle did not, it occurred to him, look as victorious as she ought to. After all, she'd bested a famous security man today. Him. There were professional thieves and murderers and swindlers who couldn't make that boast. "I'll go inside if you tell me."

Well. That meant he was stuck. He'd genuinely thought she'd refuse, just to be contrary, and save him from his own honesty.

Dylan drew in a fortifying breath. It didn't help much.

He still wanted to bawl, right there in the doc's yard.

"I came riding in slowly," he said tautly, needing to get it over with, "because I didn't want to hurry if you were dead."

A hoarse cry escaped her. A tear dropped onto his mount.

"I didn't want to hurry if you weren't dead… and I was right about you. I didn't want to be right about you betraying me."

Marielle's mouth compressed. She lowered her head.

For whatever reason, the light he saw in her dimmed.

Probably, Dylan told himself ruthlessly, because she knew she'd been found out. Where it counted, she hadn't broken him.

Not all the way, at least. Because he was still standing.

He'd be damned if he'd give her more than he already had—more than the contemptible, shameful tears that had flooded his eyes as he'd learned the truth about what she'd done to him.

The truth about what she'd found lacking. In him.

"The whole time I was looking for you, I thought I'd be so happy to find you," Dylan felt compelled to add. He looked at Marielle's clenched hand, wanting to take it in his. Knowing he couldn't. "In the end," he said simply, "I wasn't happy at all."

She started. "That's funny. Me, either."

Then she dismounted his horse into his waiting arms, carefully holding herself distant from him. She waved to Doc Finney and his wife, both of whom had emerged from their house.

"Goodbye, Sheriff Coyle," Marielle said. "Please don't trouble yourself about waiting for me. I'll manage on my own."

Demonstrating it, she gingerly stepped away from him. She stood, wobbling faintly in the waning sunlight, until the doctor and Mrs. Finney reached her. Then Marielle walked away forever without a single look back—leaving Dylan with nothing to do except ride away himself, off to collect his things and move on.

Just the way he always did. Just the way, he now knew, he always would…whether he wanted to anymore or not.

Chapter Thirteen

In the end, Dylan did not leave town. Not right away.

Not because Marielle came to him and took everything back. Not because she apologized or begged his forgiveness. Not even because she, with typical contrariness, wagered with him that he could not live in the same small town as she did without losing his mind—which, more and more, felt positively true. No, in the end it all came down to the Morrow Creek Men's Club… and the emergency meeting its members called a few days after the marshals had hauled away the Sheridans to Yuma Prison for good.

Since seeing those murdering criminals properly punished—and having the town's overdue taxes rightly paid—Dylan had become more celebrated than ever in Morrow Creek. Not that he could take any pleasure in the accomplishment. He knew he could have done the job better, faster and more efficiently if he hadn't gotten himself caught up in feeling so many tender things toward Marielle. With her near him—purposely distracting him, as it turned out—Dylan had never been less effective as a security man. While living with Marielle, he'd gotten soft.

The townspeople didn't seem to agree, though. Everywhere he went, his friends and neighbors saluted him. They gave him warm smiles, respectful congratulations and even offers of lodging—albeit confused ones, upon hearing he'd left the Millers' place.

No one in town seemed to understand why Dylan hadn't stayed there. No one doubted Marielle, either, despite the damaging things Charley Sheridan had said about her...and the damaging things Marielle had alluded to herself. In the few days that passed between Dylan leaving Marielle at Doc Finney's house and then turning up himself for the Morrow Creek Men's Club meeting—provisionally held at Cooper's livery stable—he encountered more people making more excuses for Marielle Miller than he'd ever encountered trees in a forest or clouds in the sky.

Where he found her scheming and heartbreaking, others found her charming. Where he insisted she was deceitful, others claimed she'd acted under duress. Where Dylan wanted nothing more to do with Marielle and the way she'd broken his heart...others kept on jawing at him about her. They grinned with ghoulish glee, wanting to know how Marielle was, what their plans together were, how long it would be before they had children and how many. It was downright intolerable. How could any collection of people—previously so personable and bright—suddenly have become so dense? So gullible? So blindly loyal?

Yes, Dylan knew that Marielle and Hudson had lived in town for a long time. He knew that she *seemed* affable. But no one else understood how she'd used him. No one else knew how she'd splintered his heart and left him to spend his days alone.

He couldn't go to Murphy's saloon for solace, because it reminded him of her. Also, because the one time he tried, interfering Jack Murphy had simply refused to quit pestering him about moving back in with Marielle "for her protection." By the time his opinionated wife, Grace, had joined in, Dylan had had enough. The only place he'd found any relief was at the elegant Lorndorff Hotel—and that was only because its owner, Turner, gruffly instructed all the meddlesome staff to leave him alone.

Of course, those instructions didn't preclude Griffin himself from harassing Dylan. And that was how he came to be dragged along, with one foot planted in never-ending gloom and the other stuck in righteous indignation, to Cooper's stable.

Inside, the members of the men's club were

already assembled. They gathered amid the stabled horses in the blaze of multiple oil lamps, holding ales and whiskies and cigarillos. The place smelled of hay and leather, horses and liquor. From his first heavy-booted footstep inside, Dylan improbably started to relax.

He'd never been to a men's club meeting before. Until now, he'd expected to be moving on soon. He hadn't seen the point. More recently, he'd been busy with Marielle and with proving himself as sheriff. But now those things were finished—and Griffin wasn't letting up on him, either. With a grumble of impatience, Turner grabbed Dylan by the arm and pulled him farther inside.

Amid the rumble of male voices, broad, squared shoulders and hearty guffaws, Dylan felt his own tense shoulders ease. This was a place, he realized quickly, where men gathered to be themselves, with no intrusive womenfolk nearby—and no "civil" constraints on toughness and rough talking enforced, either.

Around him, the coarsest of the Morrow Creek men stood shoulder to shoulder, engaged in serious conversations and jests alike. He recognized lumbermen and businessmen, butchers and blacksmiths, saloonkeepers and ranchers and a detective. He recognized gamblers and nodded at cowboys. To a man, everyone present was indisputably masculine—which only made sense,

Dylan reckoned to himself. Because it *was* the men's club. It was one of the few local assemblies that women still hadn't penetrated, despite Grace Murphy's persistent efforts to the contrary.

Amid backslaps and welcoming handshakes, Dylan accepted a whiskey. He drained it, then took another. He couldn't think of a single damn reason not to cut loose at this meeting. There would be no one there to judge him—no one there to encourage him to be soft, to indulge his feelings, to let himself be hurt.

Here, if someone tried to hurt him, Dylan knew what to do. The remedy involved his fists, a few cusswords and maybe his gun belt. Here, problems were easily solved. They wouldn't be talked to death or cried over, studied like books or moped about. Because men fixed things. Men solved problems. Men didn't let themselves get carried away with wanting and needing…and yearning to crawl under the fancy coverlet at the suite Turner had provided at the Lorndorff Hotel and never come out.

Frowning, Dylan took another smile of whiskey. After this, he swore to himself, he would move on. He would turn in his sheriff's badge tonight, while all the town leaders were in attendance to hear his resignation, and then he would head for Sacramento the way he'd originally planned. Once he did, nobody would bawl or protest. Nobody would look at him with big, bright, wounded-looking blue eyes and let her lips quiver in a sorrowful, affecting fashion. He would be able to leave Morrow Creek the way he'd come, with his dignity and respect intact.

Neither of which he'd have, Dylan knew as he swigged again amid the menfolk and their brawny melee, if he did what his heart had been nagging him to do and ran back to Marielle.

Dylan swore for good measure, just to revel in his manhood. He knocked back more whiskey, then talked with Griffin and Miles Callaway. Hearty guffaws surrounded him. So did boastful talk.

This was better, he told himself as he scoured the room with his usual instinctive watchfulness—which was, admittedly, somewhat blurred by the liquor he'd already consumed. It was *far* better than reading by Marielle's fire, passing time with boring conversation, gazing into her eyes and stroking her hair, making her laugh and sharing stories. Those things weren't for him.

If he was honest, he decided, they never had been.

Which did not explain the persistent ache inside him, even as he watched Owen Cooper stride to the repurposed mounting platform at one end of the crowded livery stable, step up, raise his arms to quiet the boisterous men, and then begin to speak.

Curious to know exactly what rowdy goings-on

took place at the town's secret men's club meetings, Dylan leaned nearer.

"In a minute," Cooper said, "I'm going to let Jack Murphy speak to you all." Murphy was, Dylan had learned from Turner, the current leader of the men's club. "But first..." The usually taciturn and somber stableman flashed a smile. "Let's all have a big thank-you to Mrs. Daisy Cooper for her help tonight."

At his suggestion, everyone hooted and hollered.

Bowled over by their unruly response—not to mention Owen's request—Dylan frowned. The first order of business at the men's club meeting was acknowledging a woman's help with things?

"Without my wife's good cakes and cookies, none of you would have the strength to tackle the important business at hand," Cooper added. "With help from Mrs. Copeland, of course."

More roars of approval sounded. Marcus Copeland bowed, admitting the contributions made by Molly's nearby bakery.

Flabbergasted, Dylan glanced around. Yep. He wasn't dreaming. Every last rough-and-tumble man in Morrow Creek was currently shouting out their glee over frosted spice cakes.

Well, that was normal, he assured himself sternly. After all, there wasn't a man alive who didn't like a sweet sometimes.

But tarnation—he didn't have time for this gibberish. He was a serious man with serious concerns. He hadn't even had any damn cake. Or a single godforsaken cookie. He wouldn't, either.

Apparently noticing as much, Griffin Turner shoved a slice of cake at him. *Served on a fine china plate.* It wasn't even cut crookedly or falling apart. Instead, it sat picture perfect on that tea party plate, ready for someone to take a damn nibble.

Roughly, Dylan shook his head. Turner waggled his eyebrows, wordlessly insisting as he waved the cake under Dylan's nose.

"Back off," Dylan complained. "Does the rest of the world know the Business Brute is a sucker for a slice of cake?"

"Eat it. It's good."

Dylan ignored the plate. But he snatched up the cake, wolfed down a bite with his bare hands and chewed grumpily.

Sugary spiciness exploded in his mouth. *Mmm.* He moaned.

Hearing himself even amid the men's uproar, he clapped his hand over his mouth. But it was too late. Turner heard.

He grinned. "Told you so. Now listen up. Here's Murphy."

Hoping for some genuine business at last, Dylan glanced toward the front. The saloonkeeper stood there in Owen's place, raising his arms for quiet. For a meeting of men, it occurred to Dylan, there were sure a lot of calls for peace.

It made him want to mix up the whole thing and cause some damn trouble, just for the hell of it. Maybe, he thought in a whiskey-fueled haze, he ought to finish his cake first, though.

"...so that's why we're here tonight," Murphy was saying when next Dylan paid attention. "To honor that commitment. Because, as we all know, there's nothing finer than a home and family."

What the hell? Abruptly brought up short, Dylan choked on his last bite of spice cake. Spewing crumbs, he listened while Turner helpfully and brutishly pounded him on the back.

"...so welcome, all of you, the latest of us to make that promise. It's by one of our own, to my sister, Miss Corinne—"

Dylan gawked, hardly able to credit his own hearing. He shot a dubious glance around him. But all the assembled men seemed to find nothing peculiar about Murphy having commandeered their men's club meeting to suddenly wax poetic about family.

"—Murphy, who's gone and promised herself to someone we *never* thought would get his damn oversize head on straight—"

A chorus of rowdy laughs met Murphy's statement, but Dylan could only shake his head. *Not this. Anything but this.*

"—but he did, because he officially proposed

and she said yes." Murphy beamed. "Which, as you all know, means a special meeting of the men's club. This meeting. So come on up—"

Still shaking his head, Dylan cast another appalled look at his manly compatriots. A few of them seemed downright moved.

Did that mean he *wasn't* the only man who was soft on the inside? If all these hardened men were sniffling over this…

"—Hudson Miller!" Murphy finished. "Come get yourself honored, you son of a bitch." He laughed, then hugged Hudson.

At their embrace, Dylan boggled. *This* mushiness was what went on at the men's club meetings? Engagements? Hugs? Sniffles?

"I'm leaving." Dylan brushed the cake crumbs off his hands.

Someone shoved a napkin toward him. He scowled away that assistance. He didn't want any dainty napkins or genteel manners.

"You can't leave," Miles protested, appearing insensible to the problem altogether. "This is the best part, coming up."

"That's right," Turner agreed. "This is what *all* of us went through. You might as well know about it beforehand."

That stopped him. "Beforehand?"

"Before you make up with Marielle, of course," Miles said.

"And get busy settling down with her, like you

want to do," Turner added in his deep, imposing voice. "Go on. Listen up."

But as Dylan hesitated and heard Murphy take charge again, he found his resolve redoubled. Because the first words from the hardy saloonkeeper were, "Hudson, here's your wedding advice."

With a muttered swearword, Dylan bolted for the stable's doors. There was no way in hell he was staying for this madness.

It was difficult to create a joyful saloon dance, Marielle learned not long after she'd parted from Dylan forever, when a person felt certain she was about to die of heartache.

All day, every day, a cloud of despair clung to her. More tenacious than nonstop territorial sunshine and more bothersome than the most grabby saloon customer, her misery refused to abate. At first, Marielle tried ignoring it. With the steeliness borne of having made her way West, forged a career dancing and provided well for herself and her brother, she tried to pretend that nothing whatever was wrong. But that didn't work.

Mostly because tears kept overwhelming her, at odd moments and even less predictable hours, making a farce of her attempts to prove that she was fine. *Just fine!* Even Hudson noticed.

"Why don't you try again to explain to Dylan?" her brother urged. "He'll understand this time. He was just upset before."

But Marielle knew that was impossible. Because the way Dylan had looked at her—callously and irredeemably—was emblazoned on her heart forever. The way he'd purposely misled her niggled at her, too. Because why would he have done that, knowing it would put her in danger with the Sheridans?

"He didn't know it would do that," Hudson argued when she said so, displaying a rare dose of clear thinking. "He couldn't have. He never thought Charley and his brothers would get you. It's not as if Dylan ever meant for you to be kidnapped and forced to bargain what you knew to try to get yourself free."

That made sense—and *almost* made a dent in Marielle's indignation and hurt. But only almost. Because a part of her wanted Dylan to trust her and love her unreservedly…no matter what happened. It was a viewpoint she shared with her brother.

"Even though you didn't trust him?" Hudson prodded.

And that was when Marielle was forced to employ tactic number two—staying ruthlessly busy. Determinedly, she bandaged her ankle in the way Doc Finney instructed and then went back to work at the saloon, trying to bury her pointless longing for Dylan beneath sampling Harry's meager cooking and making up new dances. For Jack Murphy had, at Marielle's instigation, agreed to pay her to choreograph shows for her troupe of dance hall girls, and she had an awful lot of lost time to make up for.

Privately, Marielle believed that Murphy merely felt sorry for her and would eventually cut short her new job. But until then, she meant to make the most of her opportunity. Because, as Jack had mentioned, better dances would prove a benefit to his saloon, making it a worthy competitor to more famous locales.

Unfortunately, that plan had not so far come to fruition. Thanks to the men's club meeting that evening, the saloon was nearly empty. Most of the boisterousness present, in fact, came from Grace Murphy's Ladies' Aid Society meeting upstairs.

Glancing upward as another round of laughter made its way from that assembly, Marielle put away her pencil and notes.

So far, she'd supervised two of the new dances she'd devised, but they both needed more work. When her ankle had mended more thoroughly, she knew, she'd be able to demonstrate the proper steps herself. Doc Finney had promised that her ankle wasn't badly reinjured. In fact, he'd gallingly suggested that although Marielle's injuries were genuine, she was making them worse by *languishing around, feeling sorry for yourself.*

Still annoyed over that declaration, Marielle frowned.

How dare Doc Finney suggest that her heartache was somehow frivolous! It wasn't as though she could simply snap her fingers or apply a bandage and make everything all right. She was sure that time would *not* heal the gaping wound Dylan had left in her.

Without him, everything felt…ludicrously empty. *Why* couldn't he have believed her? Trusted her? *Stayed* with her?

Maybe, a small part of her suggested, because she'd assumed—openly—that he never would. Her obvious doubt must have hurt Dylan. A little. But that reasoning voice of hers was drowned out by the sound of chattering feminine voices as the meeting upstairs broke up and all the women clattered down again. They clustered with the dance hall girls for a moment.

Next, purposefully, they all approached Marielle with Grace at the lead. It was almost as if… they'd been meeting about her?

"It's time," Grace announced as she reached Marielle's chair, "that you did something to deal with this situation."

"I can't!" Marielle objected. "My hands are tied."

If Dylan wouldn't listen and he wouldn't stay… what more could she possibly do? Grace and the others didn't understand.

"If that were true," Sarah McCabe said, "you would not be a confirmable Morrow Creek woman. And you are. So get up."

More of her friends approached. Good-naturedly, they eased her to her feet. Molly Copeland collected her reticule.

They began bustling her with them out of the saloon.

In the doorway, Marielle caught hold. "Stop! You can't all just hurry me out of here. I have a will of my own, you know."

"Yes, and your will is being thwarted," Grace observed. "That simply can't be allowed. That's why we're going."

Marielle held on. "Going where?"

Rosamond McGrath Dancy blinked with apparent surprise. "To the men's club meeting, of course. It's what we decided tonight, during our own meeting."

Ah. Relaxing at last, Marielle let go. She'd misunderstood. This had nothing to do with her personal disaster. This was merely another one of Grace Murphy's famous suffragist causes.

Since she needed diversion anyway, she agreed. "All right."

After all, what could possibly go wrong? Grace knew what she was doing. She had the backing of at least two dozen other women, to boot. Between them all, they would at least have fun.

"Now you can waylay Dylan," Olivia Turner added as they all reached the raised plank sidewalk outside the saloon and started walking, "and get to him before he turns in his sheriff's badge.

A man like that, once he's quit, he's quit for good. Griffin tells me that's Dylan's plan, too. So we have to hurry along."

Caught short, Marielle dug in her heels. Or tried to.

Despite her resistance, the horde of women carried her along, jollily and determinedly. "We did not all wind up happily settled by happenstance, you know," Daisy Cooper informed her pertly. "It took effort on our parts. You can't quit now."

"You, Marielle, are on the verge of wonderful happiness!" Violet Foster enthused, her plain face made beautiful with joy. "All you have to do is get past your stubbornness and try."

"Stubbornness?" In no physical condition to truly put up a fight, Marielle let herself be coasted along down the town's main street. In the near distance, Cooper's livery stable rose two stories high, glowing with lights. "I'm not being stubborn!"

"Of course you are," Adeline Davis argued. "We all were."

"Until," Molly said, "we got brave enough to move past it."

Marielle couldn't believe her own ears. Had they all actually met tonight to discuss her and her problems? Truly?

"You know you want to," Jobyna said, grinning at her.

"*I* want to," Corinne Murphy put in stridently, her gaze fixed on the livery stable. "I hear they're handing out marriage advice to Hudson tonight. I want to know what they say."

A general hum of agreement swept through their group.

But Marielle wasn't convinced. "I'm right to stay away!" she insisted. "I should not have to be the one to go to Dylan."

"Would you rather be right? Or happy?" Nellie Trent Bannon posed this question with her usual journalist's inquisitiveness. She was famous for it. "Because sometimes you can't have both."

"Pish posh." Grace waved them all off. "Be right!"

Befuddled but tempted, Marielle bit her lip as they continued down the street. For days now, she'd been anguished and miserable, missing Dylan. Was her pride worth all that?

Because that's largely what it was, she realized. Her pride was hurt. She was upset that Dylan hadn't instantly forgiven her. But of course he'd been overwhelmed and confused. Just look at what he'd been through that day! A wedding, a kidnapping, a pursuit, a shootout, two dead men, stolen money, two arrests…

"I'm not right, Grace," Marielle admitted. "I hurt him."

"Then tell him and he'll forgive you," Savannah piped up.

Startled to hear her expectant friend's voice, Marielle glanced to the edge of their bustling group. Savannah was, indeed, coming along with them, expanding belly and all.

"He's probably already left," Marielle assured them all in a shaky voice. She cleared her throat, watching uncertainly as the livery stable drew closer. She could have sworn she heard husky male laughter coming from inside. "He's a drifting man, after all. He can't wait to leave. He's probably on a train."

"He's in the men's club meeting," Olivia insisted.

"Is he?" Savannah asked with a typically analytical aura. "Is he a drifting man? Because it looks as though he's decided to stay put." She smiled. "He hasn't wired Sacramento yet."

"He hasn't?" *But that disproved all her theories about him wanting to leave her.* Fraught with foolish, burgeoning hope, Marielle pulled up short for one last stand. "You're all so meddlesome! Why can't you leave me alone to be unhappy?"

As one, her friends gave her united sympathetic looks.

She felt dangerously close to being crushed by a huge hug.

At the last instant, Grace stepped up with her usual take-charge manner. "Because it's not necessary that you be unhappy," she stated with certainty. "Not while there's still hope. And there's *always* hope, according to me. So gather your courage—"

"And fix your hair!" her sister Molly advised giddily.

"—and follow me," Grace finished. "Because tonight, we're crashing the last bastion of masculine secrets in Morrow Creek!"

Her rallying shout drew cries of support from the women.

But Marielle couldn't help frowning. "You're using me as an excuse to beat down another of the town's barriers to women," she accused Grace. "You've wanted to do this all along, haven't you?"

"Yes," Grace said crisply. "I have." Then she smiled. "But that doesn't mean I don't appreciate the very convenient excuse you've offered." She grabbed Marielle's arm in an affectionately no-nonsense way. "So take a deep breath and throw out your excuses. Because tonight, for Marielle's sake, we're going in!"

Everyone cheered again, louder than before.

But Marielle saw her last excuse standing in the night. She pointed at the stable doors, securely closed and doubtless bolted shut from within. "They're locked. Oh, well. Never mind."

She wheeled around, intending to wallow in her heartache awhile longer—at least as long as it took for Dylan to be the one to come begging for her forgiveness instead. But Jobyna identified her pretext...and wouldn't stand for it, either.

"Someone has to go first," her friend said. "Make it you!"

"You'll officially be the bravest between you and Dylan forever," Sarah advised, getting straight to the sticking point. "No matter what happens from here, you'll always have that."

Now, *that* did appeal to her, Marielle decided giddily.

That she could do. It was all the justification she needed.

Boldly, she grinned. "Well, what are we waiting for, then?"

So Daisy Cooper produced a key, they all clattered upstairs to the nonbarred entrance to the livery stable's living quarters and prepared their onslaught on the until now impenetrable Morrow Creek Men's Club and all its virile, tough-talking, wholly unsuspecting secret members.

Chapter Fourteen

When Dylan first heard clattering above his head, like the sound of a hundred goats all milling around in the livery stable's upstairs living quarters, he thought he was saved.

Because if ever a man needed saving, it was him. He'd never withstood so much advice, so much cheering…so much outright twaddle all in one place. If he'd wanted reassurance that he wasn't the only softhearted man in Morrow Creek, then he had it in spades tonight. Because from the moment that Jack Murphy had kicked off his counsel to Hudson with an edict that *A happy wife makes a happy home*, the pabulum simply hadn't quit.

He'd been forced to hear it, too. Because Seth Durant and Judah Foster were blocking the double-barred stable doors. Dylan had worked with them at Rosamond McGrath Dancy's Morrow Creek Mutual Society. He liked them. So he hadn't wanted to knock their heads together. Instead, he'd stayed to listen.

Every man had stood to offer more. One at a time, each rugged, unassailable, hard-fisted man he knew and respected took his place at the front of the meeting and gave suggestions.

"...then you're gonna have to let her warm her ice-cold feet on you at night," O'Neil, the ruddy-faced butcher was saying owlishly. "Because she's gonna love you forever when you do."

Around Dylan at the bizarre meeting, men nodded sagely.

But he'd had enough. Whether the noise overhead had been rogue goats or not—and it admittedly seemed unlikely—this meeting seemed destined to go on forever. He had to stop it.

"I've got something to say," he called out roughly.

As one, the whole assembly turned to him. They grinned.

He scowled at those grins. Because they were damnably *knowing* grins—suggesting their owners thought that they'd gone and broken him...and were proud of it, what's more.

"You've come to your senses," Turner said beside him with a smile and a nod. "Good. I thought *I* was stubborn, but *you*—"

"You're in a category all your own," Cade judged, wearing an irksomely knowing look. "If I'd been as cussed as you, I would have never searched Simon Blackhouse's private train car to find Violet. And I'd be a sorrier man for it, too."

Dylan grunted. "You're both drunk." He weaved as he pushed his way forward. Maybe he was drunk, too. Maybe that explained the goats. Because no one else—no one without his finely honed gunslinger's hearing—seemed to have noticed it. "Here we go."

His mumbled pronouncement caused murmurs. His ascent to the mounting platform that doubled as a speaker's dais drew cheers.

These men, Dylan knew, did not know what they were in for.

Drawing in a breath, he glanced at Hudson's shining, expectant face. As the man being honored, Hud occupied a place of privilege near the front of the assembly. In his hand, he held a whiskey. In his heart, he held the love of a woman who'd agreed to be his. Forever. At the realization, Dylan felt consumed by all the emotions he'd tried to deny till now.

Knowing he had to push them back, Dylan told himself, cynically, that Hudson and Corinne's commitment would waver. That Marielle's unreliable brother would mess up their love. That they were doubtless only getting married just to irk him, on purpose, because they knew their happiness would hurt.

But it was no use. Dylan was forced to surrender before he'd given his usual resistance a fair try. Worn down by the buoyant optimism and generous encouragement in the room, Dylan was unable to deny his feelings. Or how they pained him.

A devastating wave of sadness washed over him.

Because even fickle Hudson, with all his faults, had found someone to love him. And Dylan hadn't. Or he had, and he'd lost her. It was a wonder that Hudson had gone through with his proposal at all, given how long he'd waited for Marielle to be settled herself. Hudson must have thought, must still think...

...that Dylan and Marielle would make things work somehow. Otherwise, he never would have risked leaving his sister alone.

Struck by the thought, Dylan hesitated. If everyone else believed Marielle was blameless—believed he ought to go ahead and forgive her for what she'd done—was he really justified in hanging on to his bitterness? If every man in Morrow Creek was secretly softhearted on the inside—and every woman knew it—wouldn't Marielle simply wind up with another man just like him?

Just like him...but *not* him. The idea rankled sorely.

He knew Marielle hadn't truly wanted Charley Sheridan. The man was a criminal and a liar. Yet Dylan had taken his goading words over Marielle's. Too upset not to, he'd buckled under them.

He'd been unable to hear Marielle's reasoning… or her love.

If, he persisted in telling himself, *it had ever existed*.

"I've come up here," Dylan made himself say, partly so he'd quit brooding about what couldn't be changed, "to turn in my badge." He yanked off that tin star and showed it to everyone.

The general grumble of discontent surprised him.

"I can't tell you I don't want to be sheriff," Dylan went on in a raw voice, "because I do. I like Morrow Creek. I found a new start here— and a home, too. I'm powerfully glad for that."

"Why are you leaving then?" Thomas Walsh yelled.

Dylan half expected to find the *Pioneer Press* editor with a pencil and notebook in hand, ready to take down his answer.

But all he saw in the crowd were confused masculine faces.

"I can't stay," Dylan went on, "because I can't give you all what you deserve—and that's a good sheriff. My head's not in it. Neither is my heart. Here, I'm too damn distracted—"

"That's 'cause of all the fine women in town!" someone shouted, drawing a chorus of ribald cheers from the crowd.

"—and I can't rightly say when that's going to quit, either," Dylan went on doggedly, gazing out at the rapt, disgruntled-looking crowd. "Turns out, I can't sleep. I can't eat. I—"

"*I* know when that problem's going to quit, Sheriff!" a feminine voice rang out. "I know just how to fix it, too."

At that unexpected ladylike sound, every head turned.

Marielle Miller stood at the bottom of the stairs leading to the livery stable's living quarters. Her back was straight, her chin high, her expression defiant. Behind her, women clustered on the stairs and gathered on the stable floor.

All of them, he saw, looked downright triumphant.

Most particularly, Grace Murphy, aptly at their head.

"If you'd like to come over here and listen," Marielle challenged him in a tremulous voice, "I'll tell you, too."

Dumbstruck at the sight of her, Dylan blinked.

He truly *had* to be dreaming, he knew. Because not only had this farce of a men's club meeting become a gossipy advice session, but also Marielle was there. Just the way she'd been in his thoughts, from moment to moment and breath to breath.

He wanted to run across the stable, take her in his arms and never let her go. But that would be ludicrous. Because this Marielle was a figment of his imagination, brought on by drink and duress and despair. She wasn't real. She couldn't be.

Proving otherwise, Marielle said, "I'll come up there to you and do it instead, if you'd prefer. Which will it be?"

Duly challenged—twice—Dylan frowned. All the men's heads swiveled toward him, waiting for his response. He clenched his sheriff's badge until his hand hurt, hoping to wake himself up.

It didn't work. Because this was real. It was now.

It was Marielle, typically trying to beat him at this.

Well. He'd be damned if Marielle would fix up their lost love all on her own. Not while he was there to do it for them.

He was a man, after all. Men fixed things. Didn't they?

Knowing they did, Dylan scoured the crowd with a hard look, mutely daring them all to disagree with his silent assessment.

No one did. They were too caught up in the events of the evening—the same way they'd been caught up in Dylan's attempt to hand over his badge and leave Morrow Creek behind…the same way they'd been caught up in listening and had not even noticed the two dozen or more women infiltrating their secret men's club.

He had, it occurred to Dylan, unwittingly become an accomplice in the women's undoing of the club's sanctity.

"Miss Miller," he said, finally meeting her

gaze with a determined one of his own, "we are *not* doing this in front of everyone."

"Not even me?" Hudson piped up, characteristically flip.

"Not even you," Dylan confirmed sternly.

Then, amid a whole passel of his male friends' and neighbors' frustrated groans, he strode across the stable floor, swept Marielle along with him and guided them both outside into the starry night beyond…with one brief, all too irksome stop to intimidate Judah and Seth into finally unbarring the stable's double doors beforehand. That effort slightly spoiled his exit with Marielle, Dylan admitted confidentially—but what waited beyond would, he hoped, be absolutely worth it.

In the darkness beside the livery stable, in a quiet alleyway beneath the territorial stars, Marielle looked up at the man she'd come for and prayed she'd done the right thing.

Just as he had before, at the creek bridge, Dylan seemed stern. Severe. Possessed of an authority she could only have given him by lending him her heart…and her future along with it. But the only thing she needed from him now was his forgiveness.

Anything else, she told herself, would be a bonus.

That didn't stop her heart from hammering madly, however, as Dylan released her arm and stood before her. It didn't stop her palms from growing damp or her knees from quaking. She was afraid, in that moment, in a way she never had been before. Because Marielle intended, as a last-ditch effort, to be utterly honest with him—to explain herself and her feelings completely.

Instead, compelled by an urge she didn't understand and didn't much care to contemplate, she touched Dylan's face. She went on gazing into his eyes as she cupped his stubbled jaw.

She raised herself and pressed her mouth to his, silently and surely. Beneath her lips, his mouth felt like warm stone.

Slowly, just the way she'd hoped, he kissed her back.

She knew then that there was hope.

Even after all that had happened between them.

"Hello," Marielle whispered, desperately wanting a homecoming between them.

"Hello," Dylan murmured back, giving nothing away.

In the distance, meandering hoofbeats sounded. A faraway voice rang out, then was answered by someone else. But in her unexpected haven with Dylan, Marielle didn't care about that.

"I heard," he said, "that you have a solution for me."

Oh, yes. A solution to his problem of not sleeping, not eating, not being able to do his job as sheriff. She'd promised him that, at the bottom of the stairs inside the meeting.

Marielle smiled. "I do have a solution. But first, let me—"

Touch you some more. She'd longed to do that again even more than she'd known. Now that he was within reach, tall and real and just as handsome as she remembered, Marielle was possessed with an urge to crush him to her and never let go.

She settled for stroking his face again, lovingly and yearningly. But Dylan grabbed her hand. Closed his eyes. Pressed her palm against his face and then pulled it away. Opening his eyes again, he fixed his gaze on hers. Hoarsely, he said, "If you're toying with me, Marielle, just…don't. I can't stand it."

"Toying with you?" She blinked, startled. "How could I—"

"How could you not? You're here, all beautiful and kind and *here*." He frowned. "I'm still half convinced I'm dreaming you."

"Then I'm not the only one." Feeling her gaze soften, Marielle shook her head. "The thing is, Dylan, I can't sleep, either. I can't eat. I can't do anything that requires caring about anything at all. I think that part of me is broken."

His face grew somber. "Marielle, I'm sorry. I never—"

"No, *I'm* sorry," she insisted. "I'm sorry I hurt you, and I'm sorry I let you think I wanted something other than what we had together." She remembered his hurtful accusations that she'd conspired with the Sheridans for adventure, money or thrills. "I didn't know what I wanted, until I met you. Then I wanted—"

"For me to leave you alone and quit bossing you around?"

Marielle grinned at his perspicacity. "—to believe that *I* could have what other people have. That *I* could have love, and a future, and someone to stick by me. I wanted that *so* much. But because I'm me, and because so many people have left me—"

"I'm not those people," Dylan vowed. "I never will be."

"—I was afraid to tell you so. It was as if voicing it aloud would make all hope of it happening vanish," Marielle said. "At the same time, I had Charley Sheridan threatening me, *threatening Hudson*, and I couldn't just do nothing! I held off Charley as well as I could. I didn't tell him a thing until the day he and Peter took me from the church. I swear that's true."

Somberly, Dylan nodded. "You should have told me. You should have told me what was happening. I'd have protected you."

"How could I?" Marielle protested. "At first, I didn't know you. By the time I did, I had too much at stake to risk it." She caught hold of his hand. Squeezed. "I didn't want to lose you.

If you'd known that I'd cooperated with those outlaws, even a little bit, what would you have thought of me? The worst!"

"Never." He squeezed back. "I never could. You're good and fine, Marielle, and I did you a disservice by forgetting that, even for a minute. But somehow, Charley got to me." Dylan looked irate with himself for admitting it. "I was scared and furious and surprised, and it all seemed to make sense. Then, it did."

"And now?" she asked, hardly daring to breathe.

"Now?" Dylan arched his brow, gazing at her in the starlight. Fortunately, there was a moon sailing overhead, too. It carved his features in light and shadow. "Now I know I was wrong. Everyone told me so. I should have listened."

"Well, now. That wouldn't be like you at all, would it?"

He stared. "You're *joking* now?"

"I'm *giddy* now," Marielle corrected, stepping nearer. She put one hand on his coat, where his badge should have been. "Because already you've given me more than I hoped for, just by staying to listen." She drew in a deep breath. "I'm sorry, Dylan. I'm truly sorry I hurt you. If I could take it back—"

"You don't have to take it back."

"—I would, but I can't. So all I can do is kiss you again, and give you my heart, and say goodbye to you the way I should have before but was too stubborn to do." With tears welling in her eyes, Marielle pressed her mouth to his. She felt like sobbing. "Everyone told me you're staying in town, but I know better than to hope that's for me. Besides, I just heard you turn in your badge!" Wildly, she gestured toward the livery stable looming behind them. "You're a good man and a good sheriff. There's no reason *I* should drive you away—"

"Drive me away? Marielle, you don't—"

"And I don't want to cost you a good job," she went on, desperately clutching his lapel now to keep herself from crumpling with the effort it took to deny herself another kiss. She cleared her throat. "So, I want you to know that I promise not to interfere with you in any way. You can stay in Morrow Creek and keep your job and keep protecting people here."

Dylan didn't say anything as she struggled for more.

Why wasn't he speaking? Didn't he know how difficult this was for her? Her friends might think she'd have no trouble, but Marielle knew better. Saying goodbye to him was impossible.

"You should get some sleep for a change, too," Marielle rambled on, churning her arm as she sought the right things to say, "and maybe have something to eat now and then—except *not* Harry's beans with bacon, because his 'secret ingredient' is unutterable," she warned with a headshake. "You'll be happy. I just know it." Somehow, she mustered a smile. "There. Done."

There was a long pause, during which the sound of singing filtered from inside the livery stable. Then, "You sound as though you've got things all figured out for me," Dylan said.

"Well." Marielle sniffled. "I want you to be happy."

"But how can I be?" Dylan asked. "Without you?"

Dizzily, she waved. "That's easy. You'll put on your badge. You'll find a nice little house. You'll start courting someone…"

At the notion of him loving anyone else, anyone at all, Marielle gave a choked sob. She simply couldn't help it.

"Will that house have a tumbledown picket fence?"

Confused, she blinked. "If that's what you want."

"Will it have a broken window that still needs fixing?"

She frowned. "Your notion of a happily ever after is extremely questionable. But if you *like* broken windows…"

He did enjoy fixing things, Marielle recalled hazily.

"Will it have a woman with laughing eyes and open arms?"

Now she felt downright murderous. "You don't have to taunt me! Yes!" she cried. "Blonde or red-head, curvy or skinny—"

"Brunette and thickheaded?"

Marielle's frown deepened. *Argh*. This was anguishing.

Why was he making her imagine his future without her?

"I honestly don't think," she said in the calmest voice she could manage, "that you would be happy with someone simpleminded. But if you have your heart set on a stupid woman—"

"It's *you*, Marielle." Dylan's broad smile stopped her argument. "I have my heart set on *you*. I always have. That's why it hurt so much when I thought I'd lost you."

Dazed and befuddled, she blinked up at him. "Me?"

Broad shouldered and strong, he nodded down at her. "You."

"But it's *never* me," Marielle protested, disbelieving. "I try to be good, and I try to be nice, but it's never enough in the end. Nobody stays. Nobody...*wants*. Not like I do. I never—"

"Today," Dylan said with a serious look, "it's you."

She still couldn't fathom it. She shook her head.

"Tomorrow," Dylan went on, "it will still be you."

"It can't be. I only came to apologize. I got

carried away with boasting!" Marielle gestured toward the livery stable. "You won't believe how persuasive Grace can be when she gets going."

"Next week," Dylan said, undeterred, "it will be you."

Another headshake. "I want that *so* much, but—"

"Next year, in ten years, a whole lifetime from now," Dylan continued, his voice growing huskier, "it will always, always be you. For me, Marielle, there could never be anyone else. Until you, I felt broken. With you, I feel whole. I had a home with you, for a little while, and it was the best thing I ever knew."

"But you always wanted to fix everything!"

"I wanted to be better. For you. *More*, for you. But—"

"More?" Marielle blurted. "How could you be more? You're wonderful, just the way you are! I love you, Dylan. I do. I love you in a way that won't seem to leave me, no matter what I do."

"You're not trying hard enough then." Dylan sucked in a breath. He squared his shoulders, appearing to steel himself for…something. "Maybe if you remember how soft I can be, how prone to fits of emotion, how fond of bringing you flowers—"

"But those are the things I love about you."

Skeptically, he studied her face. "You can't."

"I can. I do. I will. Forever and ever. If you'll let me."

He seemed overcome. Inhaling anew, he looked away.

"Then if I tell you," Dylan said in a raw voice, "that I love you with all my heart and soul, you won't balk?"

Marielle wanted to laugh with joy. "You love me?"

"If I tell you that I dream of you, that I need you, that I don't want to go on another minute without you—"

"You do love me," she pronounced with gleeful certainty.

"—you won't think I'm weak?" he asked determinedly.

Too late, Marielle realized that Dylan was truly afraid.

Her heart went out to him. Because she was afraid, too.

Together, they were both trying to overcome that fear.

"I'll think you're *strong*," she told him. "Strong enough to know what you want, to know who you are, to stand up to me."

At that, he laughed. "If you think I'm soft all over—"

"How could I?" she offered an impish grin. "I know better."

At her reminder of the intimate times they'd

shared, Dylan seemed to relax. He shook his head at her. "Now you know all."

"I know all and love all," Marielle amended. Had he really been afraid, all this time, that she'd turn away from him? "I wish I could devote all my days to making sure you know it."

"I think you'll find that's *my* job—making sure you feel loved and appreciated and wanted and needed and cared for."

"All that?" In the moonlight, Marielle gave him an arch look, wishing she could kiss him again. "That's a tall order."

"I'm a tall man."

She couldn't help laughing. "Well, your word *is* law around here, Sheriff. Who am I to argue?"

"You're not to argue. Not tonight." Dylan kissed her, longingly and assuredly. He pulled her even nearer, then gave her a provocative look. "Not even if I order you to turn right around, walk over to the Lorndorff Hotel and take up with me there in my very fancy suite, where the bed is big and cushy—"

"Sheriff Coyle! That's scandalous!"

"—and the man who's accompanying you there is *very* eager to make up for the time we've lost over the past few days."

His intent expression made her heart flutter. But Marielle wasn't giving in too easily. "I like a fancy suite," she told him, "but I'm afraid you don't have the authority for this."

Dylan looked surprised. "I sure as hell do."

With a smile, she slipped his forgotten badge from his hand. She pinned it on. She patted it. "There. Now you do."

"Now will you come with me, then?" he asked.

"I have a better idea." Marielle clung to his lapels, then kissed him again. "I want you to come home. Please. Come home."

For a moment, Dylan looked awestruck. "I have a home?"

"If you'd stop dawdling, yes." Marielle tugged him a few steps down the alleyway. She didn't only want kissing. "You do."

"I have a home. With you," he repeated.

She puzzled over his rapt expression. "Again," she said while gesturing, "you'll have to walk there with me."

"We're really going to be together?" Dylan asked.

At that, Marielle realized what was going on. She turned to delve her fingers in his hair, then gave a sturdy yank.

"Ouch!" Dylan rubbed his head. "What did you do that for?"

"To let you know you're not dreaming."

He grinned. "I think you need the same lesson."

"Oh, no, I don't!" Marielle backed away.

But Dylan caught her within seconds.

Dratted ankle. It had brought her and Dylan

together…and now it was helping to keep them together, too.

Well, maybe it wasn't all bad. Not really. Not in the end.

"Go ahead." Valiantly, Marielle screwed up her courage. She shut her eyes, getting ready to have one of her own hairs pulled out in fair retribution. "Show me I'm not dreaming, either."

Dylan came closer. He steadied himself with his hand on her shoulder. She felt his warmth, his nearness…his intention to gain the payback he deserved. Breath held, Marielle tensed.

Gently, very gently, Dylan kissed her. His breath feathered across her face, stirring all her memories of them together.

"You're not dreaming," he said.

As she opened her eyes and took his hand, as they examined the livery stable where the rollicking men's *and* women's club meeting was going on…and then chose to round the corner and travel toward the luxurious Lorndorff Hotel instead, Marielle knew it was true. Wonderfully, she wasn't dreaming.

She'd found true love with Dylan, against all the odds.

She'd had to be brave. She'd had to risk everything. But she'd done it. From here on, there would only be *more* bravery, *more* risk and *more* effort— there would be, if they wanted to keep their happiness growing for the next decade or five.

They did. Dylan himself had told her so. She agreed.

As the two of them traveled through the moonlight toward the rest of their lives together, Marielle knew it would be worth it. All the effort, all the vulnerability, all the kisses and the hopes she and Dylan shared would blend into a love that was rare and recovered, and all the more precious for it.

"I hope you like weddings," Marielle said, "because I don't know if you're aware of it or not, but Hudson and Corinne are—"

"Getting married," Dylan surprised her by saying. He tossed her another devilish grin. *"Believe me*, I know it."

He aimed a signifying glance over his shoulder at the livery stable. Then he mused aloud, "I think, if we try, we can beat them to it and save ourselves a whole lot of trouble."

"Why, Sheriff Coyle." Marielle batted her eyelashes at him. "Are you trying to evade the overall wisdom of the Morrow Creek Men's Club? But the members are so very eager to give it!"

"You *knew* about that?" Dylan asked, walking faster.

Evidently, he was just as impatient as she was to sample that cushy bed in his suite at Olivia and Griffin's hotel.

"Of course I know about it. All the women do. Every woman reports what she knows." Marielle waved. "Do you think everyone in Morrow Creek is happily settled just on happenstance?" she asked, mimicking Daisy Cooper. "It takes effort."

"And love," Dylan amended. "A whole lot of love."

"Plus some shared wisdom. Some match-making. And friends—and brothers—who are meddlesome…and often right." Shrugging off the chill in the air, Marielle looked around at her peaceful, starlit community. Most of the house-holds had settled down now. The saloon was quiet. The Lorndorff Hotel stretched upward nearby, promising untold wonders with Dylan. All of that still lay ahead for her, but right now, overall… "I love this town."

"Me, too," Dylan said. "Because it has *you* in it."

Then they ascended the hotel's steps and went into the ornate lobby, ready to begin their new life together with a reunion, a hurried-up wed-ding and probably a lot of advice.

Because that's how things were done in Mor-row Creek.

Lovingly. Sweetly. Meddlesomely…and won-derfully.

* * * * *

MILLS & BOON®

HISTORICAL

AWAKEN THE ROMANCE OF THE PAST

A sneak peek at next month's titles...

In stores from 1st January 2016:

- **In Debt to the Earl** – Elizabeth Rolls
- **Rake Most Likely to Seduce** – Bronwyn Scott
- **The Captain and His Innocent** – Lucy Ashford
- **Scoundrel of Dunborough** – Margaret Moore
- **One Night with the Viking** – Harper St. George
- **Familiar Stranger in Clear Springs** – Kathryn Albright

Available at WHSmith, Tesco, Asda, Eason, Amazon and Apple

Just can't wait?
Buy our books online a month before they hit the shops!
visit www.millsandboon.co.uk

These books are also available in eBook format!

MILLS & BOON®

The Billionaires Collection!

This fabulous 6 book collection features stories from some of our talented writers. Feel the temperature rise with our ultra-sexy and powerful billionaires. Don't miss this great offer – buy the collection today to get two books free!

Order yours at
**www.millsandboon.co.uk
/billionaires**

MILLS & BOON®

Why shop at millsandboon.co.uk?

Each year, thousands of romance readers find their perfect read at millsandboon.co.uk. That's because we're passionate about bringing you the very best romantic fiction. Here are some of the advantages of shopping at www.millsandboon.co.uk:

* **Get new books first**—you'll be able to buy your favourite books one month before they hit the shops

* **Get exclusive discounts**—you'll also be able to buy our specially created monthly collections, with up to 50% off the RRP

* **Find your favourite authors**—latest news, interviews and new releases for all your favourite authors and series on our website, plus ideas for what to try next

* **Join in**—once you've bought your favourite books, don't forget to register with us to rate, review and join in the discussions

Visit **www.millsandboon.co.uk**
for all this and more today!